W9-CPO-815

Praise for the Work of
Mary Curran Hackett

"*Proof of Heaven* belongs on any keeper shelf. It's beautifully
written, mesmerizing and tragic, thought-provoking, and a
reaffirmation of faith. The story of a mother's love for her son
was touching . . . but it was the tale of one boy's search for
heaven that brought me to tears. I loved this book."
—Shelley Shepard Gray

"*Proof of Heaven* is a remarkable first novel that explores the
intersections of science and religion, medicine, and faith. . . .
Reminiscent of Carol Cassella's recent work, this is an emotionally
fulfilling, spiritually inviting, thought-provoking novel."
—*Booklist*

"Does heaven exist? Are our loved ones waiting to reunite with
us? Can near-death experiences offer proof? In Hackett's debut
novel, everything hinges on an intriguing young boy, Colm,
whose rare medical condition repeatedly causes him to die and
return to life. Indeed, Colm physically manifests the dilemma
each character in this novel faces: How can brain and heart,
reason and faith, speak to each other?"
—*Kirkus Reviews* on *Proof of Heaven*

"Colm's journey will move and charm readers who are also
searching for answers to their own questions of faith. Hackett's
lovely debut is a good choice for Melody Carlson devotees."
—*Library Journal* on *Proof of Heaven*

"A stirring and remarkable, life-affirming debut. . . . Kudos
to Hackett for presenting a real world, gritty yet soaring tale
in which humans must make personal choices between hope
and hopelessness. . . . And rest assured that once you've
finished . . . you may well look at life and its inevitable
conclusion in a new way."
—*New York Journal of Books* on *Proof of Heaven*

PROOF
of ANGELS

Also by Mary Curran Hackett

Proof of Heaven

PROOF
of ANGELS

MARY CURRAN HACKETT

WILLIAM MORROW
An Imprint of HarperCollins*Publishers*

PROOF OF ANGELS. Copyright © 2014 by Mary Curran Hackett. All rights reserved. Printed in the United States of America. No part of this book may be used or reproduced in any manner whatsoever without written permission except in the case of brief quotations embodied in critical articles and reviews. For information address HarperCollins Publishers, 195 Broadway, New York, NY 10007.

Designed by Diahann Sturge

ISBN 978-1-62953-243-1

For all the real angels among us, especially my own father, Phil Curran, and all the brave firefighters like him, who walk through fire so that others may live

Go forth and set the world on fire.
—St. Ignatius of Loyola

Angel came down from heaven yesterday.
She stayed with me just long enough to rescue me.
—Jimi Hendrix

The golden moments in the stream of life rush past us
and we see nothing but sand; the angels come to visit
us, and we only know them when they are gone.
—George Eliot

❧ Prologue

If you live in the dark a long time and the sun comes out, you do not cross into it whistling. There's an initial uprush of relief at first, then—for me, anyway—a profound dislocation. My old assumptions about how the world works are buried, yet my new ones aren't yet operational. There's been a death of sorts, but without a few days in hell, no resurrection is possible.

—Mary Karr, *Lit: A Memoir*

SEAN MAGEE WAS ON FIRE. THE FLAMES LICKED HIS neck and then disappeared over his fire-retardant jacket as he crawled on all fours trying desperately to find his way out. He was staying below the dense black smoke, but it was already impossible for him to see. As he moved across the large, seemingly endless space, he could feel the heat radiating up through the floorboards and he could tell the entire room would consume him if he didn't escape in the next minute, possibly seconds.

Breathe. Breathe. Breathe. That's all he wanted to do. Even though he knew the mask and the oxygen it was pumping to him was the only thing keeping him alive at this moment, he nevertheless had the desire to rip it off and inhale deeply. It defied logic. He knew this. But he couldn't help but feel that the mask wasn't working, that he was suffocating. If he had given in to this particular primal urge, as he had given in to so many other urges in his life, he would die. One inhalation and his lungs would become filled with the deadly smoke and would knock him out. He knew the heavy tank on his back and the mask that it was attached to was the only thing saving him now. But even the oxygen in the tank was dissipating.

As he groped in front of him for a hint at where an exit might be, he felt at once both the sinking feeling that no one was coming for him and the relief that he was alone in this. He didn't want anyone to be there with him. It would be suicide for anyone to come for him. He hoped no one had tried, because that meant that someone was already dead and was now burning in the furnace below him that was once a room. He also knew what the guys outside watching were already thinking, because they were thinking the very same thing he was at this precise moment: *Magee's a goner.*

Again, Sean fought back the urge to rip off the mask. Instead, he lifted his burned hand and tightened the suction of the rubber grip that sealed it to his face. He then put his hand gingerly down against his ax handle to keep his unprotected and damaged palms from the hot floor and continued to walk on his knees, hoping to find a corner that led to a door that led to a way out.

Despite the rising temps, the fire burning the small exposed areas of his neck and his hands, uncovered because of an earlier false sense of safety and calm, and the black void closing in all around him, Sean Magee tried to keep his cool.

His body temperature was rising. The heat surrounding him was making it impossible to sweat. Another primal urge arose: he wanted to shed his jacket, his boots, and the heavy tank, but to give up all that would mean his entire body would burn. He couldn't beat fire with fire, no more than he could cool off by cooling off.

Sean knew one thing better than anything else: how to survive. And this essential truth was what he often reminded himself of: *The key to surviving anything was to ignore every basic instinct one typically has to stay alive. Case in point,* he often said when espousing this long-held tenet, *instinct tells you not to jump out of a burning building. There is nothing instinctual about plunging to your death. But if you don't, you burn. Your chances are better on the ground than in fire. If you're drowning, your instinct is to scream. But if you give in to that instinct and cry out for help, you swallow the water and sink. Moral of the story? Whatever you think you want to do to survive, do the exact opposite.*

Sean wanted to scream for help. But he knew better. He didn't speak aloud. He didn't want to waste what little air he had left.

He heard his friends calling for him over the radio. "Magee? Magee? You hear me? Get the hell out of there."

He listened to his own breath rise and fall inside the mask.

Breathe. Just breathe. One breath at a time. One day at a time.
This was his solemn prayer. His only prayer. His meetings
were his only true religion. He groped in the darkness for a
way out. He heard the tiny voice coming from somewhere in
the nether reaches of his memory, the parts he'd spent the
past three years trying to push away.

There's always a way, Uncle Sean.

But Sean had lost his way. Somehow, he'd lost his way
again.

I can't, Colm. I can't do it.

You have to. Come on, Uncle Sean.

Sean was lost now because he had blacked out earlier, right
after the explosion initially engulfed the room. He was trying
to remember how he'd even gotten here. He thought if he could
just find the precise spot he'd started from, where he was before
the fire took hold, he would figure out how to save himself.

*Just get back. Get back to where you were. Get to where you
were . . . before. Come on, Sean. Come on. You can do this. You
have to do this.*

He mentally backtracked. He remembered why he'd initially climbed the stairs of the house. He was the ax man. His
captain had sent him up to tear open the knee wall on the
third floor and make sure no fire was behind it or between the
archaic wall framing that rose from basement to attic without
any of the fire-blocking mechanisms that all new houses had.
Sean guessed that the house had to be over a hundred years
old. It was built from basement to roof with the same line of
studs. It was essentially a house full of chimney flues. Since
the fire had started in the basement, there was a chance it had
spread up through the walls.

When Sean and his engine company arrived on the scene, he had been told by his commanding officer that the fire had been contained to the first floor and was almost out. It was just precautionary that he go in and look the place over. The hose man stayed below to keep dowsing the first floor with water. Sean, heavy with gear, ripped off his gloves and walked slowly up to the second floor, feeling every wall for the heat that could be burning within them as he made his ascent. Once he scanned the entire second floor, he opened a door that led to the attic stairs and he lumbered up to the attic with his heavy gear and repeated his task.

The attic ceiling was arched, like a Gothic cathedral. Buttresses were exposed, but drywall had been applied to the arching walls to make it look modern and to cover the original wood panels. The renovated attic now served as a little boy's playroom. Sean looked around at the familiar-looking Lego sets and puzzles that were strewn on the floor and a moment of panic seized him. Though he'd been told no one was in the building, he was always on alert. As always, Sean needed to see for himself to believe it. He bolted around the room and pulled off his mask, announcing his presence affably, "I'm a fireman, buddy. I'm here to help. If you're hiding, you can come out. You're safe now. I got ya." But when no one answered, Sean spun around and opened closets and tossed their contents in case the child was still frightened and somewhere in the room. He bent down on all fours and looked under and around furniture. It took less than a minute, but he assessed the room as clear. There was no one there. He exhaled in relief, and continued his job.

Sean tried not to remember the boy. *Not now. Not now.* He

tried not to get distracted with thoughts from the past. He knew there was no stopping the memories once they came. So he kept walking and fought them back. As he stepped over a train set, his large boot landed on, and then crushed, a tiny steam engine. He kicked it out of his way and heard it hit the wall beneath the only window in the room. Distracted by his surroundings, the memories, and the thought of a lost boy, Sean forgot to feel the south-facing wall of the house. Instead, he walked along the western wall and put out his hands.

He felt nothing. He heard no sound.

There was no fire up there after all, Sean thought, just another fool's errand in a day of false alarms and similar dispatches. The end of his shift was in ten minutes. He never liked days like this. He liked to see action. Have something happen. He turned around and walked back to the south wall. Even though he felt certain there was no fire, he had to be absolutely sure before he could go back down and report it to his captain. He was sent in with an ax to check it out and that's what he was going to do. It was his job. And he loved it.

No one would have ever guessed that the floor just below where Sean was standing, and right above where his lineman was hosing, would flash over. Weeks later, Sean's captain would still be apologizing for sending Sean in. He would still be answering to criticism from his superiors and the OSHA investigators. *The house had balloon framing. Textbook. It was a flashover waiting to happen. Shouldn't have been up there alone and without a hose.* They would all say the same thing: *Magee had no business being in there.* But even Sean could never have guessed the power of the fire that was building beneath him, that lurked behind those walls.

Unbeknownst to all, just as the floor below was enveloped in fire, Sean raised the ax above his head and then threw all of its weight forward and let it fall into the wall. It was like tearing open the door to hell.

Sean never knew what hit him.

As the ax ripped a hole through the drywall, oxygen filled the interior wall and fed the fire. Large billows of orange and blue flames and plumes of black smoke exploded up from between the studs and blew Sean and his ax across the room. After several minutes of being unconscious, Sean came to inside a black abyss. He had no idea where he was or how to get back out. He pulled his mask back up over his face, and then reached out and felt for the ax beside him.

As he struggled to regain his strength and get his bearings, he remembered the stairs. He remembered the window on the far end of the room. He remembered the toy engine he'd kicked and how it had landed beneath the window. If he found it, he would find his way. He just needed to get to the window.

Just find your way, Sean. Find it, dammit. How hard can it be?

But Sean was lost now. He had been turned around somehow in the darkness. He had no sense of direction. He had no idea where to go, what to do next.

This was precisely the time, he knew, one begins to bargain. A long time ago he told himself if he ever came to a point where he would be near death, he would not be one of those last-ditch-effort petitioners or hypocrites who declare their love of the lord. He would hold it together and accept his fate. He would be at peace. He would make his sister proud. He would be as strong and as brave as he had seen others who went before him. But here he was, on his way out. He had no time left at all. And after minutes of trying to play it cool, keep his head on straight, he could no longer resist the urge. He felt the words coming out of his mouth.

"If you get me out of this . . . if you help me outta here . . . I promise I'll be better. I'll be a better man. A better brother. A better friend. I'll even . . . I'll even do that thing I said I was gonna do, but never did . . . I'll do anything . . . Just get me the hell outta . . . ," Sean prayed and the radio picked up every word.

"Magee? Magee! You're still up there? Jesus, man, where are you?"

Sean could think of only one person now. One name. He thought he had only seconds and so he didn't bother responding with his location. If he had only a few last words to say, he wanted them to be these: "Tell Chiara Montanari that I am sorry. I am so sorry."

"What? Sean? Magee? You can tell whoever you want whatever you want when we get you the hell outta there. We're headed around the north side of the house. There is a window. Get to the north side of the house. We'll get to you. We're on our way."

"I can't see. I can't see. It's so dark. I don't know how to get out of this. I'm sorry. I'm sorry. I'm so sorry."

And just then Sean saw what he would, in the weeks immediately following the fire, forget, but then, like the apparition itself, remember quite suddenly. And he would find it impossible to ever forget it again. The smoke seemed to break and curl away, making a straight path for him and a bright, magnetic force pulled him forward. Sean succumbed to it. If not for the mask he was wearing, Sean would have rubbed his eyes. He would have tried to clarify the inconceivable scene playing itself out before him. If he didn't know better, he would have thought he had seen an angel, surrounded by an incredible all-encompassing light. He had seen it before. He would know it anywhere. It lighted the way. He wanted to go to that light. It made all the sense in the world. Suddenly, the only urge he had was not to keep cool, was not to breathe, it was simply to follow. All of his physical desires fell away and Sean followed the light the angel had made for him, that once again made it easier for him to find his way. Then as quickly as the apparition had seemingly materialized, it disappeared. And before him he saw the window. He raised his ax and smashed through the panes. He slid his legs through and stood up on the baseboard running around the length of the gabled roof, hoping to see his friends below, there to catch him.

But Sean was all alone. The men had not made their way around the house yet. And the alley was so small, he knew there would be no ladder coming for him. Flames shot out of the window behind him, burning his neck.

Sean Magee had only one option to survive. He didn't want to jump, so he knew that was exactly what he had to do.

Just a few months shy of his thirtieth birthday, on the ledge of a three-story house in Los Angeles, Sean Magee finally stepped out of the darkness that was about to consume him, and he did something he had never done before.

He leaped.

✿ Part 1

Nobody's perfect. We're all just one step up from the beasts and one step down from the angels.

—Jeannette Walls, *Half Broke Horses*

❧ Chapter 1

SEAN FELT THE COOLNESS OF THE AIR WASH OVER HIM as he descended. There was no time to think about the fall when he jumped. He just knew he had to do it. To resist. To fight. To go back. Everything was behind him now. And the impact was coming. For a split second the realization hit him that he was going to land feetfirst. His body was so large and heavy there was no way for him to tuck, roll, or switch positions in midair like a diver. If he survived, his legs would be shattered.

Sean never felt his femur bones snap, the vertebrae in his lower spine compress, or his head hit the pavement when he landed. *Legs, back, head.* Later people would tell him how lucky he was he had not landed headfirst, that if he had, he would be dead. His legs and girth had spared him. *Lucky is one of those relative terms,* he would often joke. But it didn't seem funny after the fall. Not much did.

After several minutes of being unconscious once again,

this time on the ground, Sean came to and heard the commotion that surrounded him. Several people were talking to him at once. There was a flurry of activity in the alley. He heard both men and women shouting orders at each other and into radios. He couldn't see what was happening, but he could tell what they were doing. He had been on the other side enough to know.

It took several of them to cut the tank straps, remove the clothes from his body, and slide him onto an orange board. He opened his eyes to look around him, but he couldn't see anything. He knew his eyes were open, but he couldn't see.

"I'm blind. I can't see. I can't see. I can't see," he gasped under a small oxygen mask that now replaced his melted one that lay beside him in a heap with his uniform.

"Magee. We got you. You're gonna be fine," the medic said, placing Sean's head into a neck brace.

Another was strapping Sean's upper arms to the side of the board. "Hang in there, buddy. Hang in there."

"Where did she go?" Sean weakly muttered.

"Sean, there was no one else. You came out alone. You're gonna be fine, Sean. You're gonna be fine. We got ya, man," his friend James reassured him, patting his chest.

"I . . . saw . . ."

"Save your strength. You in any pain?"

"Uh-huh," Sean said, trying desperately to see what was going on around him. His blue eyes were bloodshot. Blood flowed out of his nose and ears. His face was black with soot save for the tracks of blood that cut tiny tributaries over his cheekbones and square jaw. The flesh on his hands was black-

ened and charred and smelled like overcooked steaks. Sean
caught a whiff of his own burned flesh and his stomach con-
tracted. Vomit forced its way up his esophagus and he began
to choke.

James snapped the oxygen mask off Sean, and then with
the help of three other men took the orange board and lifted
it sideways.

"Oh god, oh god," Sean gasped, "oh god."

When Sean was done retching, the men flipped the board
again and laid it flat on the ground.

"Goddammit. Goddammit," Sean whispered.

"We'll get you something for the pain, man. We'll get you
to the hospital and get you something. Stay with me," James
shouted nervously.

"I can't . . . ," Sean said weakly, barely audible and whispering toward James, who knew his secret. "I can't take
anything. I am not supposed to take anything." Yes, nearly
burning alive and then falling from a window did not pose as
much of a threat to Sean's life as did the possibility of jeop-
ardizing his sobriety. He would rather die than go back to
nursing the bottle or sneaking pain pills.

"Man, you're gonna need a whole lot of something. Trust
me. We'll take care of you," his friend James said now, nervously, feverishly patting his friend on the chest. "Don't
worry about that bullshit now. Stay in the moment, man.
Booze is the least of your worries. You make it out of this, you
have a free pass to drink for the rest of your life. You got me?
You're gonna live. You got me? We'll be hitting the swells together. You and me. Back on the boards in no time and we'll

be fishin', too. And after that, we'll hit the clubs and start dancing with all the ladies. Just like ol' times. You just hang on. You just hang on, man. Hang the hell on."

"No. No. You're not listening to me . . . No . . ." Sean shook his head and started to shake. If he had been on the other side, he would have thought the patient was in shock. But Sean was not in shock. He knew exactly what was happening.

James grabbed his upper arm, the only part of Sean that was not burned. "You listen to me, brother. You're not going anywhere. Not today. Not on my watch. You got that? You shut up and quit fighting me on this one."

Sean couldn't see James's ruddy, round, and panicked face. He didn't need to. He knew what that fear looked like. He didn't need to see what he knew James was feeling. His friend was desperate. Afraid. Sean had been there, too. Sean had been the one to grip tightly, hold on, shake, beg, and plead for someone to come back. All Sean wanted in this moment was to assuage his friend's anguish. He wanted to make them all feel better. He wanted to tell them it would be okay. He wanted to thank them. He understood his nephew Colm now. *It's okay, Uncle Sean. It's okay. Just let me go. Please just let me go.* He understood it so well. To want to hang on. To not let anyone down. Even when it hurt so badly. And Sean didn't want anyone to suffer. Not on his account. In fact, that's all he'd ever wanted—to relieve others' suffering. He wanted to help people. He wanted to see some proof that he was making a difference. A smile, a lifted finger in appreciation. A pulse. A heartbeat. Some proof. Not proof of heaven. Not proof of something beyond him. That was always his sister's and nephew's quest, not his. He just wanted proof of what was right in front of him. He wanted proof of life. It made all the difference in the world. He wanted to do that for his friend James especially, who at this very moment was yelling at someone about a falling heart rate and low pulse–oxygen level. He wanted to give James a little grin. Tell his friend, *Thanks, I'm doing great.* But instead, he said, like his nephew had just three years earlier, "Just let me go, please. Please. I've had a good run of things. Just let me go, James. It's all right. It's all right."

With the last bit of energy he could muster up, Sean smiled and closed his eyes.

𝒴 Chapter 2

W HEN SEAN AWOKE IN HIS HOSPITAL ROOM ONE
morning, two weeks after being revived from an
induced coma to heal his brain swelling—which
came four weeks after recovering from five surgeries to reset
his back and legs, not to mention the skin grafts from his
stomach for his hand and face and neck—he noticed the union
president, his battalion chief, the Light Force engine captain,
and his buddy James all standing at the foot of his bed.

As foggy and confused as he had been these past two weeks
since waking, doped up on pharmaceutical cocktails of morphine and oxycodone and whatever else they had to numb
him into a state of sweet oblivion, he still had the wherewithal
to understand what was about to happen to him. He knew the
union president didn't take time out of his busy day to make
small talk. Sean had a feeling the men were here to tell him
what he had heard them tell other firefighters Sean had witnessed in similar situations—lying on their backs in hospital

gowns, burned, or otherwise damaged beyond repair. Sean took one look at them and knew he was getting his walking papers. The union owed him. Disability. Permanent retirement. This was the drill. He had seen it all before.

"Look who is up: our miracle boy," the captain said cheerfully. "How ya feelin' today?"

"Like I just fell off a three-story building."

"At least you haven't lost your sense of humor. John Davis is here to talk, Sean. You up for it?"

"Guess so. You guys have a captive audience. Whatever it is: Shoot. I can take it."

"All right, Sean. We'll only be a minute," the union president announced, pulling out some files from a worn satchel.

Sean was grateful that the captain wasn't apologizing today. He had been coming every day with James and others from the department to make sure Sean wasn't angry with him for sending him up into the middle of a tinderbox.

Sean took in the surroundings. He had witnessed this scene play itself out: people standing in the doorway talking about what to do with the patient next. It felt like déjà vu, only it wasn't. It was real back then, with his nephew lying helpless in a bed, and Sean looking for the right time to get the hell out.

Before this accident, he hadn't set foot in a hospital in over three years. The last time, he was with his sister, Cathleen; her son, Colm; and his best friend, Dr. Gaspar Basu. They had arrived together in L.A. after a cross-country trip from New York City. They had all come to help save Colm by getting the boy the medical help he needed for his unpredictable heart, a heart that for seemingly no reason just ceased to beat and sent him into cardiac arrest seven times in seven years.

They all entered the hospital in L.A. as supposedly one unit, but they each came out of the journey different people. When they returned to New York, Sean decided it would be best if he left his position in the FDNY and struck out on his own somewhere else. And even though he was seemingly light-years away from his nephew now, L.A. somehow made him feel closer to him. Though that wasn't what he'd told his sister when he'd decided to move.

"I love L.A. Hot chicks, beaches, cars, and no more crappy winters or familiar watering holes begging me to come back in," was how he'd sold it to Cathleen to make the move easier on her. But Cathleen was no dummy. She knew Sean better than he knew himself, and she knew exactly what her brother was doing. He was running away. Again. He had done it before. He had dropped out of school and gone to Italy after their mother died. And then when something had happened in Italy, which to this day Cathleen had no idea what it was, he came running back to New York. And so, Cathleen knew, Sean was once again on the run.

"You're always welcome home, Sean. You know that. I'll always be here for you," Cathleen told him. "Don't be a stranger."

But that's what he had indeed become.

L.A. swallowed him whole. Not in the way that New York did or could, but in an entirely different way. In L.A.—away from his family—Sean could essentially be alone, and alone was what he wanted. It's what he'd wanted more than anything else. He wanted to start *over* in a place that welcomed re-creation and self-reinvention; a city where people liter-ally could and did change their faces. He wanted to be where people could go entire days on their own, where they hid inside their cars and drove to work, the mall, school, wherever in complete isolation, not butted up against each other breathing in each other's air on subways, not sitting skin to skin on packed bus benches, not huddling under awnings keeping dry and warm on rainy, cold days, and not pushing through doors en masse. He didn't want to be involved in people's lives and he didn't want them involved in his. He didn't want his sister just *popping in* anymore. He didn't want her to worry. He didn't want to worry about her. He'd had his fill of loving and losing. And seeing her with Gaspar and their now happy family made it all the more real. *He didn't belong anymore*. It was best that he kept his distance. In fact, if he had to be completely honest, the past eleven years since his mother's death and his ill-fated trip to Italy had been too painful, too hard. And then came Colm. The beautiful boy with the broken heart, who, no matter how much Sean loved him, he could never fill the place of the boy's missing father. Sean could never fix him either. New York was no haven for the brokenhearted. It was a living scrapbook. Every moment of Sean's life there had been cut, pasted, and pressed indelibly into the pages of his memory. New York. New York. New York. Home of his dead mother and father. His sick nephew Colm. Every time he turned a corner he saw them as they had once been. Alive. Beautiful. Walking. Laughing. Hoping. It was impossible. Impossible to stay.

And there was another reason, a reason that he could barely speak aloud. It had always been there—his unspoken desire to be free. It came in gnawing aches in his stomach and sometimes full-blown panic attacks. Sean had always, since he was a boy, felt trapped in the tiny apartment where his mother raised him and his sister. He spent countless hours in the tight space as a boy and often imagined he could fly—spreading his arms out, he dreamed of crashing through the walls and flying out of his apartment, out of New York, and out of his own skin. And as he grew, the buildings, the people, the noise in New York surrounded him and crushed him. In elevators, in stairwells, in subways, in hospital rooms Sean felt like howling: *Get me the hell out of here! Just get me out of here.* When he drank, the panic he often felt dissipated. He felt in control. The rooms seemed manageable. The people in them did not seem so oppressive, so loud, so overwhelming. But when he was sober the spaces caved in on him. He wanted grand expanses. He wanted mountains. Valleys. Oceans. He wanted distance. He wanted to be as far as possible from the old life. And when Sean had stood on the shore of the Pacific Ocean in Santa Monica with Colm, his sister, and Dr. Basu three years before, he knew. He knew this was where he would build his life. His new life.

A new life, Sean thought to himself now. That's what he'd wanted when he'd moved to Los Angeles. And he sure as hell was going to get it. An *entirely* new life. Once again forced to start all over from zero. As if he had nothing left to lose, because he thought there was nothing left that life could possibly take from him. Only there was always more to take. *Always.* "Don't get too comfortable, Sean," his Irish-Catholic mother would often say. "That other shoe, well, it's always waiting to drop."

Sean didn't want to have to call his sister and tell her this.

He didn't want this. *This new life.* Whatever this new life without the fire department meant.

"So give it to me straight, Davis. What am I dealing with? Disability? Pension?"

"Let's not get ahead of ourselves, Sean. We came by to see how you're feeling. You've been out six weeks. And you're awake now, so we can talk. It's just standard. They were able to fix your back and your leg will heal. It's your head everyone is worried about."

"What's new about that?" Sean said with a grin.

"Back to yourself. I like to hear that," the captain said again, nervously.

"I am looking at my legs in traction. I have steel rods and screws inserted into my back. My hands—under these gloves—look like leather mitts. From where I am lying, I am calling this one as I see it."

"We can give you a dispatch position. Or you can train to become a marshall or a training officer. Or you can take the full pension for disability."

"How much time do I have to think about it?"

"After your short-term disability expires."

"So no more riding on the engine? No more fires? No more runs?"

"No, Sean. Would you want someone like you to have your back in a fire?"

Sean inhaled and didn't respond. He didn't need to. He'd been here for six weeks. Short-term disability lasted only a year, and it came with strings. He would be examined con-stantly. And he knew what the doctors would report: He was unfixable. He wasn't going to be able to go anywhere in *three* years on his legs, let alone one. He shook his head. Even though they were giving him options, he knew they wanted him to be the one to say it, to be the one to come to his own conclusion, and relieve them of the dirty work of taking away a man's life. Because that's what it was: a life. Every firefighter knew it. This wasn't just a job. It was a life. *A life. His life.* The only one he saw fit to live.

"I am not fit to do anything else. I don't know what else to do. I'm a firefighter. It's all I know how to do. It's all I want to do," Sean said to no one in particular.

"Come on." The captain walked over and put his hand on Sean's exposed shoulder. "I know this is hard to take. But you're going to be okay. Do you know what a lucky break you just got? You fell three stories and survived. You're a goddamn tank, for Christ's sake. You're lucky you're going to be able to walk. This is one of life's wins. Take it."

"So I've got no other options?"

"Sean, you know we can't put you back on an engine or a ladder. You can still be in the department. You'll always be a brother to us. You'll get full benefits. You'll be able to feed yourself. Take care of your family."

"I don't have my own family to take care of," Sean said curtly.

"Well, now you'll finally find some time to change that, won't you?"

Sean swallowed hard. He was thirty years old. He hadn't had a serious girlfriend in eleven years. Most of his buddies in the department were married and had kids already or were on their way. He'd spent his twenties taking care of his nephew with his sister—and he was well aware it was her family, not his. Besides, she had married and moved on. And what were his chances now of starting a family? Of even thinking about it? Who would find him attractive now? Useful? His face and neck were half burned off. His hands were basically useless to him now. If he wasn't in so much pain, he'd laugh. So he joked instead.

"Yeah sure, Captain. I'll get right on that. I am sure girls will be lining up down the hall as soon as they hear a disfigured burn patient who can't walk is ready to start a family. Get me a profile started on Match.com."

"Sean, I didn't mean to . . . ," the captain said, trying to apologize.

"Nah, it's all right. I am joking. I'm joking."

❧ Chapter 3

SEAN WOKE UP AT 4 A.M. HE COULDN'T FALL BACK TO sleep. And he knew he wouldn't be able to unless he made the dreaded call. All he had to do was buzz the night nurse in and have her bring over a phone and a pen so he could put it between his lips and use it to punch the numbers. But he couldn't bring himself to call Gaspar. It had been months since they'd spoken, when Gaspar called to tell him his sister was expecting twin boys who were due any week now. He'd be an uncle again. And the only time Sean had spoken to Gaspar or his sister before that was to congratulate Gaspar and his sister on the birth of another boy, their second in just three years of marriage. Three pregnancies in three years. *Always the good Catholic girl*. His sister didn't waste any time.

"We have named him a noble and worthy name: Sean Magee Basu. Cathleen would like you to be his godfather," Gaspar announced with his usual Indian accent and formality to Sean when his first child with Cathleen was born.

"What were you thinkin'? It's got no ring to it! How's he gonna catch the ladies with a name like that? Should have named him after you," Sean joked.

Gaspar took it as the best compliment he would ever get from his friend. "He'll do just fine. Like his uncle. I assure you. Now come home. Meet him. Your sister worries about you."

"What else is new?"

"That's not fair. She has a right. You give her no reason to think you're fine. You don't call. You don't write. You don't visit. Poof. It's like you disappeared." Sean could even picture Gaspar using the hand gestures of a magician on the other end of the phone, when he said "Poof." Gaspar Basu had a tendency to speak every word as if delivering a Shakespearean soliloquy on a stage to a jam-packed theater of eager audience members.

"Don't be so melodramatic, Gaspar. I am fine. I go to work every day I am scheduled. On time. I go to meetings every day. Haven't had a drop in over three years. I haven't set foot in a bar. I go to the beach now. I took up surfing and fishing. You should see me, Gaspar. Cutting up the waves . . ."

"I'd love to. You should invite us all out to see your place," Gaspar said, uncharacteristically direct and without a hint of flourish.

"All right. All right. Layin' it on thick. Quit it. I'll be there. Send me the invite to the baptism. Tell Cathleen to quit her worrying. She's got enough on her plate. Tell her this is how normal siblings behave. They go their separate ways. Live their lives. Call on Christmas. The end."

"Yes, but you don't . . . call . . . ever . . . and you don't return our calls . . ."

"I will. I'll be better. I'm just so busy," Sean lied.

"Have you met someone? Someone who is keeping you busy? Is that it? Come on, tell . . ."

"Okay, great catching up with you, Gaspar. Catch ya later!" Sean hung up and never did attend the baptism. A shift came up. He took it.

Now they didn't even know about the fire or his fall. Sean thought it best if he didn't put Gaspar or Cathleen down as his emergency contact. Not only did he not actually believe he'd ever be injured or killed, he also didn't want them to come running to his side if he ever should find himself in a difficult predicament—say the drunken bender he was once notorious for back in New York. That was the last thing he needed: to fall off the wagon and wake up one day to find his indignant sister at his bedside in some California hospital. So James, his surfing buddy and fellow firefighter, was put down as Sean's only emergency contact. That's how he wanted it. Sean believed, however erroneously, that being independent and strong meant being alone.

Sean tried adjusting his position in the bed, but there was no way to get comfortable. He resigned himself to the pain for a second, but then pushed the little red button that was attached to his self-administered morphine drip and let the preset dosage flow. It was weaker than yesterday. They were tapering him. He could tell. But it was enough, for now. It was so easy, he thought. It was so easy to slip back into old habits. And so hard to break them once they got started. Impossible even. He knew there was no ending it. Once he got out of the hospital he knew he'd be hunting down the stuff, alcohol, oxycodone, whatever, just to feel this way all the time. It terrified him. And yet . . . and yet, he pushed the button again. Nothing came out. He knew it wouldn't. But still, he wanted it. It was a good reminder to him. How easily one could, quite literally, push one's own self-destruct button.

After a few moments, when he felt the morphine do its work, he leaned his head forward, and with the pen pursed tightly between his lips, tapped the phone number and TALK button before letting the pen fall on his chest and lifting the phone to his unmelted ear.

✺ Chapter 4

I N ANOTHER GOOD SAMARITAN HOSPITAL ACROSS THE country, Dr. Gaspar Basu was standing in his scrubs in the middle of a dimly lit hallway just outside the door of a patient's room. He was poring over an ultrasound of a congestive heart failure patient when he felt his phone vibrate in his chest pocket.

He pulled it out and recognized Sean's number. He lifted up his wrist and checked the time. It was only 7:00 in the morning in New York City. Gasper inhaled and held his breath and braced himself for horrible news.

"Sean? Are you all right?"

"Why do you always expect the worst? Is that any way to answer a phone?"

"You're right. I am sorry. It's just that you only call once in a blue—"

"Is this a bad time?" Sean cut him off, not needing to be reminded that he was a terrible friend every time he called.

"I'm on my presurgical rounds. I head into the OR in an hour. Just trying to check in on my patients. But I have a few minutes," Gaspar said, closing the laptop and walking down the corridor to find a spot to sit.

"So, how are things? Cathleen's due any day now? Right?"

"No, she has about four weeks from being full term. But she has gone early both times before."

"That's good. That's good. How are the kids?"

"Fine. Everyone's great. Exhausted, but great. House is full. Kids are healthy. Knock on wood as you say."

"Good. Good."

"Sean, what's going on? You sound, I don't know, tired? It has to be four A.M. in L.A. You're stalling. What is it?"

"Gaspar . . . I hate to do this. But I just don't know what to do. I don't know what to do."

"Sean, are you drinking?"

"No, no. It's nothing like that," Sean said hesitantly, and breathing hard to muster up the courage to speak again. "I don't know how to say this." Sean paused again, searching for the words. "I was hurt. Injured pretty badly in a house fire."

"When? How badly? Do you need me to come out there? What's going on?" Gaspar asked urgently, without revealing a sense of panic. Though he went into physician mode, asking for the facts, as Sean's friend he couldn't help but feel worried.

"Six weeks ago," Sean finally exhaled.

"Six weeks! And I am only hearing about this now? Why didn't anyone call us? Why didn't *you*?" Gaspar's voice turned almost angry.

"I couldn't exactly. I never told my commanding officers about you. They saw my parents as deceased and that I had no wife and kids on my records, so they didn't call anyone. I was in a coma most of the time, because of some swelling in my head. And I had a few operations for my legs, back, hands, and face," Sean said, feeling the thick bandage around his head as he spoke the words.

"My god, Sean. What happened?" Gaspar's voice dropped suddenly to an almost inaudible whisper after he heard the words *swelling in my head* and *few operations*. Gaspar knew instantly Sean's injuries could have been fatal.

"I jumped out of a three-story building that was about to explode. Landed feetfirst. They say I got lucky. Had I landed on my head, I'd be dead," Sean said matter-of-factly.

"They're right. In fact, it's a miracle." Gaspar stood shaking his head. Still in disbelief. "Tell me. How did the surgeries for your burns—for your legs—go . . . can you . . ."

Sean heard the anxiety in Gaspar's voice and knew what Gaspar was going to ask. "It's okay, Gaspar. It's okay. I will be able to walk. Yes. I mean, at least they say I'll be able to. I haven't tried yet. Been on my back and rolled around mostly. But I have a shitload of pain. They tell me that's good, because that means I'm not paralyzed. I'll probably have a limp. I have a rod and screws in my back. I have them in each of my legs, too. I had some skin grafts for my hands and face. I'm looking at physical therapy and then—"

"Disability? Do you think they're going to pension you off?"

"Maybe. They gave me options. I could have a desk job if I want it. The union guys came by yesterday to pay me a chummy visit. But I just don't see myself trapped in an office all day or on dispatch. I don't know if I can do that. Honestly,

I don't know what I am going to do, Gaspar. I feel so, I feel so . . ." Sean's voice cracked. He hadn't spoken the words out loud to anyone. He wept softly and then small waves rippled up through his chest and he began to sob. "I feel so, I feel so . . . alone. Alone. Gaspar. I know that's what I wanted. I wanted to come to L.A. to just be alone. I know that . . . But I can't do this. I can't. I can't do this alone. I thought I could. I thought I was strong enough. But I'm not. I feel lost and alone."

Gaspar listened to his friend cry on the other end of the line and felt helpless. He had never seen or heard Sean cry. Not even during those horrific days beside Colm when everyone, including Gaspar himself, found it impossible to hold it together. Something inside his friend had changed. He knew that. There was a desperation he had never heard. A sense of hopelessness Gaspar had known himself. These were not the words his friend would ever say. If Gaspar could fly there this moment, he would. Nothing pained Gaspar more than being helpless in times of need. "Sean, I am so sorry. I don't know what to say. I'll come out there immediately. You won't be alone for much longer. I promise you that. I'll get to you."

"No!" Sean suddenly stopped and inhaled, pulling himself together, using the back of his burn-glove hand to wipe the tears from his eyes. "I'm being an idiot. These drugs they have me on are making me depressed as hell. I am acting like a baby. Just forget it. I'm just tired. Please. Forget it. My sister and the kids need you."

"Sean, you're not being a baby. Stop it. You're right, though, those meds are horrible. And being trapped in that room alone can't be good for you either. I'll make arrangements. Let me worry about that. Not you. I know your sister will want to come, but she can't fly right now. She's too close to her due date. She'd be on the next plane out there if she wasn't pregnant. But I can come. I'll handle the logistics. And I'll try to be there by tomorrow. I'll move some surgeries around next week and get someone to cover for me."

"Thanks. I didn't want to do this. I didn't want to make you guys have to adjust your lives again for me."

"That's what family is for. Sit tight. I'll tell Cathleen. Expect a call from her. In the meantime, I'll make arrangements and call you when I need more details about where you are."

"Gaspar?"

"Don't even ask me to lie to my wife—your sister. She loves you. So, no, I won't. She has to know about this, Sean. I don't know why you shut her out. I won't be a part of it. I will tell her. I'll do it in such a way that she doesn't get too worried. But this is the last time. You two should talk. Really talk. It would do you both good."

"Not now, Gaspar. Please. Not today. I just need a friend, that's all. I need some help. I'll talk to Cathleen. I will. It's just been so hard."

"I know. You're right," Gaspar said, resigned and not wanting to upset Sean further. "Get some rest and I'll see you soon."

❧ Chapter 5

SEAN PUT DOWN THE PHONE AND LOOKED OUT HIS window for a long time. His eyes had fully healed, he thought with relief. He could see things clearly. He watched as the dark, predawn Los Angeles sky transformed slowly until a sliver of iridescent golden light just over the horizon broke through a purple-gray haze. The diminishing darkness was punctuated by buildings and streetlights, not to mention a few faint stars that were hastening to disappear as the golden light expanded and spread across the sky.

It was magnificent. It was the first time in weeks he had felt such a moment of peace.

He loved the sunrise. It had always been his favorite time of day. As a child, he remembered watching his small Irish mother, her dark hair pulled tightly back in a ponytail, sitting by the window in her rocking chair, saying her rosary as the sun came up behind her each morning. As a boy, he often woke up to this sight and climbed on her lap, snuggled into her neck, and rested there sleepily, while listening to the words rise up through her chest cavity and fill the room with her Irish accent. *Hail Mary full of Grace, the Lord is with you . . .*

Then as a teenager, he watched the sunrise each morning while he ran through Central Park with his sister, Cathleen, who was a college student though still living at home. He hated to run. His large body wasn't built for endurance running. But Cathleen, small and slender and light as air on her feet, loved it. Their mother, ever the worrier, wouldn't let her only daughter go out alone in the park in the dark morning. So it was Sean's duty, as the man in the family, their father having died in a fire before Sean was even born, to protect his sister. And so each morning with sweat pouring down his head and soaking his T-shirt through, he ran beside his tiny raven-haired sister with alabaster skin who never seemed to break into a sweat as they ran full tilt into the park. Every step pained him. But the farther inside the park they got, the more it seemed as though the city disappeared and they only heard their inhalations, exhalations, and the sound of their feet landing in unison on the worn paths. He knew she was a much faster runner than he was, but she kept pace with him. Step by step. They usually never spoke on their runs, but one day, Cathleen said, "Look!" Sean did, and saw that she was pointing to the ground, where the sunlight had dappled the dew-covered orange and yellow foliage. "It's like we're running on a million golden stars, like a path to heaven itself."

Later, whenever he was angry with his sister or frustrated by her constant worry and nagging, he remembered that moment. He remembered how big her heart was and how the

very thing he loved most about her was the very same thing
that saved him. *She noticed the little things*. First, it was things
like leaves on the ground, but then, just as easily, she noticed
his lies, his cover-ups, and his breath. It was also the best
trait she passed on to her son Colm, the very same trait that
made Sean want to protect the boy, wrap his arms around
him, and never let him go. The boy saw everything so clearly
when Sean had been so blind. Like during his drinking days,
when he was so intoxicated he could barely make it home.
Some nights, he would just sit on the Manhattan side of the
Brooklyn Bridge and watch as the sun arched and rose over
it, swallowing the whole of the bridge, and on many occasions
hoped that it would swallow him, too, as it rose and took its
station above the jagged, obliterated skyline. And even later
still, he loved the sunrise. Even after AA and L.A. had cured
him of his late nights and blindness, he wanted to be the first
one on the waves to watch, while perched on his board, as the
sun rose behind his apartment, a few minutes earlier than in
the City of Angels behind it, and which rose three hours earlier over his sister and her boys back in New York, and which
rose five hours before that over Chiara Montanari all the way
in Florence, Italy. Everyone, it seemed to Sean, saw the light
before he did. Though it didn't stop him from trying to get
to it first.

He could not only see things better now, he could feel
things better, too. With the tapering of his dosage, he was
feeling less groggy by the day. But everything felt raw. He felt
as if someone had splayed him open and left him exposed.
Every moment he lived with the realization of what his new

life would be like felt as though someone poured a fresh dose of saltwater on him. Burning him over and over and over again. And there was no relief, save for God and fire itself.

For as long as Sean could remember, his life had been bookended by these two desires: fire and God. The former he believed he'd inherited from his father, a firefighter like him, and the latter from his mother, a devout Irish Catholic. He had spent his early life in the shadow of the monumental grief that the absence of a father brought to him, and he spent his twenties trying to run away from the pain that his mother's death bored through him. He thought, however irrationally, that by being close to fire, close to a higher power, that he would somehow find his way to them both again.

He had lost God once. Lost the fire inside himself, too. And just as he was making his way back to God, back to the fire, he could feel himself losing both all over again. Faith and hope, Sean knew, were not things that one acquires with a lifetime guarantee. They are not a gift-with-purchase when buying into God. They are acts that take practice, patience, and fortitude. And he was tapped out of all three. Each time in his life that he thought he was close to having it figured out, close to being certain and resolute, life sent him to the back of the line.

Sean was feeling a new ache. It wasn't in his leg or back this time. It wasn't in his head or neck. It radiated deep within him. He couldn't put his finger on the sensation, but he was starting to think what he was experiencing was a sort of death. He inhaled and exhaled, hoping that breathing would give him the answers he was looking for; would assuage the pain building up in his chest. He felt like he was losing everything.

He had no idea what he wanted out of life. He had no idea what he was capable of doing. He had no idea what he was supposed to do without his job, the only life he had known for the past decade.

Fire, like God, had saved him once. If it were not for the fire department, the friends he made, the daily purpose the job gave him, and James's friendship especially, he would be dead by now. The men and women who cared for him, looked out for him, both the ones during his drinking days and the ones now who made sure he didn't drink, made him believe there were people out there besides his sister, besides his nephews and Gaspar, who cared about him, who thought he mattered. Who believed his life meant something to someone.

Sean had been looking for a place his entire life. He wanted to find that place where he belonged and stay there. He didn't want much. He was not a materialistic person. He was content with the life that he had, and if he had his way, it would have kept on going in the way he had come to know.

Fire. God. Meet. Repeat.

But in a few weeks he would have to hobble out of a hospital and start his life all over again. He would have to find something else. *Where?* He didn't know. *How?* He couldn't even guess. *What?* There was nothing he could imagine he would ever want to do.

Sean shook his head in despair. Five years ago he might have yelled and strung profanities together in such a way that they would make a seasoned sailor blush. He might have thrown a punch at someone; made someone bleed. Drink. Drink till his lips and fingers tingled, his liver burned, his mind blessedly dislodged itself from his cranium and floated somewhere above it all. God, he wanted a drink. The thirst never left him. But the new Sean, shattered and broken, did not move or cry or shout. He looked out over the vast city and suddenly remembered something he had promised to the darkness the night of the fire.

. . . I promise I'll be better. I'll be a better man. A better brother. A better friend. I'll even . . . I'll even do that thing I said I was gonna do, but never did . . .

Sean jolted in his bed with the realization and felt the sharp pain radiate down his back, through his leg, and down to his feet.

Sean remembered the light. He remembered what he had to do. What he must do. He remembered his prayer being answered. The light that guided him to the window. And he remembered the promise he had made to God in exchange for sparing his life.

"I'll even do that thing I said I was gonna do, but never did," he said aloud to the rising sun.

❧ Chapter 6

GASPAR PULLED HIS SUITCASE BEHIND HIM AS HE walked briskly toward the taxi line outside the airport baggage claim at LAX. Once at the end of the line, he stopped, jammed the handle down on his suitcase, and sat on it. Finally at rest, he pulled out a handkerchief to wipe the sweat sluicing down over his caramel-colored cheekbones, collecting in his five o'clock shadow that appeared to be much grayer than his jet-black hair.

The past two days had been a blur of surgeries, patient complaints over rescheduled procedures and appointments, Cathleen's cries and worries over her ailing brother, babies crying in the night, airports, mad dashes across terminals all to get here. *Here. Los Angeles. Again.* It hadn't really hit him till he exited the sliding doors of the airport. Till he inhaled the air, though it was not so different from the noisome air he'd left back at LaGuardia. He hadn't fully embraced what it meant to be back in the city that brought with it so many memories, not to mention the life he now had. The life he could hardly have imagined for himself just five years earlier.

Ever since he'd met Cathleen, her sick boy Colm, and her brother Sean, life as he knew it had been a similar blur—a mad dash from one destination to another. From ER to ER. From New York to Italy. Then New York to Los Angeles. Then back to New York. Then India. Then marriage. And all of it was leading him to this moment. Every moment he now lived as a husband, a father, a friend once again could all circle back to a moment on a hillside in Los Angeles. Everything he had now—this new life—Cathleen, the boys, a marriage, a home. Every blessed thing was because of what had happened on that hill that overlooked the city.

Gaspar remembered it all.

He didn't recall it being so damn hot though. But then again, the last time he'd arrived here he wasn't wearing cashmere. This time he had left on an exceptionally cold New York spring morning. The thick purple sweater that covered his lavender plaid button-down—both items Cathleen had laid out for him for the trip—were far too heavy for the scorching L.A. heat.

"You'll get cold on the plane, Gaspar," Cathleen insisted as she pulled clothes out of their closet and nervously packed Gaspar's bag, and added things Gaspar knew he wouldn't wear or didn't need. But Gaspar never felt the need to disagree with her anymore. He had learned early on that whether or not Cathleen was right, she always seemed to win. By not arguing with her, he was saving himself time, and the world much needed oxygen.

He laughed at what she would say now if she saw him like

this. He looked ridiculous amid the women in stilettos and short skirts, grown men in skinny jeans and ripped T-shirts. L.A.'s hallmark, he thought, was not the beach, the movies, or celebrities, but its inhabitants' eternal state of adolescence; the summertime of everyone's life.

It was sweltering, but it would be undignified if he stripped down in front of everyone. He was hoping the cab line would move, and soon he would feel the AC. He was anxious. His foot tapped on the sidewalk. He looked at his watch over and over. It was nearly 2 P.M. It would be 3 P.M. by the time he got to the hospital. There was no reason to rush, really. Sean had been lying alone in a hospital bed for six weeks. *Six weeks*. Gaspar shook his head as he rolled the words around in his mind. An hour, a half hour, it probably didn't matter much at this point. But it mattered to Gaspar. He wanted to be there now. Sean's self-imposed isolation had gone on long enough.

Although it was unlike him to force his way through a line, Gaspar stood up, pulled sharply on the handle of his bag, and walked past the head of the taxi line and out into the driving lane, holding his hand up as any New Yorker would.

A cab swooped in beside him. Gaspar, wasting no time, threw his bag in the backseat and shouted, "Good Samaritan, 1225 Wilshire Boulevard." As the car sped away past the open-mouthed and indignant passengers waiting for cabs, Gaspar tore his sweater off and ripped off his tie.

He wasn't in New York anymore.

Sean had been asleep when Gaspar walked in. The first thing Gaspar did was look at Sean's vitals. Everything appeared normal. But then he looked at his friend's face, and there was nothing normal about him. Lines had deepened around Sean's eyes over the past three years. His flesh was no longer soft and boylike. His oceanic waves of auburn hair had been shaved for the surgery that released the pressure in his skull and exposed the burned flesh on the outer edges of his face and neck. Gaspar could picture what the scar beneath the bandage wrapping Sean's head looked like. His right ear appeared to have melted into the side of his head. But Gaspar knew it looked worse than it was. The swelling would subside, and after a couple more surgeries he might even have an ear that looked somewhat normal. Both of Sean's hands were in bandages. His legs were both in casts, but one was elevated. His head and back were in a stabilizing brace.

"Rest, Sean. Rest," Gaspar whispered.

Gaspar put his hand on Sean's chest. He was not doing so as a doctor, as a person looking for a heartbeat or a sign of life. Gaspar needed no such proof. Gaspar wanted Sean to know that someone was there. That someone knew Sean's heart. That he wasn't alone any longer. But if he had to be honest, Gaspar wanted some reassurance, too. If he had his way, he would have hugged him, wrapped his arms around his wayward relative. But Sean could not be embraced. There was no part of Sean that any person could wrap one's arms around.

Sean felt the hand and woke to see Gaspar standing over him.

"Took ya long enough," Sean said with a smile before opening his eyes to even see it was Gaspar.

"I tried, but you know that L.A. traffic," Gaspar said with a mock shrug.

"I thought it would be days, maybe a week. How'd you get away?" Sean said weakly, barely getting the words out.

"Are you kidding me? I had no choice. As soon as I told your sister what had happened she all but dragged me out of the hospital. And believe me, if she could have, she would have launched me here on a rocket. Once the plans were in her hands, I'm afraid, I lost—"

"Control . . ." Sean finished Gaspar's sentence, and they both laughed until Gaspar stopped suddenly and seriously added, "She worries about you. We all do."

Sean didn't say anything for a few minutes. It was a heavy silence. Gaspar could tell that Sean was holding back what he desperately wanted to say. Gaspar felt the same way. It hadn't always been this way. Talking used to come easily to the two friends, but both were tired of jokes and false pleasantries. It would be pointless. Both knew neither man would say it. And instead they would fill the air with vacuous words. If Sean said, "I'm fine," Gaspar knew it would be a lie and Gaspar would argue it, and eventually Sean would have to concede that he needed help. A lot of help.

"I'm scared, Doc."

"I know, Sean."

Gaspar looked down at Sean and took in the whole of him. He was still massive, long and wide. There was nothing diminutive about him. Even after all the surgeries, the coma, the weight loss, Sean's basic structure was mammoth. His shoulders jutted out wide, taking up the majority of the hospital bed. His legs looked even larger, the width of small tree trunks in their casts.

A gentle giant. That's how Cathleen had described him to Gaspar a long time ago. But Gaspar knew better.

A small tear crested from Sean's eye. It made a track

behind his ear and flowed along the edges of his bandaged head before falling on the pillow.

Gaspar pretended not to see. Sean pretended not to have shed it.

"I'm broken, Gaspar."

Gaspar nodded. A lump swelled in his throat. If he spoke now, he would reveal all his cards. Show Sean he had been bluffing the whole time. That he wasn't up for any games. He wasn't as strong and as funny as his friend thought he was.

Gaspar swallowed hard and composed himself. "Bones heal, Sean. They take time. Six months, maybe a year, you won't even remember feeling so badly. You'll be back on them sooner than you think."

"I'm not talking about the bones."

"Sean, it is just going to take time."

"That's all I got, Doc. From here on out. It's just time. Me until the end of this life. Nothing but time in between. And I'm broke."

"Sean, I thought you said they'll pension you. You'll have a paycheck."

"I'm not talking that type of broke. For a guy who gets paid the big bucks, you're not too quick on the uptake, ol' man."

"I blame it on age, the children, and lack of sleep."

Sean smiled and then tried to shake his head, but remembered he couldn't.

"Kids." Sean coughed. "Kids."

"Sorry . . . I . . . Sean . . . I don't know what to say . . . how to make this . . . better. Tell me what you want. What can I do? What can make your life better?"

"You know, I've been thinking a lot about that lately. In

fact, all I do now is think about that question. God knows I've got the time to think about it," Sean said, waving his bandaged hand around the room. "I sort of came to a conclusion. I sort of figured something out."

"Oh?" Gaspar said, grabbing a chair and pulling it up beside the bed.

"Long before this fire, long before all that we went through with Colm, not just back in L.A., but all the years before then, I was broken. Something wasn't right. I mean, I walked around. My arms worked. My legs worked. My mouth sure as hell worked . . . ," Sean said with a wink.

Gaspar smiled and nodded.

"But I didn't. I didn't work. Something was fundamentally broken in me. I've been sitting in here and thinking *what if . . . what if . . .* I don't know . . . God . . . or whoever is calling the shots upstairs . . . knows it already, too. Knows I am just a screwup. Knows I am broken all the way down to the studs. I was formed like that old house I jumped from. I was just an explosion waiting to happen."

"Sean, you've been through a lot. You're just feeling down," Gaspar said, trying to assuage his feelings.

"No, no. It's not that. I've been depressed before. I've been sad. This isn't like that. I just know this. I know this. No matter what I try to do, what I try to be, wherever I try to go, it's always the same answer: *You're broken, Magee. Call it. Throw in the towel.* The universe has been givin' me signs. Year after year. Screwup after screwup."

"Are you saying you're suicidal? Sean . . . if you are . . . we can help you. Cathleen and I can help you . . . the hospital can help you."

"No. No. I'm not finished yet . . ."

"I'm sorry. I'll shut up now. Go on," Gaspar said while adjusting his tortoiseshell glasses with his forefinger, pushing them back up on the bridge of his nose, though they were already perfectly placed.

"I've been thinking. I have been broken. But I've also been thinking I can get better. I can *be* better. I think I can finally do something—really—do something about it. For a long time I haven't been honest. Not with you. Not with Cathleen. Not with anyone. Not even the people at my meetings. I'd tell them I am an alcoholic. I've been giving different reasons to different people for so many years for why I do what I do that I actually started to believe my own bullshit. I actually convinced myself that I drank because of nine/eleven, or because my mom died, or because I didn't have a dad, or because of this bs or that bs. Me and everybody else, right? Doesn't everybody have their own bag of crap they have to carry around? Look at my sister. The girl never complained. Never drank. She was in the same apartment with me. Lived the same life, and in some ways she had it that much harder, and she didn't drink. She didn't feel sorry for herself. And I've never told anyone this. No one, Gaspar, not a soul, so I am telling you now: I think I know what is breaking me. Keeps breaking me. What's keeping me broken."

"Sean, it's okay. It's okay." Gaspar tried to calm Sean with a gentle pat on his chest. He could hear the increased beats of Sean's heart on the monitor. He could see the sweat brimming over Sean's eyebrows. "Whatever it is, Sean, it's okay. Just stay calm. Okay?"

Gaspar feared something awful. Had Sean killed someone? Raped someone? Beaten someone? He knew a side of
Sean that his wife, Cathleen, didn't often see. He knew that
beneath Cathleen's seemingly "gentle giant" lived a volatile,
mercurial man whose temper had been known to explode.
Shortly after Colm's final collapse in L.A., Sean had admitted to Gaspar that he had unleashed a torrent of hateful
things on his nephew. Sean had been so angry with the boy
one day for running away from and scaring his mother that
Sean screamed at him and accidentally shoved him to the
ground. Sean told Colm that his real father wasn't coming
for him and that his father didn't love him. Sean regretted
the words as soon as he spoke them. But he couldn't help
himself. The anger was so raw and so real, he was helpless to
stop it. Gaspar remembered Sean being inconsolable about
the event. He blamed himself for Colm getting so ill and for
taking such a turn for the worse shortly thereafter. He felt
like his outburst had broken the boy's heart once and for all.
Gaspar tried to tell Sean that's not how the heart works, but
there was no convincing Sean. He blamed himself. He told
Gaspar of other times over the years he'd lost his temper. It
happened mostly in bars when he was drunk, and he usually
took his fury out on hapless strangers.

*What type of thing could a man do that would so paralyze him
and keep him from living his life, drive him to nearly drink himself
to death at points, drive him away from his family, compel him to
think he was so fundamentally broken that he was beyond fixing?*
Gaspar almost didn't want to know. He didn't want anything
to come between him and the love he felt for Sean. He didn't

want to judge him or have to hold something against him. Most of all, he wanted to be able to honestly say, "No matter what it is, Sean, you can be forgiven."

But he didn't. Gaspar said nothing and braced for what Sean felt compelled to tell him.

"Remember when I wouldn't go with Cathleen to Italy? Remember how hell-bent she was on all the religious mumbo jumbo, and I said I wouldn't go dragging Colm to the far reaches of the earth for some voodoolike healing ritual, Catholic or otherwise?"

"Yes. I do. That's why I went. I knew someone had to talk some sense into her," Gaspar said and nodded.

"Truth is, Gaspar, I wanted to go. I really thought the trip was going to kill him, and I was worried. I was really worried. I wanted to be the one to protect him. I was glad you were there. I was glad of that. And I guess it all worked out in the end for you and Cathleen and all. But still, to this day, I've felt guilty for not going. I sometimes think he wouldn't have gotten so bad if I'd been there. I would have told her it was enough. That he'd had enough. She wouldn't have pushed him so hard. And then maybe I wouldn't have pushed him so hard. But the truth is, I didn't go because I was scared. I was ashamed. I didn't want to remember."

"What happened in Italy, Sean? Your sister told me that a long time ago you moved there, right after your mother died. She said you were going to be a priest, but you came back . . . excuse me . . . a drunk."

"She's right on all counts. But she doesn't know everything."

"What happened, Sean?"

Sean looked out past Gaspar. He knew there was no going back now. He had to tell him. He needed to tell him.

"There was this girl . . ."

Gaspar's eyes widened and relief fell over his entire face, even his tense shoulders slackening. "Oh, that's all."

Sean looked embarrassed. "Forget it. I shouldn't have said anything."

"No! No. I am sorry. I just thought . . . with that buildup . . . that you were going to say you killed someone. That you were evil or a serial killer or something."

"Too much *Dateline*, Doc. You and my sister watch too much television."

Gaspar exhaled a laugh. "Enough. Tell me more about this. I want to know. Does Cathleen know?"

"No. It's not like I ever told her. She was going through her own thing back then. It was almost eleven years ago. She'd gotten pregnant. Colm's father had already taken off. It wasn't exactly the best time to tell her that I'd pretty much done the same thing. Not exactly. I mean Chiara wasn't pregnant or anything, but I messed things up. I didn't realize how badly until I saw what Cathleen was going through and how unfair Colm's dad had been to her by taking off. I was so hard on him, but then I—I wasn't any better. I thought I was different. I thought I was better somehow, that I had a legitimate reason for breaking someone's heart . . ."

"Sean, people leave and break up every day for lots of reasons. Things just don't work out. That's life. You can't carry that guilt around forever. What can I do to make you feel better about this?"

"Lots."

"What?"

"There is a bag with my things right in that locker over in the corner. Could you pull out my wallet?"

Gaspar walked across the room, opened and then looked inside Sean's locker. For a second Gaspar had a flash of an altogether different scenario. He saw himself standing in a morgue and being handed a plastic bag:

> One wallet
> One set of keys
> One watch
> Two sticks of chewing gum
> One ticket stub to a matinee movie
> A sobriety chip

How different it all could have been. Gaspar took the wallet over to Sean and asked, "Now what?"

"Open up the wallet, Doc. There should be a piece of paper in there."

Gaspar pulled out a faded pink scrap. "It's just a receipt for a cup of coffee?" Gaspar asked, confused.

"Turn it over."

Gaspar flipped the receipt over and saw a list of crossed-out, handwritten names:

> ~~God~~
> ~~Mom~~
> ~~Cathleen~~
> ~~Gaspar~~

And then two that weren't:

Colm
Chiara

"What's this about, Sean? It's a bunch of names."

"Those are all the people I hurt . . . either when I was drinking or using or when I was trying to get clean and everything in between. I've tried to make amends. And I thought I got to a good place, at least a place where I wouldn't hurt anyone anymore."

"You did, Sean. You did. You've done beautifully. You don't have anything to make up to anyone else. You must stop this . . . this guilt you carry, especially about Colm. You have nothing to feel ashamed of or guilty about. Everything worked out for the best. For Colm. For your sister. For me. For you. Please. Please stop this. But I must ask, is this name, Chiara, the woman you're talking about from Italy?"

"She is. And I made a promise to myself that if I got out of that house, if I got out of that fire, I'd man up and I'd finally go back and make it right. Fix what I broke."

"And in the meantime fix you, too?"

"That's the plan."

"But how? I don't understand. What could you have done? You were just a kid back then."

"I was. But I was old enough to know better. To do better. I didn't."

"Sean, you can't beat yourself up over these things. We've been through this. You have to let some things go. To move on, you just have to let stuff go. These AA meetings, these twelve steps and whatnot, I know you think they work. I know you think by turning yourself over to a higher power, by repenting and feeling guilty and ashamed, you're somehow healing yourself. There are other ways. Alcoholism is a disease, Sean. It's not something you can pray away or repent for, no more than I can pray away and repent for my high cholesterol. I eat right and take a pill. I don't pray and regret all the years I ate too many sweets. It doesn't make me weak because I take a pill. No more than you would be weak if you just tell people you have an illness. Addiction is an illness. You're not at fault. You must stop this self-flagellation. You must. For yourself, for your sister, for me. You must."

"I can't, Gaspar. I can't. Not about this. Not about Colm. Never. I could have been better to him. And I can't forget about her. I just can't. I tried. For years I tried."

"I know, but you're an adult now. Sometimes it's best to just move on."

"But don't you think it means something? Don't you think it's some sort of sign?"

"I don't follow."

"I mean—of all the people to think of—just as my life was about to go up in smoke, I thought of her. I thought of *her*. It was her name I thought to speak. I promised myself if I got out of that mess, I'd be a better man. And, Gaspar, I think she holds the key."

"That's a dangerous assertion, Sean. She doesn't know she holds so much power. It's not fair to her. That's a lot of pressure. She's probably moved on. Have you thought of that?"

"It doesn't matter. I have to tell her I am sorry. I have to do this. I do."

"Sean, how do you know this isn't one of those lies you tell yourself? You said you've been lying to yourself for so long, how do you know if this isn't one of them?"

"It's not. You know, there was a point when I was trapped, I couldn't see my way out and I had this sense that if I could just get back to the spot where I started from—find that place, that center—I'd find my way home. And Chiara is that place. I realize that now. If I can just go back and make it right . . ."

"Then what? Live happily ever after? Sean, this is too much. You know who you sound like right now?"

"Don't even say it. Don't even bring his name into this." Sean spat the words out angrily.

"But I will. Because you were the one to bring him up first, and you know it's true. You sound just like Colm. Remember? If he just got to L.A., if he just found his father, if he just got to see him once . . . then everything would be perfect for him. His dad would be there waiting for him and tell him he loved him and would be part of his life . . ."

"That's not fair."

"What's not fair? You were the one who kept telling Colm what a mistake it was. You were the one warning your sister that she was setting the boy up for heartbreak . . . and what happened? You remember his face? Do you remember how heartbroken he was when he saw where he was? When he realized his father wasn't there and wasn't coming for him? When he finally realized his father wasn't the man he had built him up to be in his imagination? Do you remember what it did to him? Do you? Because I do. I do. I'll never forget it for as long as I live. No matter how long I live and how much I do in life, I will never ever be able to erase that pain he felt."

Sean's face grew red. Tears collected in the cracks around his eyes. "Shut up. Shut up. You hear me, Gaspar? Don't say another word. Shut up."

Gaspar stepped away from the bed and tried to give Sean space to collect himself. Looking out the window, Gaspar shoved his hands in his pockets and shrugged. Neither man said anything for a few minutes, until Gaspar broke the silence. "I'm sorry, Sean. I am. I didn't mean to upset you. It's just that, as your friend, as your brother-in-law, I don't think I can help you do this. You're injured and you're ill. You need to focus on getting better. If you must, pick up the phone and call the woman. Send her an e-mail. Make your peace. But I know what you're asking me to do. I already know what you want. You're asking me to get you out of this hospital and take you to Italy. You're basically asking me to help you bring back the dead. Make what died in the past alive in you again, and we both know that is never going to happen. Stop this, Sean. Stop it now. Just come home to New York. Come home to us. Let Cathleen and me take care of you."

"Just go. It was a mistake to call you. I was an idiot to tell you anything. Please just go. Take my keys. You can stay at my place tonight, but then just go back to my sister and the boys. They could use you more than I could at this point."

"Sean . . . I didn't mean to upset you. Please . . ."

"Thanks for making the trip. Take care. And if you can do one thing for me, please don't shoot your mouth off to my sister about any of this," Sean said, swallowing hard and then closing his eyes.

❧ Chapter 7

AFTER GASPAR LEFT, SEAN FELL INTO A FITFUL SLEEP. He had hoped to dream of Chiara. He'd been having dreams of her almost nightly since the fire, but he never saw her face. He could make out scenes of the two of them together in Italy. He saw her small hands in his. Her fingertips covered in pastels were swallowed completely by his large hands. He could see their feet together, walking in unison across the Ponte Vecchio, where throngs of tourists were pushing past them.

As they walked through Florence, he saw the ancient, smooth cobblestones, the black soot and dirt along the foundations of ancient buildings, but he could not for the life of him look down and see her face. He felt her hand slip out of his. Pulled away from her by the crowd, he lost sight of her for a second. Then as the crowd parted, he could see the back of her head. Waves of burgundy curls bounced as she ran from him. He chased her for miles, in and out of alleys and streets.

He found her and then lost her again in the piazza outside the Duomo. Its facade of elaborate polychrome marble panels, arranged in squares with shades of rose and forest green and white, reflected the afternoon light and blinded him momentarily. He held up his arms to block the light as he scanned the piazza looking for her. His eyes darted between the Baptistery of St. John and the giant cathedral with its iconic and gigantic octagonal brick dome. Between the two buildings he saw the Nigerian merchants wrapping their illegal knock-off Louis Vuitton and Gucci bags into large blankets and running with their bundles from the *polizia,* whose sirens Sean could hear approaching from close behind. For a moment he thought he saw her enter the stairway that led to the tower overlook, which was located inside the museum gift shop. He looked up and could see the top of the Duomo, and he remembered the day that the two of them stood on the viewing tower looking down over the rolling hills, the red-roofed homes, and Santa Croce in the distance. Her body was warm. Her arms were wrapped tightly around him.

It could always be like this, Sean. It could.

It was stolen time. He wasn't supposed to be there with her. He was never supposed to be there. His seminarian collar was shoved in his pants pocket. A jacket covered his black-collared shirt. But he was with her. He climbed up the dark, cavernous steps, feeling the cool stone walls as he made his ascent. The steps became narrower as he neared the top. His large body squeezed through the passages. It seemed to take an hour to get to the top and he struggled to catch his breath. Finally, he reached the summit. He could see Santa Croce to the southeast—its distinct terra-cotta roof and white *facciata* that looked like a child's game board from so far away. He turned. There she was. He could see all of her. Her large amber-colored eyes staring right at him, her thin lips pursed into a pout, the kind a spoiled child would make after being denied a treat, the type that was impossible to sustain. He smiled at her and her pout gave way to a laugh. Her nose crinkled with the facility of a bunched-up sleeve of a linen shirt. The dimple in her right cheek appeared with the grin. Sean reached for her, but she ran by him and disappeared back down the stairs. He couldn't keep up with her anymore. All he wanted was for her to turn her face toward him. One more time. All he wanted was to see her face. Hold it in his hands. Look into her eyes a bit longer and feel what it was like to be looked at by someone who loved him completely. He shouted her name, and she disappeared. He lost her somehow to the sea. It confused him for a moment, but he got his bearings. *California*. Somehow he was no longer in Florence.

A giant ocean opened up for him at the edge of the piazza. Sean grabbed his board, waiting for him in the sand below, and before he knew it he was back on the water. Sitting on his board, he looked back toward shore and watched as the sun rose behind the mash-up of old-Bohemian homes and ultramodern mansions and storefronts that lined the Venice Beach seashore. Sean could see the window to the one-bedroom apartment that he rented just a block behind Ocean Front Walk on Venice Beach. He looked past the initial row of jam-packed properties, glass-enclosed apartments, and store-fronts. He tried to find her face among the people walking up and down the walk. He turned and noticed throngs of other morning surfers out, too, vying for position alongside him. Sitting like Sean with their legs wide over their boards, their torsos bobbing up and down in rhythm together, they appeared to Sean to be in some sort of worshipper trance. *A new type of morning mass.* For a moment, Sean forgot Chiara. He forgot what he was chasing.

Sean saw a wave far out on the horizon before anyone else. *Jackpot!* he said to himself. He swung his body around and paddled hard. His broad shoulders were wider than the board, and he knew he could make time faster than men half his size. His forearms bulged under his wet suit as he pushed, hard, away from the group of other surfers. After just a few more hearty strokes, he looked back and noticed that no one else was going for the wave. He was the only one. *Impossible.* He shook his head and laughed at the others who just sat and waited. As he reached the swell, he popped up in one fluid motion. His arms extended out as he balanced on the board. He swung the board to the left and directed it into an oncoming wave. He disappeared under the crest. He held his fingertips out and felt the water swallow him.

Sean could hear his friend James talking to him. He couldn't see him, but Sean could hear his voice: *There is a moment in every swell, man, and in every wave caught, a moment when the water could take you, man. Or it can spit you out and send you flying across its surface. That's what you want. You want to get spit out. It defies logic. But you do. It beats the alternative: being swallowed and digested. Believe me. But the moment is so fleeting that most people miss it. They miss the subtlety of it. Every good surfer knows what to do when that moment comes. And once that moment passes, there is no going back. What is done is done. Sink or soar. The moment when the wave meets the board, wraps itself around it, and invites it to come in. One hesitation—even the smallest gesture at all of unwillingness—will let the wave know that you're not ready. It's all or nothing with the wave. She wants you all in, man. So you need to find that perfect moment between the rise and the fall. Right there; that's where you'll find it.*

Sean felt the moment. It swelled. Expanded. Not just the wave, but time. Sean could see the tip of his board, and could feel the speed and force building below him. He could feel her—this wave—pushing him toward the light and making her way toward the shore as he glided through.

Sean could feel its perfection. *What a ride.* And it was glorious. The morning sun from the east illuminated the white foam crashing outside the crest so it appeared as if a halo of sacred water surrounded him. His hands felt the coolness as the wall of water enveloped him. He was whole and perfect. Alive. For the first time, he thought, if only for a second, he wasn't missing his moment.

The moment was his. *This is life. This is life. This is all I need.* "Yes!" he shouted.

"Yes!"

But Sean looked back and the water was turning colors behind him. It was no longer blue. Behind him a swirl of orange and red was chasing him. He looked down and saw the flesh on his hands burning, turning black before his eyes, the flesh melting and dripping off the bone. He was touching fire. He heard cries outside the flames. Everyone on shore and in the water was screaming at him to get out.

Just get out.

Sean's legs buckled. The pain was extraordinary. He felt

it all the way up his spine, where it settled in the base of his neck. He fell off his board and continued to fall and fall and fall. There seemed to be no end to it.

Until there was.

Sean jolted awake in the dark room. He looked at his hands, wrapped, secure, and burned; and, he was sure, still disfigured underneath the bandages. He felt the throbbing ache in his head and looked around at the four walls surrounding him, closing in on him with each passing second. He pushed his morphine button. Though he knew only one dose was allowed and nothing more would come out even if he tried, he pushed it again. Like the addict he was and would forever be, even if he never had another drop to drink or popped another pill, he would always be chased by it. He knew this. And he, too, would always be chasing it. The moment. *The aw, man. The yes, yes, it-could-always-be-like-this moment.* He pushed the button again and again and again and again and again— hoping to chase that ephemeral and intangible moment before the sobering burn set in.

ℋ Chapter 8

G ASPAR TURNED THE KEY, ENTERED SEAN'S APART-
ment, and dropped his bag by the door. It had all gone
wrong. Cathleen had asked him to do one thing: convince her brother to come home. And all Gaspar managed to
do within a few hours of landing in Los Angeles was to get
kicked out of Sean's hospital room. Her request was going to
be more difficult than he had anticipated.

Thirsty and hungry, Gaspar headed straight for the kitchenette that opened into the small living space. He opened the
refrigerator and was instantly assaulted by the fetid smell of
rotten meat. *Not one person*, Gaspar thought, *had the sense
to come here and take care of Sean's place. Take out the trash,
pick up the mail.* "What if he had a pet?" Gaspar wondered
aloud how one could become so isolated, so removed from
others that they didn't have anyone to sort their mail, clean
their fridge, and take out the trash. From the looks of the
fridge, Gaspar had to guess Sean had gone grocery shopping

the day before the fire. It was stocked with a week's worth of steaks, eggs, vegetables, club soda, and limes that had grown fuzz and collapsed inward. Gaspar quickly shut the door, and covered his face with a towel he grabbed from the counter while rummaging through cabinets and drawers looking for a garbage bag and some bleach to begin cleaning.

As Gaspar threw the contents of Sean's refrigerator in the trash, he grew annoyed. Something besides the smell gnawed at him. Gaspar threw a half-filled jar of tomato sauce so hard, he missed the trash can altogether and it smashed against the dishwasher door. Sauce spattered all over the cabinets, on the porcelain tile, and as far away as the door to the apartment. It wasn't until Gaspar heard the glass shatter, saw the cabinets appear as if they were bleeding, as if they, too, felt cut open, that he was even aware of his anger. He wasn't just angry at Sean's friends, or lack thereof, or at Sean, or God, or anyone else he could see fit to blame if he really wanted to. He was angry with himself. He should have known something was wrong. He should have tried harder to be a better friend. Gaspar grabbed a sponge, turned on the faucet, and let hot water pour over his hands. He stood for what seemed an infinite time, letting the water run, the steam rising up in front of his face, fogging his glasses. He wanted to feel the burn. Wanted to feel just a bit what Sean was feeling right now. But he couldn't take the pain. He shut off the faucet and pounded his fist on the countertop. "Dammit! Dammit! Dammit! Dammit!" Gaspar yelled. It felt so good to let it out. He did it again and again.

After he calmed himself by shouting one expletive after another, which he'd never before uttered in his life, he collected himself and tried to decide what he had to do next. "Where does one begin to clean up such a giant mess?" Gaspar asked himself aloud, reaching into the sink and wringing out the sponge, then giving it a hearty shake. *On one's knees,* Gaspar thought to himself. *On one's knees.*

While Gaspar scrubbed, his anger dissipated. There was something so therapeutic about the act of cleaning, wiping away remnants of the despoiled day. Even if hot water couldn't do it, he could erase it all just by sheer will. He could wipe away every sin, every transgression, every regret. His own. His friend's. And so Gaspar set out to scrub away Sean's past six rotten weeks, or at least the parts he was capable of expunging, on his knees, one scrubbed tile at a time.

After an hour of frenetic cleaning, Gaspar realized the apartment was filling with a pink glow. Putting down his cleaning supplies on the lone table in the living-dining-kitchen area of Sean's infinitesimally small apartment, Gaspar looked for the source of the light, crossed the room, and pulled back a set of linen curtains. As he did, Gaspar noticed for the first time just how close Sean was to the Pacific Ocean. He pulled the sliding glass door and walked outside. He stepped out on the balcony and inhaled deeply.

Gaspar could see that Sean had set out one chair, and beside it was a small table with a little potted plant that had wilted in the hot sun. A book, *The Perfect Day,* lay on the table next to the plant. From the look of the placement of the bookmark, it appeared that Sean was just beginning the book. Gaspar picked up the book and flipped through the pages that included several pictures of surfers in various positions on their boards, not unlike the cover of the book, which depicted a surfer being dwarfed by a giant wave. It was difficult for Gaspar to picture Sean—his pale Irish skin, his immense legs, his bearlike physique, popping up on a surfboard, let alone living among tan Californians. Gaspar shook his head and put the book back down.

He stood for as long as his tired legs would allow him and looked out at the horizon. Eventually he succumbed to his exhaustion and sat down to try to see what Sean saw. He tried to envision Sean's life. It wasn't a stretch for his imagination. Gaspar had a pretty solid idea of what Sean's days were like.

He remembered all of his own early years in New York. Alone. Sitting. Waiting. Waiting for what, he was never sure. But there came a time when he had lost hope he'd ever find anyone else after losing his wife, Niranjana, to suicide after their only son, Dhruv, had succumbed to malaria. Yes, Gaspar Basu knew what it was like to resign oneself to a life alone. To resign oneself to sleepless nights looking at stars and ruminating on one's place in the cosmos, to days spent picking up and working extra shifts, to working oneself to the point of exhaustion, if only to fall asleep a little quicker, to feel just a little less—less tired, less scared, less lonely, less hopeless, less wanting.

But then one day all that changed. Cathleen Magee arrived with her sick boy and a fifteen-minute examination turned into a life. One appointment, one chance meeting held the possibility of turning one's entire world around. *How many times did it happen in a day, a week, a year, a century?* Gaspar marveled. Strangers meet. Smile. Laugh. Hold hands. Time and an accumulation of shared experiences turn into love and then marriage and then children. Just like the Big Bang. From out of seemingly nothing comes an entirely new universe. Just like that. Over and over again. The multiverse theorists and quantum physicists had a point, Gaspar knew. The possibility of more than one universe made sense, just as humans had an infinite capacity to multiply, expand, illuminate, and even collapse, leaving behind dark matter and energy. It happened every day.

How quickly Gaspar's life had changed since that day in his office. He'd been so lonely just a few years ago and then, as if instantaneously, his life had become so abundant. So busy. So filled with people and their problems and their needs and their love. It made those years he'd spent alone, without a friend, let alone a family all his own, seem all the more distant, all the more lonely.

Yes, Gaspar knew exactly what Sean's days were like.

Was this, Gaspar wondered, *how the universe really worked? Did there need to be a balance in the universe of loneliness, too? Were only a certain number of people permitted to find joy at the same time?* It was ridiculous to wonder it, but he wondered all the same. He had been alone for so long, and then suddenly, from out of nowhere, he absorbed, like the process of osmosis, simply by proximity and a need for balance, the love of a family. Was his gain Sean's loss?

Until this moment, it had never occurred to Gaspar what price his new life came with. That for every love gained someone else has to learn to let go. Someone else had to say good-bye to the way of life they had always come to know. A father kisses his daughter good-bye on her wedding day. A mother watches her boy take her car keys; watches her very own heart disappear into grown-up oblivion. A friend watches as her best friend marries or moves on. One's gain is another's heart-break. Cathleen had been Sean's world; Colm, his universe. And then they all drove to Los Angeles, hoping for a miracle, hoping for some sign that the universe made sense after all, and right before them the universe shifted once again. And nothing made sense. And yet it all did.

But no matter what, sense or no sense, Sean was the one left sitting alone and waiting.

Gaspar stood up and walked around the apartment. There were several pictures on the wall. From what Gaspar could make out, they were photos that Sean had taken of the waves crashing at dawn and dusk, of sunburned surfers carrying their boards out to the shoreline, of palm trees seemingly black against a setting pink sun, of rows of silk floss and jacaranda trees in full bloom lining suburban streets, of skaters with odd haircuts and brightly colored and intricate tattoos, and of beauties spilling out of bathing suits and wearing large, expensive, bedazzling sunglasses. Sean had somehow saturated the colors, Gaspar guessed, so they appeared more vibrant than they would in real life. He accentuated the details and the contrast, so the pictures had an element of texture, too. It was as if Gaspar could feel the fabric on surfers' wet suits and the sand in their hair; touch the soft petals of the blooming jacarandas. Gaspar was incredulous. He'd never taken Sean for an artist. Not in a million years. There was nothing famil-iar about this new Sean.

He remembered something Cathleen had said to him many years earlier. "He has a way of changing, Gaspar, only you can't see it happening because it is so gradual. And just when you get used to one version of him, he emerges as someone entirely new, like a phoenix rising from the ashes over and over. He was a wild kid who wanted to be a pilot back then but ended up this studious philosopher type, then a seminarian, then a drunk, then a firefighter, then a drunk again. It took him so long to find his place. I used to worry all the time that he wouldn't find his way, but now, I know he'll be okay. No matter what happens, I know he'll be okay." Gaspar couldn't wait to tell Cathleen, *You won't believe this, hon. He takes pictures. He's quite good. He even surfs now. You don't have to worry. He'll find something new again . . .*

Gaspar scanned the room and took it all in as if for the first time, as if he hadn't been there for an hour cleaning it. Two custom surfboards—one long, one short—hung on metal wall racks. Books filled a series of well-made, though worn, oak barrister bookcases. Gaspar saw no television or radio, and let out a small laugh at the realization: without Yankees games, neither the radio or TV would be of much use to Sean. Gaspar took a mental inventory. He knew his wife would ask, "What's his place like? Does he need anything? Has he got enough clean towels? Good pots and pans? What's his couch like?" Gaspar noted the midcentury maple table and its lacquered surface. It had all the markings of a secondhand-store purchase. Four faux-antiqued and French Provincial–painted chairs surrounded it. An overstuffed, eighties-era leather love seat was so worn that the deep espresso-colored leather faded into beige splotches where the cushions met and flattened in the middle. None of the furnishings seemed to match the other. The entire place was a hodgepodge of decorating styles that would make the interior designer in his wife cringe. It was utilitarian at best, institutional at worst. But totally Sean. Gaspar knew that Sean simply never cared about *stuff.*

Gaspar walked into Sean's bedroom. His bed was made with military precision, the corners tucked tautly. The top sheet folded crisply over the navy blue blanket. A pile of surfing and oceanography books covered with cellophane dust jackets and Dewey decimal labels were stacked neatly on his bedside table. Gaspar turned and looked in the mirror above the dresser. Stuck up in the seam of wood trim was one photo. Gaspar inhaled, put his hand up, and touched it, closing his eyes and remembering the Santa Monica Pier. Three years earlier. The night before they took the boy, who hoped to see his father, to the hill with an observatory overlooking Los Angeles. Gaspar could see the moment on the pier in real time. Sean was smiling wildly, happier than he had been in years. Colm was alight with hope and anticipation for what was to come the next day. Sean was holding the boy after a ride with Gaspar on the Ferris wheel; Colm's head was resting in the crook of his uncle's neck. Gaspar snapped the photo just as Sean leaned in and rested his own head on the boy's. A perfect moment. Sean's *A Perfect Day.*

Gaspar took the picture down from the mirror and held it in his hands for several minutes before hanging it back up.

He knew he must help Sean. He owed him that much.

Chapter 9

T HE FOLLOWING MORNING, AS GASPAR WALKED DOWN the hallway to Sean's hospital room, he felt a sense of urgency he hadn't experienced since he'd been trying to find a cure for Colm five years earlier. He wanted to tell Sean everything all at once. *I spoke to Cathleen last night. She understands. She insists that I help you get to Italy.* Gaspar couldn't wait to tell him how Cathleen said she'd go with Sean to Italy herself if she could. He didn't doubt it. *Long story short,* Gaspar thought of saying and rehearsing the words, *We're going to get you better.* He spent the morning making phone calls. He had spoken to a burn rehab specialist, a physical therapist, and his neighborhood VNA back in New York. They were going to start working with Sean immediately. Sean had a solid six months of intensive therapy ahead of him, possibly a year. They couldn't get him to Italy any sooner than that. In the meantime, all Gaspar had to do was find a private jet to airlift Sean back east. It would take him only a day or so to finalize the arrangements and then—poof—they'd all be together again.

Gaspar entered the room as the doctor on morning rounds was exiting.

"Morning, sir. How is the patient today?" Gaspar said brightly, hoping for some medical banter. But without his white coat and stethoscope, Gaspar just looked like another hospital guest.

"Looking better every day. Go see for yourself." The young doctor rushed out, barely making eye contact.

Next patient, Gaspar thought. He knew the drill. "Have a great day!" Gaspar shouted back down the hall. "Nice talking with you!"

Before Gaspar could wait for a response from the harried doctor, he heard Sean's voice.

"I thought I told you to go home," Sean said.

"Good morning, Sean. It's a beautiful day," Gaspar said, coming in quickly and pulling back the room's curtains.

"Guess so. It's not like I'll be out enjoying it," Sean said, trying to adjust his torso with a small wriggle. Moving even an inch caused Sean to wince in pain.

"Well, that's what I came to talk about. I called your sister. I told her everything . . . and . . . ."

"You what? I thought I said I didn't want your help. I thought I said I didn't want you talking to my sister," Sean snapped.

"I know what you want, Sean. Listen to me. I am sorry about yesterday. I didn't understand . . . until I did. I understand now and I want to make it up to you."

"No, you were right. I sounded like a fool. I think you were pretty clear."

"I am sorry. And no, you didn't sound like a fool, Sean. Why is it so foolish to admit something? I was a fool to laugh, to dismiss you. Cathleen and I have made some arrangements this morning. She's hired a physical therapist and a visiting nurse. She's setting up a room at our apartment as we speak, and in six months, maybe a year . . . we'll get you to . . ."

"No."

"What?"

"No, I am not going back to New York. No, I am not going to have my pregnant sister take care of me like I am some baby. No, I am not going to give up the life I've worked hard to create out here."

"What life, Sean? You're all alone and you have no job keeping you here. And as far as I'm concerned, there is no one who cares enough to even visit you, look in after you, take care of your apartment, get your mail." Gaspar stopped talking, realizing how harsh it sounded.

"It's my life, dammit. My damned life," Sean shouted.

"Sean, please. Let us help you."

"Help me do what? Huh?"

"Get better. We can make sure you get the best care. We can make sure you're not alone . . ."

Sean averted his eyes and tried not to look at Gaspar. He seemed to be bracing himself. Sweat poured down over his eyebrows. He gritted his teeth.

"Sean? What's wrong?"

"It hurts."

"What?"

"Everything. My back. My legs. All of it. The pain meds . . . they wear off and I can't take any more drugs. They have limits on them. But it just hurts so bad."

"Sean, please. Please, we beg you. Your sister wants to help you. You know her. She loves you. Come home and let us help you."

"I'm not going anywhere. I'll find my own help. I don't want to be a burden. You, Cathleen, the boys, you have your own lives now."

"Sean, you're not a burden. You're family."

"I got this. Okay? Drop it. I got this."

"What if I got you help here? What if I got you out of here and got you a nurse and a physical therapist?" Gaspar said quickly, trying desperately to appease him.

Sean's eyes turned back toward Gaspar.

"You'd do that?"

"Of course I would. I want you to get better. If you want to get better, if you want to go see this woman, Chiara, and make it right, then you have to get better."

"Chiara? So you're going to help me with that, too? You can get me to Italy?" Sean asked, confused. "But last night . . . last night . . . you basically said it was silly. You thought it was a dumb idea."

"I was wrong, Sean. I see that now. This is your life. Yours. Not anyone else's. Sometimes I forget that. Sometimes when I am doling out advice I forget that I am not the one who has to live with the consequences. Someone else does. As a doctor, I do it every day. I make informed decisions and I suggest things that make sense to me, on paper, but sometimes, some decisions can't be made by someone else, no matter how much experience, no matter how much knowledge he or she has. I don't know what's in my patients' hearts. I had a plan for Colm. I was so sure my plan would be the plan to solve everything. But you remember, Colm had another plan. I didn't know, back then, what was in his heart any more than I know what's in your heart now. If there is one thing this life has taught me it's that our choices have to be our own, Sean. Whatever we choose for ourselves, the choices have to be entirely our own, otherwise we're living the consequences of another's decision, another's judgments, consequences that the one meting out the advice doesn't have to live with five months down the road, let alone five years. And it's usually advice the giver won't even remember giving. I don't want you living your life based on what I think you should do. I think the first step in getting you better will be you owning all of your decisions. From here on out, that's what you'll do. Ten years from now, it won't matter to me in the least if you do or don't find this woman. But it could mean all the difference in the world to you. So you make that choice. You."

Sean sat for a second and said nothing. He wanted to think about what Gaspar had just said. He wanted to go back and think about how many decisions he'd made in his life based on the insights of others, based on what other people thought of him, expected from him. He thought about how many times he'd listened, and how many times he hadn't. He thought of his mother and his sister, who both gave him advice knowing they would be the ones living the consequences right along with him. He thought of his mother's voice, the joy in it, when he told her he wanted to be a priest and how that joy, that pleasing her, meant more to him than anything else in the world. He thought of the fear and pain he felt when he didn't think he could do it, and the worry he felt that even though she was dead and long gone, she would somehow have disapproved of him anyway for leaving the seminary. Sean also thought of the priest in Florence who told him that he was sinning, and told Sean that he needed to repent, told Sean that he needed to let the girl he loved go. He wondered where that priest was. He wasn't living the consequences of that choice. Sean was. Sean thought about some of the advice he had given over the years, too. His fair share, he was sure. And he shuddered, remembering how he scolded little Colm, screamed at him for being selfish, for wanting to find his real dad, and how heartbroken and lost the boy was, sobbing into his shoulder, *Why doesn't he love me? Does he know how much I love him—want to know him?*

"I know what you mean, Gaspar," Sean admitted.

"I know you do. Now are you going to let me help you?"

"Sure," Sean said in resignation.

"I have some calls to make. But I'll find you someone here. I won't be able to stay much longer than a week though. Your sister, you know she's due in a few weeks; I must be there. And my practice . . . I just can't leave it."

"I know. I understand. It's okay. I'll be okay."

"You're sure? Absolutely positive? I was at your place and it doesn't look like anyone has been by or taking care of stuff for you. Do you have someone paying your bills?"

"Not at the moment."

"I'll take care of that before I go. I'll make all the arrangements."

"You don't have to do that. I'll get somebody."

"But I do. I worry that you're all . . . alone . . ."

"Gaspar, I have some buddies out here. They're not great housekeepers. They wouldn't think to check my apartment, but they do care, Gaspar. They do. People just have different ways of showing it. Some guys visit me every day. My buddy James, for instance, was the one who taught me to surf. He showed me around when I first moved in. He's a solid guy. You know he's the one who saved my life the day of the fire? I lost my heartbeat, and he brought me back."

"Good friend to have around."

"Ya think?" Sean winked.

"So, Sean, you are sure? You are sure you're not too lonely here?"

"I'm sure. I'll be okay. I will."

"I hope so. Your sister will never forgive me if something happens to you."

"I know. Believe me, I know. I am sorry about being such an ass these past couple of days. I know it wasn't an easy trip. These meds are messing with my head. I don't feel like myself."

"Please, don't apologize. I was the one who walked in here and pushed you too hard, too soon. I had no right."

"You're all right, Gaspar. You're all right."

"So . . . ?" Gaspar asked, changing the subject, and blushing from Sean's compliment. "Let's talk about something else. I'm here to stay for a while."

"What do you want to talk about?"

"Why don't you tell me what happened the day of the fire? I still don't feel like I got the whole story."

"No? I thought we covered it."

"Not really. We got at each other's throats so quickly when I first arrived that you never told me the entire story. You never told me how exactly you got out of that fire. You said a house exploded in flames. How did you jump from a house and live?"

"It's a miracle, isn't it? That's what everyone keeps telling me."

"A miracle? That doesn't sound like the Sean I know. Now you sound like your sister, Cathleen."

Sean laughed. "Seriously, it was the craziest thing. You're going to think I am nuts . . . but . . . nah . . . forget it . . . forget I ever said anything."

"No, what? Tell me. I won't laugh this time. Promise." Gaspar crossed his heart, like Colm used to when he was a little boy.

Cross my heart, Uncle Sean! Sean could almost see him there standing in the room beside Gaspar and making the motions across his heart.

"Do you believe in . . . Aw, shit. Forget it." Sean meant to shake his head, but couldn't.

"What? After everything we've been through, everything we've talked about over the years, you can't ask me something . . . just shoot."

"I already know the answer, Gaspar. I know that you're going to think I am nuts."

"What? Just ask already."

"Do you believe in angels, Doc?"

"As in the beings with wings? Or like Clarence in *It's a Wonderful Life*?"

"I guess they can come in all shapes, all forms. Some have wings. Some are invisible. Some look like us. Some come to us as light. They're supposed to be messengers, God's messengers. They're supposed to send us messages, signs. I think the Hindus believe in them. I know the Catholics do. Muslims and Jews do, too, I think. But, do you, Gaspar Basu, believe in them?"

"Why are you asking?"

"I just want to know. Your answer will determine whether I tell you my crazy story or not."

"I can see where this is going, Sean. So yes, for the purposes of you telling me your crazy story, I believe."

"Nope. That's not a real answer."

"Sean, it doesn't matter what I believe. We've been through this. You have to trust your own experiences. Everybody has their own, his or her own truth. If they say they've seen angels, heaven, their dead son or daughter, their grandmother or best friend, then who am I or anyone else to judge them? They know what they saw, what they felt. Remember your sister? How she was so sure, so absolutely sure she could see your mother? Remember when we were in the hospital in L.A., how she claimed your mother told her Colm would be okay, would live a long life? There was no arguing with Cathleen, no telling her otherwise. We were there, too. We didn't see anything. But for her it was real. And then there was Colm, back when he was really sick . . . no matter what Cathleen said to him, assured him, no matter what priests told him, he was adamant, he couldn't see heaven. He hadn't seen it for himself . . ."

Sean cut Gaspar off. "I get it, I get it . . ."

"So you know what I am getting at. Just tell me. Help me understand what happened. What you're going through."

"I swear to God, I am not making this up, Gaspar. I wasn't on any drugs. I wasn't hallucinating."

"I believe you."

"I was sent up into this tinderbox. No one knew about all the combustibles in the basement, all we knew about was the balloon framing, which basically meant that fire could get trapped in the walls. I went up two flights to check to see if there was any damage up there or fire. We all thought the fire was out. On the surface, everything looked good. But still, in structures like those, it is procedure to knock out some walls and make sure no fire is behind them. No one actually thought the fire was up there. But there was an explosion in the basement just as I threw my ax right into a wall. The room filled with fire. The explosion threw me clear across the room. I hit my head. I was out for some time, while the room burned and filled with smoke. When I woke up, I had no idea where I was. I thought I was trapped. There was so much black smoke, I couldn't see in front of me. The floor was burning right below me. I knew the room was close to the flashover stage. Once that happens—the room is about 1200 degrees. There's no surviving that. I would have been a Sean barbecued sandwich—for a limited time for ninety-nine cents, come and get it! There was a point when I just knew I was a goner."

"Sean, Sean, Sean," Gaspar repeated like a mantra and closed his eyes, imagining the horror. *The could have been.*

"So I said a prayer. Promised myself a long time ago that if I ever found myself in a similar predicament I wouldn't be a hypocrite and declare my devotion to our lord and savior and all that crap, but I did. I said a damned prayer. Promised God or whoever was listening, angels, saints, my dead mom and dad, whoever, I'd be a better man if I got out of there, and just like that, this angel appears from out of nowhere. She was so bright, and it felt so real, and I followed her and just as I got to the window, she disappeared. She got me out of there. I got to the window and I just jumped. A second after I did, the room flashed over and the entire floor gave way. The house exploded behind me. If it weren't for that angel, I'd be, I'd be . . ."

"Dead," Gaspar finished, tight-lipped and with a nod.

"Yes. I'd be dead. But I am not. And I can't help but wonder why. And I can't exactly go around telling people that an angel saved me. Or that I have some divine purpose now, some reason to be alive today. I can't very well do that. Not now, not after all the bullshit I put my sister through telling her she was crazy all those years she went searching for miracles to save Colm . . ."

"Sean, I understand. I do. But it could be a lot of things . . ."

"Yes, that's what I want to hear. I need to hear some common sense. I need some sort of scientific reason. Tell me one, Gaspar. Please, because I feel like I am losing my mind."

"Well, for one, you said the angel led you to a window. Are you sure the sun wasn't coming through the window? That it wasn't some sort of aberration? Some trick of your eyes? An optical illusion?"

"No, I am sure it wasn't. It was black as night. The window was covered in smoke. Next try . . ."

"You said you were unconscious at some point? Did I hear

that correctly? You lost your way? Your head injury could have caused you to hallucinate. You could have been dreaming or suffering from oxygen deprivation. It could have been a stroke of good luck—that you happened to see a person—but actually you were already on your way in the right direction for the window."

Sean smiled. He liked hearing Gaspar try to reason away the unfathomable. There was a secret thrill in it. And Gaspar was so good at making the irrational so banal. But there was a part of him he wasn't going to reveal to Gaspar. *I saw her before, Gaspar. I saw this angel of light before.*

"And then there is the most obvious reason for why you didn't see an angel . . ."

"Oh? What's that?" Sean asked.

"Well, if an angel was going to go through all the trouble to save you . . . why stop there? Why stop at the window? You were three stories up. Why didn't she just carry you to the ground safely?"

Sean let out a loud laugh and slapped his own leg. "Ouch!" he said, realizing again that his hands still hurt and so did his legs. "Yeah, it was just some sort of illusion. I know. Thanks, Doc. You're right. It's all a bunch of nonsense."

"Now, now, that's not what I am saying. You asked me for logical reasons. I gave you some. But the illogical can't be ignored either. It is illogical that you're even here today talking to me. All of my textbooks, all of my experience in medicine tells me that you should be dead. So there is something there. There is space for the irrational. Always."

"So you think there's a chance that all of this—me being here—isn't just some fluke? That there is a reason bigger than me? That maybe I have a second chance for a reason?"

"Maybe. As a man who is living his second chance, I have to say it's not something to take lightly. And angel or no, the facts are irrefutable. You are here. For whatever reason, Sean, you have a second shot. And you have to remember, like you said, angels come in all sorts of shapes and forms. You have lots of angels looking out for you—here and now. And maybe *you're* the angel with a message, a purpose that you need to fulfill here on earth."

"So you agree there was a reason—why I am here?"

"Yes, my friend. I agree. But maybe you need to look at it another way, too."

"How's that?"

"Stop thinking in terms of chances—first, second, third— whatever. Think of it in terms of phases, chapters, if you will. You're just turning a page, moving on to the next chapter. Nothing to be ashamed of in the previous ones. You're just moving forward, like everyone else in the world. But now you've got the perspective you didn't have before. Now you know how important it is to savor every moment."

"But don't you have any regrets, Gaspar? Don't you ever think there was a better way? Have you ever looked back and known you so fundamentally screwed up that you can't possibly go on?"

"Of course, I think everybody does. I have many. Too many."

"So how do you do it?"

"How do I do *what* exactly?"

"How do you get up? Start over? Go on? Live out your second chance, chapter, or whatever you want to call it, knowing the people you loved once don't get to, or knowing that they might be out there living their life without you, without a second thought about you?"

"Some days I try to be a little nicer, a little more patient. Sometimes, I try to smile a bit more. I try to make up for all the years I wasn't so nice, so patient, so pleasant to Niranjana and to Dhruv. I can't go back and be kind to them. But I can be kind to others. I can't bring my dead wife back. I can't undo a lot of things, Sean. You're right. And you know that, too. You do. That's not our job. So I try to be a bit better, every day. That's all we can do."

"I regret so much though. I've screwed up so many times. I don't know where to even begin making up for it."

"Sean, stop. Just stop."

"Stop what?"

"Thinking about the past, Sean. Stop. I know it's easier said than done. But a wise boy once told me that thinking about the past can make you angry or sad, and thinking about the future can only make you anxious. But there is a space in between the past and the future. It's the present. It's right now. So rest there, Sean. Rest there. You have nothing to regret in this moment. No mistakes have been made. Nothing is about to happen. If you just stay here." Gaspar put his hand on Sean's heart and tapped it. "Right here. Stay right here."

❧ Chapter 10

GASPAR STAYED IN LOS ANGELES WITH SEAN FOR A full week as promised. It took the better part of every day for him to make all the necessary arrangements for Sean to return to his apartment and have around-the-clock care.

Sean amazed Gaspar with his progress. In just a remarkable seven days, a mere seven weeks from jumping out of the building, Sean was able to sit up. His head was removed from the stabilizer and his neck was fitted for a brace. The bandages on his hands were removed and protective gloves slid on; he could finally use his hands to hold his own drink.

Though several doctors had explained to Sean about the injuries he'd incurred, Sean admitted to Gaspar that he didn't quite grasp what they were telling him. So Gaspar called for Sean's CT scans and X-rays, and the two sat together looking at the glow of Sean's insides. Gaspar used a pen as a pointer to show Sean that he had two clean breaks in each of his femurs.

Almost identical. He showed Sean the before photos—the two femurs, snapped and jagged black lines through white bones. Sean winced in pain just looking at the films, though the initial excruciatingly acute pain of the break had long since faded to a throbbing, constant one.

Then Gaspar held up the post-op films. Each of Sean's legs now had four screws drilled into it: two at each side of his hips and two in each of his knees to support the rods placed to help the bones heal. Gaspar explained how the screws would eventually have to be removed. Sean shook his head in disbelief.

"So another surgery?"

"Sort of. You'll be awake. They may give you a twilight drug. Numb the area. No big deal."

"How come you doctors are always telling us patients that it's no big deal? Have you ever had titanium rods stuck in your body and up your ass?"

Gaspar laughed and said, "Point taken. Speaking of asses . . ." Gaspar pulled up another set of films.

He showed Sean how his bones had been fused above the coccyx and sacrum between the lumbar and thoracic area of the spine.

"And this," Gaspar said, brushing a long stroke of his pen against the film, "this is a Zielke rod placed in the L1–L3. These are pedicle screws in the L3 and L4. You're lucky your spine was not severed, Sean. It's a miracle. If it had been, you would never be able to walk again. You'll regain most motor functions eventually. Bending may be an issue, since the lumbar area is where you need the most flexibility," Gaspar warned Sean, "but for the most part, with physical therapy, you will eventually walk and regain enough to do most of your activities."

Sean looked at the pieces of himself, broken inside, now held together with rods and screws and pins that looked like a series of chains. "For once my body looks like how I feel inside. Shattered," Sean remarked quite melodramatically.

"Or," Gaspar paused, "stronger than ever. Now that you're reinforced."

"Ever the optimist, Doc."

"No, a realist. You're on your way to getting better inside and out."

"But I won't be able to fight fires? Surf? Do any of the things I love? Any of the things that make me who I am? How is that good news?"

"Maybe it's time, once again, my friend, to redefine who you are. Or better yet, stop defining yourself by what you do for a living or how you have fun, but rather by what you believe."

In Sean's first day out of bed, he was moved into a mechanical recumbent wheelchair. Gaspar and James walked alongside him as he practiced using the buttons and steering himself. Pleased to finally be out of his room, Sean took a long ride through the corridors of the hospital. They passed by nurses' stations, waiting rooms, and patients' rooms, some where patients were crying out in pain and some where only the sounds of a game show wheel spinning could be heard.

Sean hated it.

"I gotta get out of here, guys. It's killing me," Sean said.

"One more week," James assured him, "and then you're sprung."

"I've made all the arrangements," Gaspar added. "A gentleman nurse by the name of Tom, and with great luck he is also a physical therapist, will meet you and James the day after I leave. He's agreed to care for you during the day and help with your rehabilitation. I'll have a night nurse as well. James will fill in here and there. Isn't that right, James?" Gaspar nodded in James's direction.

"Yes, sir," James said, giving him a false, friendly salute.

The two men had spent a lot of time over the past week sitting in Sean's room, eating, loafing, and at times watching reruns of *Jeopardy!* and racing to answer each statement with a question.

"What is the Emancipation Proclamation?"
"Who is Al Pacino?"

Sean enjoyed watching the two competing with each other more than the program itself. It was the most entertainment he'd had in weeks. Even more so, he enjoyed seeing James, a firefighter and surfer, who replaced each period at the end of a sentence with *man,* and had a degree from a local junior college, trounce Gaspar, world-renowned cardiologist, each night.

"Lucky guess," Gaspar would say each and every time James would come in a second before him. Though Gaspar feigned exasperation, Sean could tell that Gaspar enjoyed the company of James as much as he did. James was not only smart, and obviously a devoted friend, but he worked hard. He pulled two doubles in the week Gaspar was there. He stopped in during his shifts when he could, after his shifts, and before them. He always came in with something that was the "bomb."

This veggie burger, Gaspar, it's da bomb, man.

This hummus. The. Bomb. Bam.

Hands down. Oh my god, this coffee. Da bomb! Which James followed up with an explosive gesture and crashing sound effects.

"No wonder," Gaspar said, leaning over Sean one afternoon, just before biting into a sandwich, "James didn't think to go to your apartment, the boy is always eating and or exploding."

On the last morning of Gaspar's stay, he arrived at Sean's room early to sit and go over the expected recovery plans. But just as he was about to get up and say good-bye to Sean, James peered into the room and said he had a surprise for Sean.

"Close your eyes, man."

"If it's a stripper, you're tipping," Sean quipped back.

"It's nothing like that. What did I tell you? Those joints are for losers. I don't need to pay for my lady friends," he said with a knowing smile. His bright green eyes squinted, and his lips closed as he stuck his double chin out, stretching the hanging skin and what looked like remnants of baby fat, and said, "Take a load of this face. Is this the face that needs to pay for chicks?"

"What is it then?" Sean said, covering his eyes with his gloved hands.

"Keep 'em closed. I'll tell ya when to open," James said, shouting through the doorway of Sean's hospital room.

Sean heard two sets of adult footsteps. One set was James,

he was certain. But the other, by their pacing, was a woman's. Alongside her, Sean could hear a soft padding sound, followed by tiny clacks, like fingernails tapping the floor.

"Keep 'em closed! No peeking!" James erupted when he saw Sean tilt his head back to sneak a look through the tiny slits of his closed eyes.

For a second Sean thought it was his sister, Cathleen, with one of the boys. But then he felt a soft push on his upper thigh. The only part not covered in a cast.

"Can I open them?" Sean asked.

"You can open them!" James said cheerfully. "Go on, man!"

Sean opened his eyes and saw the yellow-haired paw that tapped at and then rested on his upper thigh. Sean's eyes followed the length of the paw and saw that it was connected to the outstretched leg of a yellow Labrador. Its large brown eyes were slanted in such a way that he appeared as if he were about to cry. Each eye was surrounded by flecks of baby-fine and soft white hair that gathered and met in a peak above his large pink-spotted black snout. His ears flopped down next to his head and swung a bit as he cocked his head as if to say "Hello" when he pulled back his paw. He had a bright blue vest wrapped around his abdomen and a red collar that was inscribed with the name "Chief."

"It's a service dog, Sean," James explained. "The guys back at the house all chipped in and got him for you. There is usually a huge waiting list, like a mile and a half long, for these dogs, but because of your immediate needs and living conditions—meaning you're alone and being a firefighter hero and all—you got one! You're gonna work with his trainer, and in a few days he'll be fetching club sodas for you from the fridge. Hell, I bet we can eventually teach him how to surf. He can get our towels for us!"

Sean looked at the dog, back at James, and at Gaspar, who stood behind James smiling, totally taken with the dog himself.

"He's mine?"

"Yes, he's yours," James explained. "Well, actually Libby here is going to help you two get acquainted. She can teach you what you need to know to take care of him. But mostly he'll be taking care of you."

Libby, a tall, lanky brunette with cropped hair and a row of earrings up her right ear, and an intricate tattoo wrapping her forearm, put out her hand to shake Sean's. "I'm Libby Cartwright. Your trainer."

Sean put out his gloved hand and shook her hand gently, and held it and tried to squeeze it as if to say: *Wait.* He was staring at her tattoo. Celtic knots in green and orange seemed to be camouflaging scars on her arm. Sean took a hard look and recognized the shape and pattern. He had seen them on fellow rehab patients back in the day. They were scars of old track marks. A heroin addict's tell.

Libby caught Sean's eyes. Sean knew she knew what he saw. The two made eye contact and nodded in secret acknowledgment.

"I can't have a pet," Sean said, looking at Libby, and then at James and Gaspar.

"What are you talking about, Sean? Of course you can," James said sternly. "Don't go kicking a gift horse—"

"No, it's not like that. It's just in AA I was told I had to keep a plant alive for a year, then I'd be able to move on to a pet . . . and I can't keep the damn plant on my patio alive."

Gaspar laughed aloud.

"What's so funny?" Sean snapped.

"I saw that plant," Gaspar said with a knowing grin and nod. Libby laughed, too.

"Oh, so you're laughing now, too?" Sean said flirtatiously to Libby.

"Chief is different, Sean. He'll tell you what he needs. You won't forget to feed him or give him water. He won't let you. He'll be able to turn on lights, open cabinets, and fetch your shoes since you can't bend down. He knows over forty commands," James assured Sean.

Chief sat beside Sean and propped his warm muzzle on his lap. Sean put his hand on the dog's head and started to stroke his fur. Sean hadn't felt anything but pain in his hands in weeks. And with the protective gloves, there was no way his skin was able to feel the warmth of Chief's snout, the soft hair above his eyes, but Sean felt as though he could. For a second, he felt as if he could feel as he had before the fire.

Libby knelt down beside Chief and wrapped her sleek, ropey arms around him, rubbing his abdomen, and looked up at Sean. "He's one of the best I've ever trained. Wanna see what he can do?"

Sean nodded. "Okay."

Libby pointed across the room toward the bathroom and said, "Open the door."

Chief padded across the room, popped up and used his paws to pull down the door handle, opened it, and held it with his body.

James looked back at Sean, amazed. "See?"

"Okay, okay," Sean shushed James.

"Chief, pillow, please," Libby said, pointing toward the bed.

Chief walked over to the bed, got up on his hind legs, took the pillow with his mouth, and carried it over to Libby. Libby gave Chief a hearty pet and rubbed his ear.

Sean got the drift. He felt bad for the dog. He didn't want him running around doing tricks for his benefit.

"Hey, Chief! Get over here, buddy," Sean said and Chief turned, looked at Sean, and almost nodded in approval, as if Chief was the one making the decision about who would be keeping whom.

Chief walked past James, past Gaspar, and past Libby and lay down in front of Sean's wheelchair before propping his head on top of his paws.

"Guess he's stayin'," Sean said.

"Looks like it," Libby said with a smile.

"So he's mine?" Sean said again, incredulously. "Just like that? He's mine?"

"Well, technically, we have to work together for a couple of weeks and make sure he's a good fit for you. I'll have to teach you how to command, reward, feed, and take care of him. It seems as though Chief is quite smitten with you, so I think we're good there, but you're going to have to be released from the hospital, and in your own home, before I can really start training you. For now, do you mind if we just come and visit every day?"

"Sure, that'd be fine," Sean said, looking at her, taking all of her in for the first time. She wore little makeup, just some mascara and eyeliner that accentuated her doe-shaped gray eyes, and a hint of bubble gum pink lipstick. He was sure her skin was meant to be the color of a white peach, but it had been burned so many times by the sun that it was awash with thousands of faded brown freckles. Tiny crow's-feet gathered like party crepe-paper streamers around her eyes when she smiled. And her small, slightly upturned nose crinkled when she laughed. She had a huge, open, contented smile, the type of smile that looked as though it might give way to a boisterous howl of laughter at any moment. Sean liked it. Sean liked her. She had an easy vibe. Sean glanced over at James and could see that he, too, saw what he did. Both men were now smiling back at her.

"All right then, we'll come back tomorrow, and every day after that for a quick visit, and let you guys get acquainted," Libby said brightly. "It was so nice for us both to meet you, Sean. Looking forward to working with you. Come on, Chief. Come here, boy." Chief stood up and walked alongside Libby out of the room.

Gaspar caught James and Sean watching Libby, her long, muscular legs snugged tightly in faded jeans, leave the room with Chief.

"Thanks, Libby! Look forward to seeing you tomorrow!" James called after her.

As the door clicked behind her, James turned to Sean. "Whoooweee, I guess I'll be seeing you a lot this week."

Sean cocked his head. He hadn't been listening. His eyes were still on the door.

"Well, well, well, look who's gotten a little puppy love for his trainer," James said.

"What? Who me?" Sean said, trying to shake his head. "The trainer? No way."

"Yeah, right," James said, knocking his friend in the shoulder lightly.

"She's quite pretty, Sean," Gaspar added. "Sure you want to book those flights to Italy?"

Sean's smile fell and his eyes darted across the room to Gaspar.

"Italy?" James looked back at Sean. "Whaddya mean, Italy?"

"It's nothing, James. Nothing at all. Gaspar here has a knack for running his yap when he shouldn't be."

Sean didn't want to embarrass Gaspar, but he wanted to remind him in that moment that it was Gaspar who'd told the boy his father was in Los Angeles. It was Gaspar who'd told the boy his mother had known all along, and that she'd kept the secret from him for years. It was Gaspar's fault in the first place that the boy ran away, that he got it in his head to go to Los Angeles and find his father. If there was blame to go around, and there was plenty, Sean wanted to blame Gaspar in that moment, but knew he was equally to blame for keeping the secrets to begin with. *Can't shoot the messenger,* Sean thought and immediately recanted. "I'm sorry, Gaspar. That was a cheap shot. Even for me."

"I'm sorry, Sean, I am. I just thought, she is pretty and you'll be spending time together. And maybe there will be lots more after her. Maybe, I was just thinking, you might reconsider . . ."

"I am sorry, I don't follow," James interjected.

Exasperated and feeling as if it was pointless to keep it a secret from James, Sean explained his plan to his friend. "James, during the fire, I made a promise. I told myself if I got out of that mess, I'd be a better man. I'd make up for all the stupid stuff I've done, and I'd find a girl from a long time ago and I'd tell her how sorry I was for messing stuff up between us. I'd make things right. I made that promise, James, and I am here today, I believe, because I made that promise, and nothing, let me repeat, nothing is going to stop me. You hear me, Gaspar? Not even a long-legged knockout."

"So I can call dibs on Libby?" James said flatly, for Sean's benefit pretending to be unmoved by Sean's story.

Sean laughed. "You can call dibs. She's all yours. I've got my mind set."

Once his dibs were secured, James circled back to Sean's story. "Sounds like a hell of a plan to me, Sean. She has to be some sort of special if you've been hanging on this long, holding out this long."

"She is, James. She is," Sean said.

"I am sorry, Sean. I was just joking and I thought . . ." Gaspar shook his head.

"I know, Gaspar. No harm done. But I don't want you talking me out of it. I thought we had come to a mutual understanding."

"We had. I just hoped . . ."

"I know what you hope for, Gaspar. You want me to fall in love. You want me to get married and have babies, and make you feel a little bit better about the life you have now . . . ," Sean said, once again realizing that what he was saying was hurtful, but unable to control himself.

Gaspar shook his head as if in protest. "I know you were like a father to him, Sean. I know that. I know that you felt as if you were his father. You know that you could still—"

Sean held up his hand and waved at Gaspar as if he was shooing a bird off his balcony on Ocean View. "I am sorry. I shot my mouth off again. I had no right."

"You have every right, Sean."

James stood between the two men and searched their eyes for some sort of explanation. "I'm sorry? What kid are we talking about? Whose kid?"

"His name is Colm Magee. My sister's son. Gaspar here was just saying that I loved the boy like my own son. He is right about that. His dad took off before he was born, around eleven years ago, and I got to raise him with my sister for a little while back in New York," Sean said almost in a whisper and realized how empty and hollow it felt to say those words, to sum up seven years of his life in a few words. How impossible was it, so often in life, to sum up something so enormous?

"I got to love him as my own for a little while."

"I was a father."

"I loved a girl."

"My mother died."

"My father died."

"I used to fight fires."

Footnotes in a life, Sean thought. How many people use them to describe the infinitely huge moments that change them forever? So often those moments get nothing more than a passing mention.

"Cool," James said in a matter-of-fact tone, and shrugged.

Sean sensed that James could feel the tension in the room and didn't want to add anything further.

"I better get on my way. I don't want to get stuck in traffic and miss my flight," Gaspar added.

"James? Will you give us a second?" Sean asked politely.

"Yeah, sure. I'll be outside. Gaspar, I'll give you a ride. I don't have a shift. No sense in you taking a cab."

"Thanks, that would be kind of you, James."

"I'll be just outside," James said, shutting the door.

Gaspar walked over to Sean, grabbed a chair, and pulled it close so Sean and he could be at eye level with each other. Despite all of their brief quarrels throughout the week, neither man wanted to be the first to say good-bye.

"I'm going to be fine, Gaspar. And so are you. You tell my sister that I am doing great. Tell her it's nothing but a couple of broken bones and nothing that time won't heal. You got that?"

"Of course, Sean."

"I don't want her worrying or flying out here six weeks after she has those babies."

"Agreed," Gaspar said and nodded.

"I am glad they have you. You're a great dad and husband. Better than I could have hoped for Cathleen. Even in my wildest dreams."

"She has wild dreams for you, too."

"I know she does," Sean said, looking out the window. "Believe me, I know she does."

"James is a good man. You're in good hands."

"He's all right. And that dog, right? That dog. I can't believe he did that for me."

"It's quite extraordinary," Gaspar said and nodded. And after a long pause, he added, "You've got some great angels looking out for you. Seen and unseen. And I think my work here is done." He held up his hands in mock self-righteousness.

"Go on. Get out of here," Sean said, pointing to the door and laughing.

"Oh, Sean . . . I know I mentioned it earlier, but a man named Tom will be visiting. I've hired him to care for you, until you can manage on your own. He'll be taking you home from the hospital."

"So I don't get a say in who will be taking care of me?"

"Guess you are, as you say, *shit out of luck,*" Gaspar said with a wink, and as he stood up, "He'll take good care of you, Sean. I have no doubt. Like I said, you're in many capable hands."

"When do you think you'll come back out?" Sean said.

"When I can get away, I'll come. Perhaps after Cathleen has the babies and things settle down. Then again, when you're ready for me. And when it's time, I'll be ready to take you to Italy myself, if that is still what you want to do."

"Thanks, buddy."

Gaspar nodded, stood up, and walked over to Sean. "I would hug you, if I could . . ."

"Please don't," Sean said as he patted Gaspar on the arm. Gaspar took his other hand and held Sean's hand to his own arm for a few seconds. "I'm glad you're here. I just want you to know how glad I am that you're okay. I don't think I could have lost another . . ."

"Gaspar, it's all right. We're all right. We're all going to be all right."

❧ Part 2

If I got rid of my demons, I'd lose my angels.

—Tennessee Williams

❧ Chapter 11

THE DAY AFTER GASPAR RETURNED TO HIS FAMILY IN New York, Tom Smith appeared in Sean's doorway. He was pushing a wheelchair, and a large medical bag was slung over his shoulder. Sean took one look at the man and knew exactly why Gaspar had hired him. The man was a giant, larger than Sean himself.

Standing nearly seven feet tall, Tom's biceps and pectorals bulged out of his form-fitting golf shirt, which was tucked neatly into the equally tight jeans that accentuated his trim waist and long muscular legs. Tom was the type of man, Sean surmised instantly, who woke up at 5 A.M., downed six raw eggs in three rapid gulps, then ran a half marathon before heading to Muscle Beach for two hours.

"Crap," Sean mumbled as Tom entered the room.

"Now is that any way to greet a person?" Tom said, pushing the wheelchair alongside Sean's bed and setting down his bag.

"Sorry, it's just that I have a feeling you're one of those go-get-'em-tiger types," Sean said.

"You've guessed correctly. Tom Smith's the name." Tom held out his hand to shake Sean's.

Sean raised his gloved hand and waved Tom's hand away.

"So that's how it's gonna be," Tom said with a smile.

"No, it's just that I can't shake your hand. They are burned. They hurt."

"I know, Sean. Your brother-in-law, Dr. Basu, filled me in. I wouldn't have squeezed it hard. You can trust me."

Sean put his hand out again, and was surprised by how gently Tom wrapped his gargantuan hand around his and shook it.

"There. That wasn't too terrible," Tom said, still shaking it. "Wanna go for a walk and get acquainted?"

"Not especially. I just woke up," Sean said, pulling his hand away.

"Perfect! So we agree that you're awake! Let's go!" Tom said cheerfully, ignoring Sean's complaint.

Tom reached behind Sean's back and gently lifted him to a sitting position. Then gingerly taking Sean's legs, Tom swung them sideways off the side of the bed. Before Sean could figure out what was happening, Tom had put his arms under Sean's legs and around his back, lifted him up, and placed him in the wheelchair.

"Now that wasn't so bad, was it?" Tom said, barely breaking a sweat.

"You just lifted nearly two hundred and eighty-five pounds by yourself. You realize that?" Sean said, amazed. He hadn't been handled like that since he was a small boy.

"Two sixty-five actually. You're down twenty pounds according to your chart. We'll get you back up to your fighting weight in no time though."

"Is that why Gaspar hired you? Because you won't throw your back out while you're hauling me around for the next few months?"

"Oh, I am sure that had a lot to do with it, but mostly I think it was my good looks and charming personality," Tom said. "And the fact that I come as a two-for-one deal. I'm both an RN and a PT."

"Fantastic," Sean said sarcastically.

"So I hear you jumped out of a building and lived to tell the tale. How are you feeling today?"

"Like I did yesterday and the day before that . . . like crap."

Sean didn't want to say another word. He didn't want to tell the same version of the same story over and over again to whoever stepped into his room.

"I'm gonna be straight with you, Sean," Tom said. "I don't stand for wallowing in self-pity. Don't stand for it at all. I just want to get that out right now—right here."

"How compassionate of you, Tom," Sean shot back.

"I know what you're looking for, Sean. I've been where you are. I got hurt, too, years ago. In Iraq. I didn't think I'd ever walk again. But I did the work. I get it. You're sitting in a chair, and you're bummed because you can't move and get around and do your job, or do your girlfriend, or whatever else it is that you do. You're probably even feeling a little guilty about being alive. I bet you've been spending hours down in that lonely room of yours, just thinking that it must mean something that you've been given a second chance."

Sean turned his head as far as he could and looked up into Tom's face.

"Strike a chord, did I?" Tom said, looking down. "Well, I am here to tell you something. It doesn't mean anything. Not a thing. You had some bad luck. But let me tell you, it could have been worse. A lot worse. You know how many people I've seen who can't walk? Never will again? You know how many people who didn't get a second chance? Don't go making yourself crazy trying to attribute meaning to the meaningless. Shit happens."

Sean turned his head around quickly, and winced from the pain caused by the sudden movement.

"I know. I know," Sean added. He had been where Tom had been, too. He had, at many points in his own life, thought everything was devoid of meaning. He had periods when he felt nothing mattered and everything was a coincidence. That not one thing pointed to the next. But that was before Colm. That was before he had grown to love his nephew. He had seen what that love brought to his life. He could see how the boy's life, and all of his deaths—all seven of them when he added up every one of Colm's cardiac arrests—was another chance. Sean definitively knew that each and every one of those chances meant something. They meant something to Colm. They meant something to his sister, Cathleen, and to his friend Gaspar. But most of all they meant something to him. To erase their meaning and to simply dismiss one's life as an aberration or a magical accident didn't add up. It never would. But Sean didn't want to have to tell Tom all of this. He didn't want to fight something he knew he couldn't explain to someone who hadn't felt what he had felt. *That love. That love. That love. My god, man, it means everything.*

"So here's the deal," Tom said, pushing Sean into a large occupational therapy room at the end of a long corridor. "This is why you're here. This is why I am here. For one reason, and one reason only: To work. Work. Work. Work. That, my friend, is the meaning of life. Yours, mine, and everyone else's. Work. Sleep. Repeat. Die. The end. Got it?"

Sean gave a quick nod of acknowledgment and looked around the room that was filled with giant blue and green exercise balls, racks of weights, thick blue mats, parallel bars, and treadmills and elliptical machines, most of which were being employed by other patients in various states of recovery. There was an amputee, both legs cut below the knee, who was trying to walk on his newly fitted prosthetics with the assistance of his PT. Then there was a young woman who had lost an arm and was curling a large weight with her good arm. A paraplegic was on the ground doing triceps dips, lifting his torso up and down.

"What'd I tell ya? Two legs. Two arms. A head that works, for the most part. So don't go bitchin' to me. Got it?" Tom said quite matter-of-factly, recognizing the scene Sean had just taken in.

Sean nodded again.

"Sean, you and I aren't going to talk much about our feelings in here. Outside that door, in your hospital room, in your home, wherever else we may be you can talk a blue streak. You follow?"

Sean nodded again.

"So when we're in here, we're not going to talk much about what you can't do anymore, because all I care about is what you *can* do, and I can get you wherever you want to go if you just shut up and work hard," Tom said, pushing the wheelchair over to a large blue mat.

Sean nodded and stared at Tom for a long time, and then said, "So what do I have to do to get out of this chair?"

"First things first," Tom said, pulling Sean up and placing him on the mat. "When rebuilding a burned-up, broken-down house, it is always best to start from the ground. When rebuilding a burned-up, broken-down body, same deal. Ground up."

"Let's get on with it then," Sean said, lying flat on his back with his arms and legs spread wide, like a child about to make a snow angel. "I'm all yours, Tom."

❧ Chapter 12

WHEN TOM RETURNED SEAN TO HIS ROOM, SEAN was exhausted. The muscles in his arms and quads burned from strain. Sean hadn't felt that way since his early days in the fire academy. Though Tom's workout wasn't even a tenth of the academy's rigor, Sean felt as though he had just run a marathon, even though he'd only managed to do a few bicep curls and a few leg lifts. All he wanted to do now was sleep.

But just as Tom was about to lift Sean out of his chair and place him in his bed, Chief sauntered in the room, and Libby trailed close behind.

Sean immediately perked up, and he could tell Tom took note. "Tom, this is Libby Cartwright and my companion dog, Chief," Sean said brightly as Chief wagged his tail and propped his muzzle up on Sean's leg.

"Tom Smith, Libby. Pleased to make your acquaintance." Tom grabbed Libby's hand and shook it much more firmly than he had Sean's earlier. Sean noticed Tom looking at Libby with as much interest as James had a day earlier. Though, Sean noticed for the first time, Tom had a wedding ring on his left hand.

"Libby, this is my physical therapist and he'll be going home with me to help out for a few months until I am back on my feet."

"Perfect, then today we can let Chief get to know both of you," Libby said. "Let's get started."

Over the next two hours, Sean watched as Chief followed every one of Libby's commands. Sean followed Libby, too. He followed her hand gestures, the movement of her arms, the way she bent and snuggled into the dog. Sean tried to mimic her movements exactly, in order to have the same effect on the dog when he tried.

And Chief made it easy for Sean. Sean commanded, gently but authoritatively, and Chief complied with all of his requests. *Just like that.*

"Ask and you shall receive," Libby said. "It's that simple."

"No one has ever listened to me like this dog listens to me. It's amazing," Sean said.

"He's a good dog, Sean. If you keep a steady and calm demeanor, reward him, and love him like a family member, he'll treat you in kind."

"Makes sense," Sean said, "though I'm sure it is easier said than done."

"For most of us bipeds, you're right. But for our four-legged friends here, it is easy. They seem to just get it. No hidden agendas, no demands, no mood swings. They don't want for much—just appreciation in the form of affection, and of course, food, water, and exercise."

"Doesn't seem like a fair trade," Sean added. "I ask him to work constantly for me, and I can't do the same for him. I can never pay him back."

"Don't worry about it, Sean. Dogs are like guardian angels. A good one is always there when you need it, and will never ask you for anything in return."

"I'm sorry, what did you just say, Libby?" Sean said, turning his wheelchair abruptly around to face her.

"I said a good dog is like having your own personal guardian angel," Libby said, snuggling into Chief's side.

"I know. I just . . . It's just odd that you said that . . ."

"Hmmm? How come?" Libby cocked her head, not following Sean's train of thought.

Sean looked at Tom and remembered his comments earlier about life having no meaning. Sean could already hear the man laugh if he even mentioned his theory on second chances and the angel who had quite possibly granted him one.

"Nah, it's just that I've been thinking a lot about angels lately," Sean said, petting the dog. "But in another way."

"What way?" Libby asked gently.

Tom let out a laugh. "Oh man, here we go. Don't even say it. I've seen this a million times before, too."

Libby snapped a harsh look at Tom. "Let him finish, Tom."

"No, Tom's right. It's stupid. It's nothing," Sean said sheepishly.

Libby stared for a long time at Sean, searching for something in his eyes. Sean could tell she wanted to talk to him, to hear what he had to say, but he didn't want to embarrass himself any further in front of Tom. Cynics don't have much patience for the downtrodden in search of meaning. Cynics, Sean knew, see the hopeful as nothing more than incommodious houseflies that need to be swatted away, mere annoyances that get in the way of living their lives of certitude. He'd been there himself.

"It's nothing, Libby. You're right. Dogs are like angels. This one is for sure. It's like he appeared from out of nowhere, and he's, I don't know, not to be melodramatic, but saving my life all over again in a way," Sean said, rubbing the dog's ear and smiling at him.

"It's not stupid, Sean. Whatever it is you wanted to tell me," Libby added, looking at Tom, "you can tell me. *I'll* understand."

"Understand what?" James said, entering the room with a bag full of takeout. "I bring you great thai-dings! Get it? Thai food! Iz the scha-nizel and za bomb. Oh, hey, Libby, what a surprise! Didn't know you'd still be here . . . ," he said, winking over at Sean.

Sean shot a look at James that might as well have screamed: *I call bullshit.*

"What's going on in here? A party without me? This room is packed, man," James said. "How did you manage to swing getting so popular, Sean? Must be those good looks," he said, pinching Sean's cheek, but carefully avoiding the area where the skin graft met his jawline.

Libby laughed at James, who filled the room with a raucous energy.

Tom bristled when he saw Libby smile at James, no doubt

wondering what a woman would find so attractive in a pudgy, nonsense-speaking clown.

"Tom, this is my best friend, James. James, this is Tom, the physical-therapist-slash-babysitter-slash-nursemaid-slash-token-life-coach-slash-existentialist that Gaspar hired for me. He'll be tagging along with us for the next few months till I get up and running."

"Terrific!" James said, reaching out his hand and vigorously shaking Tom's and still talking to Sean. "This is just awesome, man. Awesome. We've got Tom, Libby, and Chief now. Sean, you're going to be back in the swells and off to Italy to find your lady pal in no time."

"Lady pal?" Libby said, looking at Sean and then following with a closed-mouth coy smile.

"Yes, I had hoped, that, well, I was hoping, to um . . . ," Sean stammered, uneasy in front of Tom.

"He's got a chick back in It'ly that he wants to get better for and make nice with. Thinks he's got a second chance at life and he's gonna go over there if he can make it with some Italian broad," James explained to Libby.

Sean looked over at Tom, who was shaking his head like a disappointed father after a son misses a field goal in the final championship game. *Not my son.*

"Aw, shut up, James. Between you and Gaspar, a man's got no hope of keeping a secret," Sean said.

"How romantic, Sean," Libby said, swooning a bit. "Do tell more," she said, pulling up a chair and resting her arm on Chief's back to stroke it while Sean stroked Chief's nose.

"Yes, please do share!" Tom said, clapping his hands in mock excitement.

"Hey, don't be an ass," Libby said, cutting Tom off. "Just 'cause you're some jaded married guy, don't go being a killjoy. Come on, Sean, I want details. Love me some good romance, so go on . . .'"

Tom's mouth dropped open. "I'm not a jaded married guy. You don't even know me."

"Well, don't go crapping on someone's dream because you think you got it all figured out," Libby said, switching quickly from enthralled romantic to combat mode. Sean realized that she went from Jo March to GI Joe in less time than it took James to chug a Coke.

"Hey, you've known me for like two seconds," Tom said to Libby.

"That's all it takes," Libby shot back. "Sometimes, all it takes is two seconds to know someone is a pompous know-it-all."

"Now, now, now, boys and girls," James chimed in. "Sounds like everyone's blood sugar is a bit low and we could all use some nourishment. I've never found a problem that couldn't be solved with some food. Let's eat!" James said, pulling out boxes of pad thai and stacking them on Sean's bedside cart.

"Why on earth did you get so much food, James?" Sean said, watching James pull box after box out of the bag.

"I don't know, I was hoping that maybe Libby would still be here and we could all nosh together," James said.

"I thought you said you were surprised that I was still here?" Libby said, catching James in a lie.

"Well, you're here now, so might as well eat with us! And you, too, Captain Buzzkill," James said, turning toward Tom and handing him a box of noodles.

"I don't eat carbs," Tom said, crossing his arms.

"Of course you don't," Sean said glibly.

Tom, as if challenged to a duel, grabbed a box and a plastic fork from James.

They all laughed and even Tom's stone face cracked into a self-conscious smile.

After Sean was released from the hospital, just a few days later, a similar version of the same scene repeated itself. The four commiserated with each other over lunches and shared time spent surrounding Sean in his chair—in his apartment, out on his balcony, down on the beach, and out at street-side cafés. As the weeks went by, Sean learned of Tom's marital problems and how his wife was growing tired of Tom's inflexibility, his constant workouts, and his day job that always took precedence over her and their two little girls. "She acts like I have a choice? How do you think the groceries and mortgage get paid for? A man has to work," he'd say, shaking his head as if he was at home finishing an argument with his wife.

They also learned about how Libby grew up wealthy in San Francisco, the daughter of a famed computer chip inventor, but somehow she got hooked on heroin while at boarding school over a decade ago. "I wasn't looking to become an addict," she insisted. "My mother and father adored me and wanted me to have the best of everything—clothes, cars, education. I had it all. I thought I would try it just once. And my god, it was like nothing I had ever experienced. And just like that, I couldn't stop. It was impossible to stop once I started. No matter how many promises I made to myself, I just couldn't. And my poor parents, no amount of begging, loving, or praying on their part could change me either. It was basic chemistry," she told the men one day while they sat sipping lemonade and eating giant burritos James had brought over. "My brain craved what the drug provided."

"So how did you get clean?" James asked gently. "How'd you end up down here and training dogs?"

"I ran away from boarding school and came down here. I got caught up with pretty bad people on the streets. I ended up in a hospital. I don't even know how I got there. To this day, I don't know who found me, who took me in. I just sort of appeared at L.A. County. A nurse told me a man brought me and left. Like some ghost."

"Or angel," Sean said with a smile.

"Oh, no, here we go," Tom said, rolling his eyes. "Jesus, give it a rest over there, St. John the Divine."

"I went to rehab after that. And while I was there, I enrolled in a therapy dog program. I was given a special dog, Mirabelle, a black Lab," Libby said, unable to control her smile when she spoke the dog's name. "She made me so happy. All I thought about was her. I knew this was all I ever wanted to do. So I learned how to train other dogs and help people who could use the companionship like I could."

"Well, you're great at it," Sean said, patting her arm in his best impression of a bona fide AA sponsor "You know it's incredibly brave, what you just did. Telling us all that."

Libby wiped away a tear before it fell over her cheek. "Thanks, Sean. Spoken like a friend of Bill Wilson," she added.

"Who's Bill Wilson?" Tom asked, afraid he was missing some important aspect of the story.

"He founded AA with the idea that individuals need others going through similar hardships to encourage each other. Basically, these groups are considered a necessity for recovery. Some members even refer to themselves as *friends of Bill*. It's like a secret message letting someone know that they're talking to a safe person. A person who understands. Everyone needs a person to understand, right, Sean?" Libby finished her explanation with a question.

Sean nodded but kept his eyes on James, who couldn't keep his eyes off Libby when she spoke.

Suddenly, and seemingly without thinking, James grabbed Libby's hand. "Man, you're tough as nails. People don't beat that stuff. But you did, and now you're doing something great for other people."

Libby put her own hand over James's. "Thank you, James," she said, looking him square in the eyes and feeling in that instant that James could see the good in her. It was the same look Mirabelle had given her. Mirabelle only saw the good, too. It was what Libby had been trying to see in herself every day in the mirror. But it escaped her. Every time she looked she saw only her mistakes. She saw only the pain she'd caused. She saw only who she used to be. But here was James, practically a stranger, who seemed to see her so clearly. Better than she could see herself. Libby's heart skipped a beat and she blushed. James saw this and squeezed her hand even harder.

"I mean it, Libby. You're a good egg." James's already ruddy cheeks flushed a hot pink. He was embarrassed by what he'd just said. He was mortified that he couldn't think of anything better to say than *You're a good egg*. He wanted to say: *You're beautiful. You're kind. I love that you love dogs. I think you're*

cool. I dig your short hair. You have the best smile I've ever seen.
But he couldn't. Words had failed him over and over. But he
was never one who could escape the moment. The irrepress-
ible moment when one knows what one must do—even if he
can't articulate it. And with that, James, forgetting he was in
the company of two grown men who might judge him, stood
up, grabbed Libby in his arms, and hugged her. "I am so, so
glad you're still here. I am so glad you're here."

Libby gave in to the hug and let James's enormity wrap
itself around her and envelop her completely. She felt instantly safe and cared for and she squeezed back to let James
know she liked the hug.

Tom and Sean looked at each other, stunned by James's
unabashed expression of emotion.

"Thank you, James," Libby said, pulling away. "I'm glad
you're here, too," was all Libby could think to add. Both, it
seemed, were at a loss for words.

As the days turned into weeks and then months, and meals
spilled over into shared afternoons and shared revelations and
intimacies, Sean had come to recognize something in each
of them, something he, too, was experiencing, a feeling he'd
had in some form or another his entire life. Each of them was
always wanting. *Something more.* Though none of his friends
had been addicted to alcohol, they each had, in their own
way, their own broken spine, their weak link. They each had
a certain crack that, like his, needed to be reinforced. For
Tom it was work. He was, Sean was discovering, incapable of
resting, incapable of the slightest imperfection. Work would
see him through this existence, even if it was the very same

thing that was destroying his life as he knew it—one wife and one child at a time. For James it was food. He buried himself in it, filling up bowl after bowl of pad thai, moo goo gai pan, pho, pesto, paninis, pizza, pasta, filling up an empty space; Sean wasn't sure even James knew how it had gotten there. And if James did, he hadn't found the words to tell anyone why. Then there was Libby, or a former version of the woman she was now. Somehow she had managed to overcome her heroin addiction, but the wanting was still there. It was in her eyes. Sean could see that there was more to the story. That there was something behind it that she wasn't even willing to admit to herself. Sean knew because he had fashioned a similar story, the story he told his sister or AA members, but then there was the one buried deep down inside him.

Everyone, Sean knew, had a demon or was once a demon, and if not either, could easily become one given the right conditions. Then again, he thought, demons were nothing more than fallen angels like himself and his new friends.

❧ Chapter 13

ONE EVENING, SIX MONTHS INTO SEAN'S RECOVERY,
Tom and his wife, Melissa, took Sean out onto Ocean
View, on Venice Beach, with Chief to meet Libby and
James at a nearby Mexican restaurant. It was James's birth-
day, and James insisted on La Cabaña that had, according to
James, tacos that were, no shock to anyone, the *bomb*.

When James spotted Tom assisting Sean, with his walker
and leg braces, coming through the door, he jolted up from
his chair and ran the length of the restaurant to his friend.
The last time he'd seen Sean walk was when he'd grabbed the
ax off the engine, tipped his hat toward James, and headed
into the house that eventually almost consumed him. James
shook the memory off.

"Happy birthday, James!" Sean said loudly, indicating to
James that standing and walking was his gift.

"Oh my god, man. Oh my god. When did this happen?"
James said excitedly, walking around Sean and inspecting him.

"We've been working on it for a month now," Tom said proudly. "Sean here wanted to keep it a secret until he was sure he could do it. He's on his way now. He still needs his chair. But he can take a few steps here and there."

Tom's wife pulled up behind them both with Sean's chair. "So this is the crew I've heard so much about?" A tall, thin blonde who looked as equally fit as Tom stepped forward and shook James's hand.

"I'm Melissa, Tom's wife. I've heard a lot about you, James. Happy birthday! Thanks for including me. Tom comes home every night with stories about you three. *Libby said this. James said this. And Sean did this* . . . I'm almost jealous. You get him more than I do. Seems like you guys have more fun than do actual work," she said, a hint of passive aggressiveness in her tone. *Almost jealous* seemed like an understatement.

"Well, so glad you could come and hang out with us," James said, surprising her with his sense of familiarity and hugging her.

James looked over at Sean. "You tired, man? Want to sit down in your chair for the rest of the way? It's a long walk to the table."

"Nah, I've come this far," Sean said, inching forward.

James stood back and couldn't contain his joy. Despite the braces and walker, his friend almost resembled his old self. Sean seemed to be putting on some of the weight he had lost. It wasn't quite twenty pounds, but close to it. The bandages had been removed from his head for weeks now and Sean's hair was finally covering the long, jagged scar that crossed his skull. His right ear was still lost, now somewhere in the melted folds of skin, but the swelling had gone down, and with the hair grown he could hardly tell he had been burned when looking at him from a certain angle.

James noticed Sean's biceps, which Sean relied on for everything, to haul his weight from chair to bed, bed to chair, and everywhere in between. The muscles were bulging out of his white shirt and his skin even looked tan. His color was returning. And not just to his arms but to his face as well. James realized Sean's hands were fitted with clear plastic gloves that almost made them look completely normal. From a distance, James guessed, no one could tell his friend had nearly been burned alive.

Yes, James had seen him every day since the fire. But he hadn't recognized the small changes. He knew Sean and Tom worked out every day. He knew Sean spent hours in the gym and James had witnessed small advances. He was there the day Sean's heavy casts were removed. He was there the day they removed the bandages around his head and showed Sean the scar on his skull and the large burned section on the right side of his head and neck. James looked away himself, repulsed and sickened by the sight and unable to witness his friend's cry when he saw his own ear, or lack of one, for the first time. But all those memories washed away when he looked at Sean standing before him. Sean had been completely transformed. Sean was well on his way to being healed. It was the best birthday present James had ever had.

"What the hell are you wearing, James?" Sean asked, breaking James's obvious reverie.

"What?" James said, feeling above his head. "Oh? This? It's a sombrero! I got one for each of us to wear! Come on. There at the table! Libby is already wearing hers . . ."

"Fantastic," Tom said, rolling his eyes.

"Oh, lighten up, hon. Have a little fun," Melissa said, patting Tom on the arm.

As the group approached the table, Libby, wearing a sombrero, stepped out of the bathroom and took Sean in, putting her hands up to her mouth to shriek.

"Sean! You can walk!" Running toward Sean, her sombrero flew off and she left it behind.

Libby, Sean noticed, looked transformed as well. She was not the same person he had grown familiar with, seeing her by day—the girl-woman who wore her faded tight jeans, faux retro T-shirts purchased from Target, and Converse sneakers like a uniform. But tonight she was wearing a short floral sundress and thin cotton sweater that covered her tattoos. She had put on a bit more makeup than usual and even taken out several of the silver hoops in her ears, only leaving a set of small diamond studs—remnants of a former preppy, boarding school life. Something else about her had changed, though Sean couldn't recognize exactly what it was at first. James looked different, too. His face appeared a bit thinner. Sean started to make out cheekbones. His Tommy Bahama shirt fit loosely over his slimmer chest, and his blond hair was a bit longer. Sean couldn't put his finger on any of it, but something was entirely different about James, too.

"Libby, you look beautiful," Sean said quietly, blushing.

James looked at Sean and then at Libby and saw, too, what Sean saw: Libby, gorgeous and smiling. Happy and clean.

"Here, let me get your chair," Tom said, coming up behind Sean with it. "It will be easier for you to cross the restaurant. Come on."

"Yeah, okay," Sean acquiesced and let Tom push the chair behind him and help position him into place.

"I just can't believe it. I can't," James said, shaking his head. "How do you feel? You okay? Tired?"

"I'm okay, James. Tom's been great. I couldn't have done it without him. He knew what I needed."

Tom shook his head. "It was all you, Sean. All you. I just told you what to do and you did it. But don't get too cocky, you have a long way to go."

Melissa nodded knowingly. "It took Tom almost a year to walk again after his accident."

"What?" James said, turning and looking at Tom.

Tom knocked on the part of his leg below his knee, under his jeans. "Iraq. About nine years ago. Transport truck I was riding in ran over an IED. Took some shrapnel. Was cut up pretty bad, but they didn't have to cut my legs off. I was lucky."

"Jesus. Lucky?" James asked. "I had no idea. I couldn't even tell. You barely limp. I just thought you had a knee injury or something."

"He nearly died," Melissa added. "We almost lost him. But he did the work, too. Hasn't stopped since, actually," Melissa said, shaking her head while recalling it all.

"Melissa, stop. This dinner isn't about me. It's about James. I'd like to keep it that way."

James, Libby, and Sean exchanged knowing glances. They knew instinctively that they would talk about this later. Would snag Tom after Melissa had gone and drill him for details.

"No wonder you're so badass," James said, squeezing Tom

by the neck. "I knew it. No one gets as tough as you without going through some shit. That's for sure."

While Tom, Libby, and Sean had ordered and then nursed their iced teas with lemon, James and Melissa had each downed three margaritas and were finding the comfortable drunk spot when one still feels optimistic and uninhibited, and not yet depressed or crapulous. While Melissa grew sleepy and rested her head on Tom's shoulder, nodding her head in and out of consciousness, James was at the stage when he felt he could say and do anything without consequences. It was his birthday after all, he kept reminding everyone at the table, and so he could order what he wanted, drink what he wanted, and ask anything he wanted and everyone had to answer. "No cop-outs," James said with a slur. "I ask. You answer. Deal?"

Tom, Sean, and Libby exchanged eye rolls in mock exasperation, but all were rather enjoying James being even more uninhibited than his usual garrulous self, which seemed impossible.

"First, Sean. Batter up," James instructed.

"What do you want to know that you don't already, James?"

"Chiara. Start talking. Tell me more about her. Tell me she's got hair made of gold and that she's a princess due to inherit a spectacular fortune. Please tell me that she has yachts, a house on the Italian Riviera, and crap like that. I want to hear all about her and why she is so damn amazing that you're willing to give up everything here to go be with her."

"I'm not obsessed. I just know what I want."

"Don't listen to the boys," Libby said, shaking her head. "They've got no sense of romance. Of possibility."

"He's obsessed," Tom added. "Sometimes when he naps, he shouts her name."

Sean looked at Tom as if hearing this for the first time. "I do?"

Tom nodded and his lips formed a long flat line across his face as he shrugged.

"Well, I want to hear all about her," Libby said. "James is right. She has to be special for you to be carrying a torch this long. I just want to understand it. What is that kind of love like?"

"I don't know if I can explain it properly. But I think we had the kind of love that knows it exists before the people in it do. It was the kind of love that, I think, would have existed here on earth even if she and I did not. It was the kind of love that has always been here and always would be for the right people who fall into it. It was already here. It didn't take long before we were both consumed by it."

"Oh my god, Sean, that's beautiful," Libby said, reaching out and touching his arm.

"It's horseshit," Tom said. "That means absolutely nothing," he added, shaking his head.

Melissa was jolted a bit awake by Tom's outburst. "I married such a romantic," she slurred before closing her eyes again and adjusting her head to find a more comfortable spot on Tom's shoulder. Tom gingerly moved his arm around her to cradle her, while explaining to the group, "She's a lightweight drinker, and on top of it our youngest doesn't sleep at night."

"Poor thing," Libby said sincerely, but then narrowed her eyes. "But how can you say that it's horseshit, Tom? Ignore him, Sean. Tell me everything. How did you meet? I love how-we-met stories. They're always filled with so much hope!" she said excitedly, pushing her fork into a triple-layer chocolate cake.

"From the moment I laid eyes on her, I knew everything I had ever known before would be different. I just knew. I can't explain it. But I knew there was something about her. I saw her one day while I was on a tour of Florence with my seminary class. I had only been in Italy a month when I was walking through the Santa Croce church and stopped suddenly in front of the gaudy tomb of Michelangelo. I was looking up at it and I thought I was standing behind a small child. But then I heard the child speak. She was talking in furious Italian to a friend. She was explaining that Michelangelo would have been horrified by the tomb, that it stood in direct contrast to everything he stood for as an artist or something like that. Her girlfriend disagreed and the two were arguing over the merits of Michelangelo's art. I knew then she was no child. No, she was not some diminutive little wisp of a person, but a force to be reckoned with. I was so busy listening in, I didn't realize how close I had approached them, and when Chiara turned sharply on her heel, she bumped into me and her angry tone dissolved into a contrite, '*Mi dispiace, Padre.*' I laughed, not just because of how quickly she could turn, on a dime, but because it was the first time anyone called me Padre. I wasn't even a priest yet, and to be honest, I was going through the motions. I didn't even want to be a priest. I was doing it out of some obligation to my dead mother, who I'd promised I would. I had one of those revelations, right then and there, and I turned on a dime, too. I knew in that moment I was hers. I corrected her, explained that I was just a seminarian not a priest, and she and I walked out of the church together, talking. I, of course, told her I totally agreed with her assessment of the tomb. We had a coffee. I thought we had talked for only twenty minutes, but four hours had passed. She missed her class. I missed my train back to Rome. Very long story short: we spent the rest of the day talking and meandering through the streets of Florence. And I couldn't bring myself to leave the city, leave her. So I didn't. By the end of that day, I'd shoved that collar in my pocket. I spent the evening with her, and then the next, and then the next, and before I knew it, just as those twenty minutes had disappeared into four hours, four hours disappeared into six months."

"Very *Thorn Birds,*" Libby said. "So juicy. Go on. I gotta hear more," she said, leaning forward and saying, "This is better than watching the season finale of *Downton,* even the one when Matthew finally got on his knees and asked Mary to be his wife."

"Nah, there's not much more to tell," Sean said, folding and refolding his napkin and then resting it on the table.

"Sure there is! Tell us what happened," Tom, surprising everyone with his curiosity, begged.

"Yeah, Sean, what happened? If you were so in love, how come you left?" James asked.

"It's complicated."

"Everyone says that." James shook his head as if to say he wasn't buying it. "Except that it's usually not. Sometimes it's as simple as one of you cheated, or one of you lost respect for the other, or one of you grew tired of picking up the other's socks, or the love you thought you'd 'walked into' just wasn't enough come time to pay the rent, man. Everyone wants to make it out to be complicated, but it always boils down to this: *me over you*. One person is selfish, and if you want a relationship to work, both have to be all in. And it always is complicated for the selfish one and simple for the one who was all in."

Libby looked at James, surprised by this rare instance of insight. "You talk from lots of experience, do you?"

"Pretty much. Un-forch," James said, cutting his word in half as he often did, as if it would have been thoroughly exhausting to come out and say the entire five-syllable word.

"But it was complicated, James. It was. It's hard for me to explain, but there came a point when I started to believe I wasn't worthy of her. She was so beautiful, so ambitious, and so filled with this energy and light. She was an artist and a brilliant student with all of these highfalutin friends, all these ideas and opinions. I felt like I couldn't keep up. I had dropped out of college. Dropped out of the seminary. I had no idea what I wanted out of life. And she did. She knew exactly. And the only thing I knew was that I wanted her. I wanted to be with her. And I felt like I was losing her. When we went out, I started to drink. Just to loosen up at first. Just to get comfortable, but then I couldn't stop. God help me, I couldn't stop. And I wanted to. I wanted to stop. I wanted to be as clean and alive and sober as I could be when I was with her. I wanted to feel every moment when I was with her, but at some point I wanted the wine more. Until it was all I thought about."

"Like I said." James nodded. "*Me over you*. It's that simple."

"But I didn't want to be selfish. I didn't," Sean shot back and then looked up at the ceiling tiles as if one of them hid his explanation and he needed to punch it out to get to it. When Sean looked back at each of them, they were locked in a communal stare. And he knew they understood. They knew. Even James put his fork down and pushed his plate toward the middle of the table.

Yes, Sean knew, they understood just how hard *the simple* really was. He knew that no matter how many meetings, no matter how many daily affirmations, no matter how many promises made to the self and others, that every simple no to the bottle, the food, the work, or the heroin was complicated. And if another person was at the table it would have been something else. Sean knew they knew. Everyone's got something that makes existing complicated. That makes them put the me-over-you in motion.

"I tried to get better though. I went to church. I thought that since it had worked before, it would work again. I went and spoke to a priest in Florence and confessed my sins. I told him about Chiara, about how much I loved her and how much I wanted to get better for her."

"So what did he tell you to do?" Libby asked.

"I thought he would say give up the wine. Do penance. But he told me to give up Chiara. He said I was obsessed. I was sinning by living with and fornicating with her and I was ruining the girl. He told me if I had any love at all for the girl, I'd leave her. I'd let her live her life, and I'd take my drunken ass back to America where I belonged. In not so many words . . . mind you."

"Well, that was some shitty advice," Tom chimed in. "You didn't take that load of crap, did you?"

Sean looked at all of them and raised his hands as if surrendering to the enemy. "I'm here, aren't I?"

"No, no, no, no," Libby said, shaking her head. "We have to make this right. You're sober now. She's an adult now. You're an adult now. You're not some nineteen-year-old kid who doesn't know better. Things have changed. If you loved each other, like you say you did, then"—Libby opened her arms wide—"then she'd be crazy not to give you a second chance. You have to go to her."

"We'll even help you," James said, wrapping his arms around Libby from behind and folding her into his chest. Libby turned and took James's hand in such a familiar way that it occurred to Sean for the first time that they were already a couple. Somehow, in the six months that had passed, they had fallen in love in plain sight, but Sean had missed it until now. *Of course they had.* They all spent hours together in his apartment. At restaurants. They often left and arrived at his place together. Sean recognized it instantly. *But why had James kept it from him? Why had Libby?* Then, almost instantly, Sean knew the answer. They pitied him. They were afraid to be happy in front of him. He imagined it was Libby's idea to keep it quiet. James wasn't the type to keep secrets. But love changes people, Sean knew. He knew it better than anyone. And James and Libby were in the part of new love that was all theirs. Just theirs. If no one knew about it, no one could taint it. They, too, had walked into the mist, and were getting consumed by it. He saw the change now in Libby's face: the relaxed laughter, the ease of her actions around James, and the glow in her cheeks.

Tom threw his napkin on the table. "Damn tyranny of the religious, self-righteous, fundamentalist bullshit artists who go around ruining people's lives."

Sean looked up at Tom and it took a minute for him to register Tom's reaction. He was still thinking of Libby and James, but then said, "Tom, I know that it would be easy for me to blame that priest. Blame anyone, but I know, in the end, I was the one who started to drink. I was the one who made the decision to leave. In a way the priest was right. I was a mess and I was messing up Chiara in the process."

"So how did you do it?" Libby asked. "How did you, you know, break the poor girl's heart?"

"I just left," Sean admitted, shaking his head in disbelief at his own actions.

"No note? No good-bye? No phone call?" Tom asked disapprovingly.

"Nada," Sean said, mindlessly pushing around his cake now.

"That's like, I don't know, harsh," James added. "Way harsh. I wouldn't want to see you."

"James!" Libby said, swatting his arm.

"I am just being honest! If you ask me, I think that's pretty weak. Pretty damn weak. No offense, Sean."

"None taken, and I agree, James. That's why I have to make this right. I owe her at least an explanation. Face-to-face this time. See, that's why it's so important that I don't write, call, or e-mail. It will appear, as you say, James, *weak*. I have to go to her and do something right for a change."

James, Tom, and Libby all nodded in agreement and reached across the table to take Sean's hand. Even Chief, who'd sat quietly beside Sean through the entire meal, leaned over and propped his head on Sean's lap in tacit agreement.

"Whatever you need us to do, man, we got your back," James said.

Sean stopped and tried to capture the moment. A moment he hadn't experienced in years. Not since he, Gaspar, Cathleen, and Colm were all together. He tried to rest there in the swell of it. He could feel his chest expanding with the enormity of what he was beginning to feel. He couldn't quite capture it, but he knew that what was happening in that moment was the beginning of something. He wasn't sure of what exactly. He had no idea how it would end or if it would end, but he could feel something was most definitely happening. A bond was forming joke by joke, shared story after shared story, forkful by forkful, smile after smile, argument after argument, secret after secret. It was a moment of fullness, of complete and utter abundance. *My cup runneth over,* Cathleen would have said if she was here. It was like feeling every possible emotion there was to feel all at once. He was exhausted but exhilarated. Scared but hopeful. Alone but surrounded by friends. Wanting but satisfied. Sad but happy. Homesick but utterly at home. And he knew that everyone at the table, somehow, at some point, had a reason for being here with him at this moment, too. *There is always a reason, Uncle Sean.* He looked at Libby's sweater that hid her track-marked arm, resting on James's back. He looked at Tom cradling his wife with one arm and pushing his plate full of carbohydrates as far as possible from himself. He looked at James tucking a fresh napkin into his shirt collar, ready to dive into the remnants of Libby's half-eaten cake. He looked down at Chief, the only one of all of them completely at peace, nodding off at his feet. He felt the swell surround him, swallow him whole and spit him out, sending him soaring, flying now, through a world without winged angels, but ones who appeared, as if from out of nowhere, and asked nothing from him in return. And yet he somehow felt indebted to them. He knew he owed each of them for getting him this far. He wanted to be the kind of friend to each of them that they had been to him. And he knew he would start right now. Today.

Chapter 14

AT SEAN'S APARTMENT THE FOLLOWING EVENING, Libby, back in her jeans and Converses, sat quietly curled up next to Chief and watched *Jeopardy!*, waiting for Sean to emerge from his bedroom.

"When's the movie, Lib?" Sean shouted from his room as he made the final adjustments to his hair, trying hard to brush the pieces toward his face to hide the scar tissue that lined his face and ear.

"Seven, I think. James texted me and said he's on his way. He's running late. We'll have to catch dinner after. So don't rush."

Sean grabbed his walker and slowly made his way down the hall. Libby hopped up with Chief and they walked over to assist him.

"I got it. I look a lot worse than I am. It actually doesn't hurt too badly to walk. I feel stronger every day."

"Tom said you're only supposed to take a few steps at a time. You're not to overdo it."

"I'm not. I got this. Go sit down. I'll be there in a second," Sean said, slowly making his way across his tiny apartment. "So you said James texted you. Do you and James talk a lot?" Sean asked, looking out of the corner of his eye and watching the answers flash on the screen before him as he made his way to the couch to sit next to Libby.

"What makes you say that?"

"I saw how you guys touched and flirted at his party last night. You're together. Aren't you?" Sean asked, collapsing slowly beside her.

Libby turned her body toward Sean. "It was that obvious?"

"Pretty much," Sean said, pulling the walker alongside the couch and out of his view of the TV.

"James wanted to keep it from you. He was worried. He thinks that maybe . . . you have a . . . oh, forget it. He is just worried that you'd feel like a third wheel."

"Nah. I am happy for you guys. Seriously. He's a great guy, Lib. But I have to ask, how did it happen?" Sean could see Libby begin to blush. "Go on. Spill it. I want to hear all about it."

"It was amazing, really. Sean, you wouldn't believe it. Without a hint of hesitation or self-consciousness, James flat out told me, 'I think you're the most amazingly beautiful woman I have ever seen.' He said it the night he walked me to my car with Chief. I guess it was right after that time he bought us all Thai food. Back when I was bringing Chief to see you every day."

Sean laughed and shook his head. "Kid doesn't waste any time. That's like right after we all met. Sounds like James."

Libby laughed, too, and nodded. "I thought he was joking. I went right back at him and said, 'Yeah, right.' No one had ever said those words to me, Sean. No one. He didn't play any games. He didn't hold anything back. All he said was, 'I want to kiss you. May I kiss you? I won't if you'll feel uncomfortable. But it's really all I can think about.' Can you imagine just coming out and asking for what you want?"

Sean nodded again. "Yes, Lib. Yes, I can. He doesn't mince words and doesn't waste time." Sean could actually picture James seizing his chance to kiss Libby. No, there were no silly one-liners for James. If he liked what he saw, he told people so. And he knew Libby, herself, was too smart to fall for some false pickup line. Women like her heard them on a daily basis. And Sean knew what James already did: if he wanted to kiss her, he would have to just tell her exactly what he wanted.

"Sean, he said it so matter-of-factly, it took my breath away. I kept telling him, 'You're crazy,' but he just looked at me with complete sincerity and waited for me to nod. And when I did nod, James put his hands on my hips—high-school-dance style, like this," Libby said, grabbing Sean's hips, "and then he leaned in and kissed me. I couldn't pull away. I just couldn't. I didn't want him to stop. Ever."

"That smooth operator," Sean acknowledged, sliding Libby's hands off his hips, feeling suddenly uncomfortable this close to her, to anyone. "Then what?"

"James said, 'We should get out of here,' and without saying anything I followed him across the hospital garage and got in his truck with Chief sitting in between us. I thought he was taking me to his place to finish what we started, but without skipping a beat he says to me, 'I know this amazing Italian place that overlooks the water. You'll love it!' Can you believe that? He didn't take me to bed. He took me to dinner . . . again . . . after we had just eaten."

"You want me to be surprised about that? About James? Of course I can believe it! James follow up a kiss with dinner? Classic. Aw, Lib. Sounds sweet. I am so happy for you two."

"Really? You're happy? You're not mad that we were sneaking around on you? Or jealous? James thinks you have a crush on me."

"Me? Have a crush on you? What are we, ten?" Sean laughed and then squeezed her hand. "You're sweet and all . . . but . . ."

"Well, you don't have to be so mean about it!" Libby joked and punched him lightly in the arm with her free hand.

"No, it's just that I really, really can't help but think about anyone other than Chiara. You understand? Right? You're beautiful. I didn't mean it that way. It's just—"

"I know what you mean, Sean. You're like a brother to me. A wonderful, kind, funny brother. The brother I never had." Libby squeezed his arm and leaned in to put her head on his shoulder.

It was Sean who was blushing now. Embarrassed and feeling unworthy of being called *brother,* Sean shook his head. He had barely been a brother to his own sister of late. "James is a lucky guy, Lib. You're a good person. He deserves a good, decent person. You both do."

"You know that night at dinner—our first date—James

said the very same thing about you. We talked till nearly two A.M. And he told me about how you guys met on the job. He told me how quiet you were, and lonely, when you came to the fire department and how he couldn't imagine being so far away from your home in New York. He said he thought something bad had happened to you back there. He's convinced you experienced something terrible that you never want to talk about. And he doesn't want to force you to do it."

Sean shook his head.

"What? Sean? You can tell me."

"It's not something I talk about. With anyone. Not even James."

"I understand, Sean. James does, too. We all have something we can't talk about. It's okay to keep it to yourself. To own it. It's okay. Keep it till you're ready. But know that James and I are always here."

"Thanks, Lib."

"No, thank James. He's the one who told me that."

"He's a pretty smart guy."

"Did you know he reads like a book a night? That he's the youngest of seven children? Grew up right here in Venice Beach and is a third-generation firefighter?"

Sean nodded.

"Of course you do, Sean. James said you spent every available hour together for the past three years, surfing mostly. He's worried about leaving you all alone . . . He's worried that I'll come between you guys."

"He's a good guy, Lib. Like I said, I'm not worried. He shouldn't be. I am glad he's got somebody. I was worried about him actually. Worried that if I ever left for Italy, there'd be no one here for him . . . no friend at least. He's got family coming out of the woodwork, but you know what I mean."

"I do, Sean. I do."

"I've never met anyone who loves life more, Lib. He enjoys every moment. Every bite of food. Every wave. He enjoys the simplest and most wonderful things and he's always reminding me to do the same. I would have been lost here without him. He's the most genuine guy I know and I've never met a guy before who just wants to help for the sake of helping."

"I know. He's almost too good to be true. He told me he became a firefighter not just because it was what his dad did, but because he couldn't imagine ever doing anything other than helping people for a living," Libby said, shaking her head in disbelief. "I mean, what's a guy like him see in a girl like me?"

Sean looked at her for a long time and a thought occurred to him. He knew that besides Libby's beauty and her heart, James probably saw someone else he could help. *Another lost soul to show the moment to.* But Sean didn't say it out loud. "You're fantastic, Lib. That's why. He knows it. I know it."

"You know what James told me the secret to happiness is?"

Sean knew, of course. He had heard James's speeches over and over on their way to catch waves. *Live in the moment. Forget the bullshit everyone tells you. The bullshit everyone expects from you. Just be here. Right now, man.*

"Live in the moment, Sean. It's like, duh. I mean everyone says that. But when he said it, it was like, *click*. I get it. Yes. Yes, James. You're so right."

"He has a way about him, Lib."

"You want to know what else he told me?"

"Should you be telling me this, Lib?" Sean said, looking worried. "I don't want you betraying his trust or anything."

"It's okay. I think you should hear it. He told me how scared he was about losing you in that fire. He said he was at the corner of the house, running toward you as you fell. He saw you land, Sean. He thought you were dead. At first the scene played itself over and over like a loop in his head. He couldn't bear to watch it. And the only thing that helped was sitting by you in the hospital and seeing your face. You were in a coma and you couldn't respond, but he talked to you every day. He told you he blamed himself. He told you he should have been there with you and that you shouldn't have been up in that house all by yourself. It was by being with you, every day, in the moment, that he could get back out of that nightmare he kept reliving when he wasn't with you."

"I wish he didn't feel that way. I wish he knew that it's not his fault. That it's not his burden. That stuff just happens."

"I think he knows that now, Sean. Seeing you recover, seeing you up and walking has really helped him, too. He told me last night that seeing you walking was the best birthday present anyone has ever given him."

"Jeez. I had no idea. I guess I forgot about that."

"What did you forget, Sean?"

"I forgot that when bad things happen to people we love, it can hurt us just as much. All this time I've been thinking about me. I didn't think about what all this was doing to James."

"It's not doing anything to him now, Sean. He's fine. But

I just want you to know how much he loves and cares about you. And how he doesn't want you thinking that he and I are going to come between what you guys share."

"I know that. But as his friend it makes me happy to know that he is happy and that he has found someone to love him. Really love him. And I can't tell you how happy I am that he's found someone he can love who will give him the love he deserves."

"You know that is exactly why I love him so much. I love him because he loves me. I love the way he loves me. He makes me feel like I matter in this world. He calls me. He listens to me. He drops whatever he is doing when I need him. You know what he said the other night? *'It is you who I want, Libby Cartwright. You more than anyone else. It's you I want to kiss. You I want to eat with. You I want to wake up next to. You I want to sit in my truck with and watch the waves crash against the rocks. It is you I want to be with. You. I choose you. Every day. It's that simple. You over me. I choose you.'"*

"Man. He's super smooth. I gotta remember that for my big moment," Sean said with a wink.

"Sean, I want to disappear into that love. Just like you said you did with Chiara. For the past few weeks I thought it would be impossible to explain to anyone else what it felt like to be with him and so I didn't even try. I didn't want to. But now I can't help it. It overwhelms me and I want everyone to know."

"Know what?" James shouted, walking through the door and catching Sean's hand wrapped around Libby's as she told him about her love for James. "What's this?"

Libby pushed herself away quickly and leaped off the

couch and wrapped her arms around James. "James! You're here, ready for the movie?"

"What did I miss?" James asked, looking at Libby and then at Sean suspiciously.

"Lib here was just telling me how you two have been sneaking around on me."

"What?" James looked at Libby. "I thought we discussed this."

"I know, James. But it's Sean. He's fine with it. No biggie. Right, Sean?"

"I'm happy for you guys. Now let's quit the bullshit and get out of this apartment. I am going stir crazy in here."

James pulled the walker from beside the couch and put it in front of Sean. "I wanted to tell you myself, Sean. I did. I just . . ."

"James, don't worry about it. Help me up," Sean said, pushing hard on the walker to stand up.

"I got your back, man. I'll always have your back," James said while watching Sean and Libby share a knowing smile.

❧ Chapter 15

A FEW MONTHS AFTER HIS FIRST STEPS TO HIS FRIENDS in the restaurant, Sean, back to his full 285 pounds and free from his chair for nearly two months now, stood up in the occupational therapy gym and took steps without the assistance of a walker or his leg braces. Holding on to Chief's leash in one hand and a cane in the other, Sean walked the length of the workout room. He had to swing one leg out in front of the other and brace himself with the cane, which made for an awkward gait, but when all was said and done, he was able to walk nearly twenty feet.

Tom cheered for and encouraged him the entire way. "You got this, Sean. You got this, man. See how easy it is getting. It's because you're strong. Those strength workouts are working, man."

"You've been hanging out with James too much, Tom.

Better watch out. Today it's saying things like *man,* tomorrow you'll be eating carbs."

"Come on, Sean. Come on. You got this. Come to papa!" Tom held out his arms and beat his chest once.

Sean exhaled hard and puffed his cheeks and let out small shouts of pain with each step, as he often did. *Acchhh.* Step. *Goddammit. Step. Goddammit.*

"That's it. That's it. Let it out."

When Sean stopped Tom caught him in his own arms and hugged him.

The two stared at each other for a second and then pulled back, repelled, as if they were both the North Poles of magnets.

"We shall never speak of this again," Tom said, standing up straight.

"Aw, come on, Tom, you know you love me," Sean said, wiping the sweat off his head and sitting down on a chair that Tom had waiting for him.

As excited as he was to go so far without a walker, Sean was still disappointed. He had hoped that by now he would be jogging. He had hoped there would be no discomfort. But with every step, he felt an explosion of pain that radiated up through his legs and his lower back.

"The pain you feel is just sciatica; the nerves are out of whack because of all the adjustments to your structure and your weird gait. You'll feel better with more work," Tom assured him.

"More work?" Sean said incredulously.

"You've come far, my little grasshopper, but you have far to go," Tom said and bowed to Sean mockingly.

"Knock it off, Tom," Sean said, snapping him with his towel. "I was just thinking that by now I'd be up and running. Gaspar said it would only take six months. It's been nearly a year."

"Gaspar's a cardiologist. I'm a PT. Would you take heart diagnoses from me?"

"Point taken." Sean shrugged. "I just gotta get moving. Not only here, but with my life. I can't be stuck inside all day. I have to figure out what I am going to do. And I can't do that if I don't get to Chiara, and I can't do that if I don't get better."

"Well, Sean, let's say, for the sake of argument, we take Chiara and this cockamamie idea to head off to Italy next month and sweep her off her feet like in some dumb chick flick, and we focus on the first part of your statement: getting you out of the house and figuring out what you want to do with your life."

"I'll know what I want to do after I see Chiara. I need to figure out what she wants me to do."

"No."

"No *what,* Tom?"

"No, that's a bad idea. Worst idea I've ever heard. No woman in her right mind wants some guy appearing on her doorstep and saying, *I'm all yours, tell me what you want me to do.* They want you to know *what you want.* They want to see that you're decisive. Because, chances are, if you exhibit signs that you know what you want and what you want to do, then she'll be pretty sure that your intentions toward her are equally decisive. I think most people feel this way."

"How's that working for you, Tom?"

"Whaddya mean?"

"Well, you seem to know exactly what you want—your job, your perfectly chiseled body—but does your wife know you want her? Does she know you've decided to fit her into your plans, your work? How about your kids?"

Tom took a step backward and walked around in a small, tight circle, as if looking for a contact that had just fallen out of his eye. When he looked up his eyes narrowed into two slits. Sean thought Tom was going to punch him, but he didn't. Instead, Tom opened his eyes and his shoulders dropped.

"What, Tom? I'm sorry. I didn't mean to hurt your feelings. It just came out. Are you okay?"

"No, no, I am not."

"What is it? Did I strike a chord?" Sean asked, using the same line Tom had used on him the first day they'd met.

"Yeah, you jackhole. You did."

"You know, Italy is beautiful this time of year," Sean said, looking out the window. "It's late spring. Northern Italy is just spectacular. And nights in Florence . . . they can be very romantic."

"What are you getting at, Sean?"

"I'm saying take your wife to Italy. Take her away. Tell her she matters. Carve out some place for her. Go a little nutty and take a few days off from working out. Heck, go home early today and take her flowers. Tell her you want to try. Tell her that your marriage means something, that you both deserve better. Your kids, too."

"Is this so you can get me on a plane to take you to Italy?"

"Maybe," Sean said with a wry smile, "maybe not. But you know, ever since I followed that angel out of that building and took that leap of faith, I've started to believe that we're all in need of angels and second chances."

Tom turned quickly and looked at Sean. "What angel? You never told me about any angel."

Sean caught himself and realized he'd slipped.

"Oh shit. It's nothing."

"No, it is not. You never told me any crazy story."

"Gee, I wonder why?"

"What is this all about, Sean?"

"Do you believe in angels, Tom? I mean, do you believe in them even though there's no real proof they exist? Other than, say, that I am sitting here and alive to tell the tale."

"I don't, Sean. I'm sorry, but I don't."

"But I saw one, Tom. I did. Clear as day. Just like you standing before me. She was real. And if she hadn't pointed me to the window, I'd be charred toast right now. I believe that with my entire body. I believe it, even if no one else does. I believe that I was spared for a reason. I believe I was spared to make my life better, have a fresh start, and make things right, especially with Chiara. Every day that I get up and work out with you, I see her. I see her at the end of every exercise. Every walk across the room. I see her. She is my finish line. My angel. My everything. She is the reason I get up in the morning. The reason I didn't give up a long time ago."

"Sean, I think the world of you. I do. And I admire your optimism. I see how hard you're trying and I don't want anything to get in the way of that, and if this girl Chiara is the carrot at the end of the stick and will get you to walk and move on with your life, so be it. But I know from experience that you can't go back. You can't undo the hurts, you can't take back the things you said and did. The hurt stays forever. Second chance or no. Angel or no angel."

"Are you talking about you? Your wife? Or me?" Sean asked.

"All of it. I am talking from a lot of experience that I earned in the world of effing-it-up."

"But have you tried? Have you really put forth an effort to be better? Have you given the same effort to your wife that you do to your workouts? That you do with me?"

Tom looked up at the ceiling and exhaled. "No, Sean. If I am being totally honest, no. But it's complicated."

"No, it's not. James is right. It's not. One of you has to make a step in the other's direction. I'm sorry, Tom, but from where I'm sitting, that person should be you. I know she loves you. I know you love her. I saw how you took care of her the night of James's party when she got a little tipsy. I've never seen you so tender. So taken with someone. I know you love her. And I know she's devoted to you. She stood by you when you were more ripped up than I was. She could have left you. You weren't married back then. She could have given up on you. But she didn't. She stayed by your side, like you've stayed by mine. That means something. That means everything. And I've had you to myself for too long. You need to start carving time out for her. You need to go to her. Just start working on it. I'm telling you there's always hope. There's always a chance to make up for lost time."

"I know you're right. I know that. But it's so hard. I don't know if I can bridge this distance between us. It's been too long. I don't even know what to talk about with her. I don't think she'll ever leave me. But I know she wants more. I just don't know if I can be the type of husband she wants. I don't know if I can be . . . I just can't . . ." Tom shook his head.

"I know you're tough, Tom. No one doubts that. I know it takes one hell of a man to go to war, almost lose a limb, come home, get married, and then go on living the rest of your life like you're strong enough to handle it all so you don't burden your wife and family. I know what you're up to. What you've been up to, because I've been there. I threw myself into work for years and I thought that would be my ticket out of the pain I felt. But it's not. The best way to get better is to walk right through that pain. You've been teaching me how to do it for months. Now you need to do it. And you need to walk to her. You need to do it even though it hurts like hell. You need to tell her she matters. She's enough. That you're not running from her, but running from yourself, your memories, your nightmares. Whatever. You just need to tell her you don't feel so tough. You need to stop running away, Tom."

"But how? What do I say?"

"Sometimes you don't have to say anything. You just need to show up. Be there for her. Start small. You have a lot of time to make up for. You can't go crazy. Just start making an effort. Start tonight. After you get me home, go to her. The best time to start, when trying to make a change, is now. Right now. Just go to her."

"But James and Libby won't be by the apartment till dinnertime. That's hours from now. I'll just wait till quitting time."

"No, Tom. I insist. Go now. I mean it. I will be fine on my own for a few hours. I still have my walker and Chief."

"Are you sure? No. Wait. I can't. Gaspar will have me fired."

"Go! Drop me at home first. I won't report you to the VNA. Then go and take her some flowers. The kids will be at school, so maybe you can use the time alone . . . you know . . . to really knock her socks off . . ."

Tom held up his hand to stop Sean from saying something he didn't want to hear.

"What? I meant fold some laundry or load the dishwasher . . . of course . . ."

Tom cracked a knowing smile. "Yeah, that's what I'll do."

"Sure you will," Sean said with a wink.

"You did great today, Sean. And you've made terrific progress these past nine months. I have no doubt you can do this. But do you really think you can do this? You'll be careful? I don't want to have to make any phone calls to Gaspar explaining why you fell in the shower and hit your head."

"I cross my heart: I will not set foot in the shower. Besides, if I want to go to Italy next month, I have to be able to be at home alone one of these days. I'll be fine. Never better," Sean said, patting Chief on his back. "No one needs to worry about me. I've got a hell of a guardian angel," Sean said, grinning.

"Sure you do," Tom said, shaking his head. "She looks like she did a bang-up job last time," Tom said, grabbing his medic bag and keys from the table. "Let's get you home."

Outside the gym, Tom walked Sean and Chief to the car. Sean looked strong. Tom barely needed to help him. With the exception of letting Sean use his shoulder to lever himself into the truck, Tom wasn't much help at all. He was just backup if Sean needed a hand or got tired. Once Sean was settled in the truck, Tom tossed Sean's walker in the truck bed with his medical bag and jumped in the driver's side after Chief.

"Gorgeous day out there," Tom said, looking out the windshield at the bright sun.

"If I could, I'd be out on the waves. Man, I miss it."

"It won't be long. In fact, there is no reason why you can't at least try."

"Nah. Still a little nervous about saltwater. I can't imagine what it would feel like on some of the wounds that still haven't healed completely."

"You can wear a wet suit. We should get you out there."

"I don't know. I don't think I'm ready. It's so weird, though. You know, I've spent the majority of my life without surfing and then it totally took over my life. Once you learn how to do it, once you catch your first wave, there is no going back."

"I know what you mean."

"You surf?"

"I did. Long time ago. I grew up out here on these waves. I haven't actually hopped up on a board in a long time. I swim though and body-board. I do just about everything else."

"Your legs?"

"Nah. They're strong enough now. It's just that . . . ." Tom shook his head, unable to finish his thought.

"You're scared to get back up on the board? To have to be a novice all over again?" Sean said.

"Exactly," Tom said and nodded.

"Me too, Tom. Me too. Nothing scarier than starting all over."

"It's a bitch," Tom acknowledged.

"You can say that again," Sean said.

Then, apropos of nothing, Tom turned and looked at Sean,

suddenly remembering a flip comment Sean had made earlier at the gym. "You know what you said back in the gym about going to Italy? You used specifics. You said you want to go *next month*. Have you made plans I don't know about? What about Gaspar and your sister? Didn't they want to take you?"

"No, I haven't made definitive ones. But I've been looking into flights. I wanted to be as good as new when I see her again. And I feel like I am getting there. Besides, I found out some stuff. It's amazing what you can find out these days. Her parents still own the same apartment they did eleven years ago. I can start there. They'll know where to find her. She's long since moved from the apartment she lived in with roommates while she was in college. Her parents were older folks who had a late-life kid."

"That's not really a lot to go on. It is 2014. You can do something totally crazy . . . and you know . . . call or e-mail the woman. There is such a thing as the Internet," Tom said.

"I told you, Tom. I need to do this in person. I never said good-bye to her. I have to do it this way. My way. If I were there I wouldn't talk to me on the phone or reply to some e-mail. Besides, I made a promise. I would be a better man. I would do the right thing. I have to do it this way."

"Okay, okay. So you know where her family is, but what about her? Did you find out anything about her? Where she works? If she is married? Has kids?"

"I know she graduated from Florence University of the Arts with her MFA a few years ago. I found some highfalutin articles published in obscure peer-reviewed journals with her name in the notes. Of course I had no idea what they said. My Italian is rusty. But still. It's something. She's out there."

"But did you find any wedding announcements?" Tom asked.

"No."

"So there is hope?" Tom smiled.

"There is hope." Sean nodded.

"Guess that's all you need," Tom said uncharacteristically. Sean could tell something in his friend was softening. It probably had been for months, but he was only now noticing it. Change is one of those things that no one notices is happening until the metamorphosis is nearly complete.

"Well, don't go do anything rash. You've come this far."

"I know. But I feel like time is everything now. I've lost so much time, and waiting a day now seems like forever."

"I know what you mean. Just be careful."

When Tom pulled up in front of Sean's apartment to let him out, Sean insisted Tom let him walk himself up.

"I'm twenty feet away from the elevator. What the hell could happen? I got this. Just go already. Get the hell out of here. There has to be a first for everything. Let me go."

Tom jumped out of the truck and grabbed Sean's walker from the bed, but balked for a moment, looking at Sean and then the door to the apartment building. "I guess you're right. There has to be a first for everything."

"I can do this," Sean reassured Tom. "Come on, Chief. Come on, boy." Chief hopped out of the truck cab and stood beside Sean dutifully.

Tom handed Sean his walker. "You're all set then."

"Good luck this afternoon with Melissa. I'll bet she'll love seeing you home early. It will be a nice surprise for her."

"Baby steps," Tom said and nodded.

"That's how we all get started." Sean laughed as he took a small step toward the door. "Go, get the hell out of here. Leave me alone. What does a guy gotta do to get some peace?" Sean said, laughing.

"Okay. Okay. Chief, buddy. Keep an eye on him."

Chief seemed to nod and move alongside Sean toward the door.

Tom walked around the truck, hopped in and sat in the car, and watched as Sean disappeared behind the door to the apartment building.

"Here goes nothing," Tom said to himself, pulling off.

❧ Chapter 16

ONCE INSIDE THE APARTMENT BUILDING, SEAN LOOKED across the lobby. He had lived here for three years, and the space had never looked quite so palatial.

"All I gotta do is make it to the elevator, Chief. Twenty feet and I'm there."

Chief walked alongside Sean, and when he got to the wall, he hopped up on his hind legs and pressed the Up button just as Libby had trained him to do several months before.

"Good boy, Chief. Good boy."

Sean entered the elevator and felt the sweat pouring down his back. He was beginning to feel lightheaded. Between the exercise with Tom during PT and now this walk, he was about done in.

"How am I going to get to Italy, Chief? Huh? How am I going to do that if I can't make it across my own lobby?"

Chief grunted as if he agreed.

"I am such a jackass. I can't do this. I can't. What am I

doing? You think Tom is right? You think I need to get my act together before I go find Chiara?"

Chief looked blankly back at him and cocked his head to the side.

"That's what I thought, buddy. I don't know what to do, Chief. Tell me what to do," Sean demanded, having grown so accustomed to ordering the dog around and talking to him that he half-expected Chief to start talking like the dog in the Bush's baked beans commercials. *Roll that beautiful bean footage.*

Just then the elevator door opened and Sean and Chief arrived outside his apartment.

Sean had put the keys in when Chief started barking.

"Settle down, boy. It's okay!"

Chief continued to bark. Unaware that the dog was trying to warn him that he was the one in danger, Sean thought something was wrong with the dog.

Suddenly, Sean felt the blood draining from his head. A hint of nausea rose from within. He thought he might faint or throw up. He was unsure which. "Quiet, boy, I have to go lie down for a minute."

As the keys went in the door Sean's body gave way and he landed with a thud on the tile floor in the foyer. On his way down, he hit the left side of his head on the adjacent kitchenette counter. The impact of the blow caused his eardrum to burst and a smattering of blood shot out of his good ear and pooled around him as he lay unconscious on the cool tiles.

Chief circled Sean calmly two times. He put his paw up on his back. If anyone didn't know better, you would think he was feeling for a heartbeat or checking Sean's vitals.

He tried to revive Sean by nudging his face with his own nose. He licked him over and over, and then put his paw up on his back again and tapped him, as if to say, "Come on, chap. Up and at 'em."

Sean didn't budge.

Chief lay close beside Sean, so that his torso touched Sean's. He propped his head on his paws and waited for Sean to wake. After some time had passed and Sean did not wake, Chief got up on all fours and walked out of the apartment, deciding it was best to wait by the elevator should a human arrive to help.

It was Libby who found Sean.

James and Libby had been relieving Tom each night for weeks. They bridged the hour and a half before the night nurse came at seven. One or both of them, given James's shift schedule, brought or helped Sean make dinner. And, if Sean had managed to make something himself, they'd take him out for a walk along the boulevard.

When the elevator door opened and Libby saw Chief, she knew immediately something was terribly wrong. "What is it, boy? What is it?"

When Libby approached the apartment, she found Sean just about to sit up and holding on to his good ear, where blood had coagulated.

"Oh thank God!" Sean said, seeing Chief walk in beside Libby. "I thought I scared him, crushed him, and he ran away."

"What happened, Sean? Where's Tom?"

"I sent him home early from the gym. I thought I could

manage taking a damn elevator ride up to my apartment myself. I thought I could do it all on my own. I'm ridiculous. I think I just passed out. Hit my head and then just fell asleep here. I think I slept the entire day. I'm no worse for wear."

"Jesus, Sean. That was stupid. Tom should have known better than to leave you alone," Libby said angrily, but still rubbing Chief's side. "You might have a concussion. We have to get you to a doctor. What if your brain is injured again? Damn Tom. That was so thoughtless."

"It's not his fault. Don't be mad at him. We were having a heart-to-heart of sorts at the gym, which we never really do. Against his own rules, you know. But I brought up his wife and one thing led to another and I told him he needed to go home to her. Seize the moment, as James would say. And you know Tom. How he can be. Not much of a talker and doesn't like to get too deep. But he got deep and thought: *It's now or never. He has to go and tell his wife the stuff he is telling me. She is the one who needs to hear this. Not me.*"

"Your own love story not enough, Sean? Now you're playing cupid with Tom, too? First James and me? Now Tom and Melissa?"

"Hey, hey, I had nothing to do with you and James. You went off and did that all without me, remember? Didn't even consult me or ask me how I felt," Sean teased.

"Oh, Sean." Libby shook her head, and with it, tried to shake the memory of telling Sean about James and her. She assessed Sean's injuries. Still seething with anger, she placed a call to Tom. "I'm getting his voice mail," she said, cupping the edge of the phone and moving about the room frantically. "Where could he be?"

"Lib, Lib, calm down," Sean said, still sitting on the ground, unable to pull himself up. "The night nurse should be here soon. Just relax."

"This is serious, Sean. Really, really serious. Do you know what could have happened to you? What if your brain is bleeding inside and we don't know it?"

"No worries, Lib. Please. I'm all right. Will you please calm down? I have you here. I have Chief. Don't I, boy?" Sean said, grabbing him in a hug.

"You could have been hurt, Sean. Seriously. And how am I supposed to get you up? Get you into a chair?" Libby said, looking around.

"Will you please just relax? What's going on with you? Something's off . . ."

"Yeah, with you. You're lying on the ground and I can't get you up."

"Just sit here with me. I'll have my strength back in a few minutes. You can pull my walker over and I'll be able to leverage myself up. No worries. If I am going to get to Italy next month, I need to be able to handle little slips like this."

"Slips? You fell flat on your face, Sean. This is no slip. And wait, wait, wait, wait a second. Hold up. You're out of your ever-loving mind. You couldn't make it across the lobby and up an elevator today without passing out, and you think you can navigate international airports? International travel?"

"Oh, come on. People in worse shape have traveled. I can do this. I am ready. I don't want to waste another minute."

"Sean, be real with me for a second. I want you to be one hundred percent straight-up and real."

"Okay. Shoot."

"Are you using? Or are you drinking?" Libby asked, propping one arm on her hip and then scanning the room for bottles, all the while tapping her toes and biting the nails of her free hand.

"God, you're fidgety today. You feelin' okay?"

"It's not me we're talking about, Sean!" Libby snapped. "Do you have stuff in here? Where is it? I am taking it with me."

"What?" Sean said with a high-pitched laugh.

"Are you?" Libby asked sternly.

"I don't know what you're talking about or why you would say that."

"Really, you don't? Look at you. You're the one whose hands are shaking. You're the one who passed out. You've got this bee in your bonnet to get to Italy. It's like you're on something. Some sort of drug. I don't know."

"Libby, I appreciate your concern. I do. I know what it looks like. I totally agree, but I assure you, I am not. I am not using. Haven't had a drop."

"But you think about it? You do?"

Sean stopped and looked at her for a long time and was about to open his mouth and lie, but then said, "Yes. Every second."

"And so this new fixation, this quest-to-go-make-nice-with-the-love-of-your-life, is your new Jameson. It gets you through each hour, each day. Am I right?"

Sean held up his hand to interject, "Hey, hey, hey. What's going on? First Tom and now you. A few months ago at James's birthday party everyone was all: *Go to her. This is a great idea. We'll help you.* And now you're all flaking on me. What gives?"

"It's just that you wouldn't be the first person, Sean . . . you wouldn't be the first person to think you had it all figured out. To think love would solve everything. You just wouldn't . . ." Libby's voice trailed off and she shook her head and patted Chief vigorously.

"Seriously, what's this about?" Sean asked, realizing she wasn't talking about *Sean* anymore.

"Let's get you cleaned up." Libby walked into the kitchenette and grabbed a towel and ran cold water over it.

"Libby, sit down," Sean said, patting the floor where he sat. "Talk to me. I'm fine."

Libby walked over, knelt down, and pushed the cold, wet towel against Sean's ear to clean him. "You popped your eardrum. You're gonna need drops for that. And it's gonna hurt for a couple of weeks," Libby said, ignoring him. "Jesus, you're lucky you didn't split your skull open again. Good god, you're the luckiest man on the planet."

Sean took her arm and held it, and brought her in close. "Look at me, Libby. Stop taking care of me, of everyone else, of James, of the dogs. Look at me. Talk to me. You can trust me with anything. I'm your friend. I won't judge you," Sean said quietly, matching her whisper with his own. "Is there something you came here to tell me? Why are you here so early anyway? What's going on with you?"

Libby looked at him and tears filled her eyes. "I can't."

"You can't what?"

"I was so stupid. I thought he loved me," Libby said, collapsing in a heap next to Sean, resting her head against his chest.

"Who, James? Of course he does! He's crazy about you. Don't be ridiculous," Sean reassured her.

Libby started to cry. Sean put his hand up over her shoulder and wrapped her in close. It had been a long time since he had wrapped his arms around a woman totally and felt the electricity between his and another's body. Chief came alongside her and put his paw on Libby's leg and tried to comfort her, too.

"Who? Chief? He'll always love you," Sean joked.

Libby sobbed even louder.

"Libby, tell me what's wrong. We can't help you if we don't know," Sean said, realizing that since Chief came along, he now always answered everything with collective pronouns. *We're going for a walk. Would you like to come with us? We need to know what's wrong before we can help you.*

"You just have to trust me, Sean," Libby whispered. "I know what I am talking about. I know how easy it is to misplace one addiction for another. I'd never tell James this. He's too kind and sweet, and I can't tell you, because you're his best friend. I can't expect you to keep this from him, or for us to have a secret that he's not in on. Everything is so complicated and all sorts of wrong. And you know James . . . he likes things simple."

"Libby, what's going on? What happened? What did you do?"

"Sean, you just have to believe me. I am worried about you. You say you love this girl. And I want to believe you. I want to believe that type of love exists, but I don't know if it does. I was Chiara. For a long time, I was Chiara."

"What? You've lost me, Lib."

"Sean, I loved a guy like crazy. I loved him and I thought we were going to get married, and we'd have doves flying out of cakes and shit like that, and then after all that we'd go riding off into the sunset on his Harley and everything was going to be all big rock candy mountain sorts of happy. We met in rehab. So of course, there's that. I know, I know. Huge red flags should have been going up faster than Old Glory on Flag Day, but you know, I thought he got me. Understood me. And, worst of all, I really believed I would be enough. I thought I would be all he needed to fill that hole inside him, the one he was filling for years with drugs. I thought I would be enough. Because he was enough for me. He was what I needed to feel whole again. But I wasn't. He started using just a few months after we got out of rehab and he just up and disappeared one day. Gone. One day he's lying beside me in bed watching Letterman and laughing, and the next he's gone. It took me two years, Sean, two years, to go on a date. Two years to have the courage to put myself out there and fall in love again. I didn't want to ache like I did after he left. But I risked it. I let James love me. And dammit, I love him. But I screwed up."

"Jesus, Lib."

"My ex came back, Sean. He came back a few days ago. Showed up on my doorstep."

"You're kidding?"

"It's like he has a happiness radar. It's like he sniffs the happiness on me. As soon as I start getting my act together and start being happy, he shows up and tries to pull me back into his dark circle."

"You told him to get lost, right?"

"I wish, Sean. He came to me with all of these lines. He said stuff that you've been saying you wanted to tell Chiara. And for a second when he was talking, I was thinking: *Yes.*

Yes. Yes. He's just like Sean. He's turned his life around. He's coming out of the dark. He's making amends. He wants a second shot. We can have a second shot. This is what I have been pray-ing for. This is what I've always wanted and wanted to believe in. Sean, he told me he wanted to make things right, that he loved me and that everything would be different this time around. He brought up all these beautiful memories, shared jokes, and hard times we faced together. He touched my face, Sean," Libby said, touching her own without even realizing it, "and I swear to God, it was like a goddamn religious expe-rience. I didn't know my body missed his so much."

"Christ," Sean said, shaking his head as if not wanting to hear anymore. "You didn't . . ."

"We did."

"Christ," Sean said again, pushing Libby off his chest. "You're right, I really wish you hadn't told me. So what are you going to do? Break ol' James's heart? Send him packing? Where is Mr. Right Now, today? You guys taking advantage of James's shifts for some lovers' rendezvous? Is he down-stairs?"

"No. God. No. He wasn't clean, Sean. He's still using and he didn't just want me, want us to work out. He wanted my money and wanted to score with me."

"Libby, Libby, Libby," Sean said, shaking his head.

"See, it's complicated. If I tell James, I kill what we have forever. I kill all the hope and innocence and love he has inside and all the love, hope, and innocence he thinks he sees in me. No one has ever looked at me the way James looks at me. I don't want to lose that. I can't." Libby's voice cracked in desperation.

"Libby, he won't. You tell him everything. Everything you just told me. You be honest with him. He's a good guy. He'll understand. Love will see you through this."

"Sean, how can you be so blind? So damn hopeful? Don't you see? Don't you see what this means for *you*? *For Chiara?*"

"No, Libby, I am sorry but I don't."

"Your obsession with this woman, it's no different from what just happened to me. You're going to go blow into her life like a tornado and rip it to pieces, just so you can feel better. Get a hit. Get some juice. Score your thrill. At least my guy was up-front, he was just jonesing for a hit, the real thing. You're worse! You're replacing your juice with her. Your latest addiction is her! And what happens when you use her all up? Huh? What happens to her? Does she get to go on living her life? Does she get to pick up with the man she is probably very happy with right now? No. No, she doesn't, because you've ruined it for her. Could you just please drop this? Drop this Chiara thing? There are a million girls right out there on Venice Beach. You're in a city filled with the most beautiful people on the planet willing to be anything you want them to be and you can't make do with one of them?"

"Chiara is not an obsession, Libby. I am sorry about what happened to you, but I am not like that dirtbag boyfriend of yours. I am not. And from what I remember of Chiara, she has more common sense than you. And I would think after all of these months, after everything you've learned about me and know about me, you'd think better of me, of James, of humanity in general. It's not rife with amoral assholes looking to score."

Libby was wiping the tears that were dropping off her face in quick succession.

"I'm going to Italy, Libby. That I know for sure. I don't know what you're going to do, but I know what I want. I have known for a while now. I don't think you can say the same. And the only person I feel badly for right now is James, because he has no idea what a pile of crap he just stepped into."

"Sean, I didn't mean to hurt anybody."

"Libby, no one ever does."

"I just wanted to believe that what we shared all those years ago was real. I wanted to be sure. I wanted it to mean something. *I* wanted to mean something."

"Libby, you know what I wanted? For a split second tonight while I was on the elevator, I had this crazy idea come into my head. I thought, wouldn't it be great if Tom, his wife, and you and James all got on a plane and we went together, we all found love together? We all got our second chances. Because that's what I believe in. That's what I think is real. But you went and fucked it all up."

"Sean, I am sorry."

"I think you should go, Libby."

"Sean, you won't say anything . . ."

"No, Libby. I won't. You should be the one to say something. I'm done breaking people's hearts."

"Funny," Libby said.

"What's so funny?"

"You just broke mine."

"James is my friend, Lib. My friend."

"I thought I was yours, too," Libby said, shutting the door behind her.

❧ Chapter 17

BEFORE TOM ARRIVED THE FOLLOWING DAY TO PICK Sean up and head to the gym, Sean went out and sat on the balcony with Chief to watch the morning surfers, swimmers, speed walkers, and joggers. "All the usual suspects, Chief," he said, lifting his coffee and watching them. "Humans and their habits, addictions, routines. They're so predictable."

Sean did not hear Tom knocking on the door or shouting, so he was startled when Tom flung open the sliding door and shouted, "Oh thank God, you're alive and still here!"

"Where else would I be?" Sean said, wiping the coffee he'd just spilled all over himself.

"I don't know. You didn't answer the door. You didn't answer my texts. And when I checked my voice mails this morning, I noticed that Libby left a bunch of messages saying how stupid and irresponsible I was. I thought you never made it upstairs or had some crazy idea to go to Italy all alone.

Libby mentioned Italy. I don't know. She wasn't easy to understand. She sounded hysterical. I panicked."

Sean looked up at him and winced.

"Don't look at me like that. What happened?"

"Well, you'll be happy to know any attempts to get to Italy
anytime soon were thwarted by my kitchen counter," Sean
said, turning and showing his bruised face and ear. "And as
for your other concern, I was unconscious for a bit, but I'm
decidedly alive."

"I knew it. I knew something bad was gonna happen! I
leave you two alone for five minutes . . ."

"Actually, it was more like all day . . ."

"Crap. Are you okay? Do we need to get you to a doctor?"

"No more doctors."

"You're sure you're fine? You don't need to be examined?"

"I'm fine. Just a little fed up. Just a little sick and tired of
everything—these legs, these hands, this ear, and now my
other ear, and being trapped here and not able to get to where
I want to be—Italy," Sean complained.

"I get it. Let's take the day off from the gym. I worked you
too hard. I have an idea."

"What sort of idea?"

"I want to take you to do something. I think you're ready. I
think we're both ready. We'll need these," Tom said, pointing
to the boards hanging on the wall.

"You can't be serious? I can't even bend down and touch
my toes."

"You'll see. I'll go get your wet suit and gloves. I hope you
have one with a hood to protect the burns on your face and
neck. Grab your walker and help me find the stuff."

"About that . . ."

"What?"

"Can we ditch it?"

"Jesus, Sean. A few days in the gym walking without braces and a walker and you think you can just throw your walker away?"

"What can I say? I believe in my own abilities even if *everyone else* around me doesn't seem to. Besides, I have a cane, too. I can use that."

Tom stopped for a moment, picking up on the stressed *everyone else* that Sean had just said. In all the months he had known Sean, not once had he said something so blasé, so passive aggressive. "Just who is this *everyone else*, Sean? I didn't say anything to you about your abilities. All I said was, you need your walker. And I know James thinks you're doing well and Libby, too."

"Huh, don't get me started on Libby," Sean said with a wave of his arm.

Tom stopped for a moment, looked at Sean, then looked back in the apartment.

"What's going on with you and Libby, Sean?"

"Nothing. Nothing at all."

"No? Then why are you sitting out here like some kid sent to sit out recess? Shoulders all slumped and pouty? Complaining about Libby?"

"Nothing, I don't want to talk about it. Are we going out or are we going out?"

"Yeah, we're going out. But before you do, do you have something to tell me? Something I should know? Are you using? Is she? Do I have to lock up my med bag when I'm around you? What's going on? I'm getting a vibe that something is going on," Tom said, assessing the room.

"It's nothing, Tom. And why does everyone automatically assume I am using or drinking? That I just can't be happy? That I just can't be upbeat without a drug? Or I can't be down, because I am down."

"There you go with that *everyone* business. Jesus, you sound like my mother."

"Is she Irish? It's passive aggression. It's an Irish-Catholic tradition. Passed down with the Waterford, Belleek, and lace curtains."

"Be serious for a solid second. What happened yesterday? How did you hit your head?"

"Tom, please, let's change the topic. How did it go with the wife yesterday?"

"*The wife's* name is Melissa. And she asked me if I was the one on drugs when I showed up at home early, with dinner."

"What? She didn't like it?"

"No." Tom shook his head and smiled. "She did. We talked all night. It was great. And then it was not so great sometimes. But over all, it was a good thing you made me go home when I did. It's a miracle really. Like, I don't know, perfect timing. Like a message from God or something, if I believed in that crap. I had no idea how close to the brink she was, how lonely she had become, how resentful she was of me. To be honest, some of the stuff she said to me hurt, but it was all true. I would say we hadn't talked like that in years. I honestly don't know what happened to us."

"Routine."

"Excuse me?"

"Routine. It ruins the best of everything. You know how many people I see take the same walking route? See that guy down there? Like clockwork, I could set my watch by him. I see him every day. Rain, shine, heat, wind. Doesn't matter. Funny thing: he hasn't lost a pound of that gut he's been carrying around. Probably eats the same four thousand calories a day, too. And look over there: that surfer goes to the same damn spot every day. Even though the tides have changed and the water is different. And I know why they do it. They just do it 'cause it's what they've always done, and they're hoping this is the time things are going to work for them. Trust me, when anything becomes routine—from church to sex, from meals to exercise, from drink to drugs—the thrill dissipates. But even after the thrill is gone, most people can't stand to change it. They can't because it's all they know, even if it is making them miserable. So you have to do something different. It's not complicated. You should know that, Mr. Muscle Confusion, making me 'switch it up' every day in the gym."

"You would think, wouldn't ya? But knowing it and applying it are two different ball games."

"Tell me about it."

"Well, you ready to break routine today? Get the hell out of here?"

"Sure. Where to?"

"How 'bout heaven, Sean?"

Without a blink or a question, Sean replied, "Hell, yes."

Chapter 18

Tom took Sean and Chief to Heaven, Heaven's Rock to be exact, located north of Venice Beach on the Pacific Highway. When they approached the beach, Sean saw a familiar large rock covered in green algae, jutting out of the white sand and taking hits from the crashing waves. Sean had surfed the swells there before. Besides being renowned for its obvious beauty, the beach was better known among surfers for its consistency. The swells ran long and hollow. The soft waves were forgiving and less powerful than at other beaches. It was a nice spot for beginners. The best part though for Sean was that during the fall months, the beach was all but empty except for a few locals and surfers. It was one of the perks of being a firefighter who worked shifts and had weekdays off: He could hit the beach all day while kids were in school and the nine-to-fivers sat in their offices. And as much as he loved firefighting, he had expressed the thought on certain occasions that it wouldn't be too awful if he never had to work and could just surf Heaven's Rock till the end of time. The cruel irony though was now that that wish had come true—he actually could surf whenever he wanted—he couldn't even climb on a board, let alone carry one to the beach.

"I haven't been here in over a year, Tom. I don't think I'm ready," Sean said, shaking his head and looking at a few old-school surfers tearing it up.

"No one said you had to hop up on your board. We're just going to paddle a bit. Work on your upper-body strength. Get your toes wet, so to speak. Let Chief here have a go of it in the water," Tom said, pulling up Sean's wet suit and zipping him into it.

"I don't think Chief's even allowed on this beach," Sean continued to protest as Tom grabbed Sean's hands to put protective gloves on them.

"I thought service dogs are allowed everywhere," Tom said, tugging the gloves and shaking Sean's arms.

"Not exactly," Sean said, pulling back.

"Today they are, Sean. Just lighten up. This is going to be fun." Tom made sure there was no gap between the gloves and the wet suit. "You're all set. No salt on the wounds today, Sean. I mean it. Come on."

"Look at the size of the waves today, Tom. How the hell am I going to get out there? I haven't paddled in months," Sean said, pointing toward the rock, where waves were crashing.

"I told you, I don't hear the word *can't*. You'll be fine, and if not, I can help you. I haven't surfed in a long time either. But I've body-boarded here with the girls and Melissa. It's a lot easier than you think. Just put one arm in front of the other. Take one wave at a time. Trust me. We'll do this to-gether, Sean. We're both ready."

"I don't know," Sean said, shaking his head doubtfully.

"Don't move. Let me bring the boards down to the surf first and then I'll come back for you," Tom explained, leaving Sean standing by the truck while he walked the boards one by one down to the water's edge.

Sean grabbed Chief's leash and leaned on his cane, watching as Tom carried the long board down to the water. The sun had just popped out from behind a large elephant-shaped cumulus cloud that had taken up half the sky and the breeze quieted; the waves were peaking just to the left of the rock. Perfect. *The Perfect Day.* As Sean was counting the seconds between waves and making mental notes, a surfer in a black wet suit like his but with a turquoise swirl on the leg picked up a swell and swung his long blond hair behind his head, snap-ping his board over the crest of the wave in one fluid motion before riding it in. Everything inside Sean wanted to run and just dive in and join him.

Sean tried to walk. He moved one foot in front of the other slowly till he reached the end of the parking lot and stood at the edge of the sandy beach. Without looking down, he felt where the long, deep scar on his right thigh was underneath his suit and rubbed it with his thumb, like a worry stone. He took a step back, feeling uneasy.

Tom came running up the sand toward him. "Ready?"

"I can't, Tom."

"What do ya mean? We're just going to get in, no pressure."

"I can't do it. I just can't. Let's go home."

"Sean, come on. We're here. Let's do this. I can help you."

Sean bristled and shook his head. "No, dammit. I can't do it. I don't want to look like a gimp walking down the sand and then be handled like a baby out there, not in front of all those surfers. I'll look ridiculous. This is stupid. Let's go."

"No, Sean. I am not letting you off the hook. You wanted to do something different. You love this. Let's do it. Stop resisting. Just stop."

"But it's different. I can't. I can't do what I used to do. I'm not the same person I used to be."

"Sean, no one expects you to be. Those guys out there don't give a shit about anyone but themselves and their next wave. How many surfers do you remember wiping out or not catching a wave?"

"Huh?"

"In all of your rides, how many surfers do you remember wiping out? What are all of their names? And how much do you think about what losers you think they are?"

"I don't think they're losers. I don't think about them at all. I couldn't even tell you a thing about any of them."

"Exactly, Sean. No one cares about you as much as *you care about you*. And the same goes for the rest of the world. Everyone is so fixated on how they *themselves* look and act that they're not paying attention to anyone else. It's sort of freeing when you think about it. When you stop worrying about what others think of you, because you know they are decidedly not thinking about you—you can do anything. You're never really as important as you think you are."

"I know, but I'll look like a fool."

"Did you always know how to surf, Sean?"

"No, I was pretty terrible at it at first."

"Then it's just like that. You're starting all over again."

"That's the thing though. I know how good I was and how good I can be. What if I won't be good again?"

"Sean, you have to try. You have to take a leap of faith."

"This coming from Tom Smith, resident cynic? You are asking me to take a leap of faith?"

"Sure. Why not? You said yourself I need to change, switch it up, try new things, right? If I can do it, you can. We'll start over together."

"Together," Sean said and nodded.

Tom put his arm around Sean's waist and Sean hooked his arm around Tom's neck and the two walked slowly down to the water. Sean had forgotten how laborious it was to dig one's leg into the sand and push. Every step engaged a new muscle. He felt like he was learning to walk all over again.

"Am I too heavy, Tom?"

"You're not heavy, you're my brother," Tom said with a wink and a nod. Sean let out a loud laugh.

"You're such a smartass, Tom."

"Pot, I'd like you to meet Kettle. Kettle, this is Pot," Tom said, pointing at Sean.

As they reached the sand where the water smoothed and packed it firmly beneath their feet, Sean got his bearings and threw his cane back up on the dry sand.

Tom picked up the board and the three walked out into the surf. Chief hopped a bit at first, running in the surf and then running back out, dancing along the edge of the water, seemingly afraid at first to get wet until he was, and then there was no going back.

Sean went out slowly and felt the wave slap his thighs and then his stomach as he moved deeper into the water. When he was waist high, he let himself fall back.

Submerged under the water, Sean closed his eyes and spun a few times, feeling the freedom of being completely weightless and unburdened by his legs. For a split second he remembered the hotel somewhere in Nevada, where Colm had come out of his room running with abandon for the water, his arms swinging as he jumped into the pool and swam to his mother. *This is what it felt like for him. This is the joy he felt. The possibility he saw then. I see now. I see it now, Colm.*

Sean broke through the surface and popped his head out just as a wave crashed into him and took him with its roll to shore. When the water abated, Sean popped his head up and shouted a child's "Yahoo!" before diving in again and breaststroking toward Chief.

"Let's get Chief up on the board," Sean shouted across the crashing surf.

"Think it will scare him?" Tom screamed back.

"Nah, we'll put him on it and you can swim him out to the waves and help him catch it. It'd be fun for the ol' boy. A little R and R for all he's done for me."

Tom wrapped his arms around Chief, lifted him, and positioned him on the board.

Chief, soaked and panting, looking for all the world like he was smiling, pushed his snout up and shook his wet ears and lay on the board.

Tom positioned his body under the board. Holding on to the back of the board with one arm, using the other he swam toward the approaching waves.

As the water swelled, Tom turned around and positioned the board in the direction of the wave. The board took to the wave and Tom let it go.

Chief's ears flapped back as the board carried him effortlessly across the white foam rim of the swell. Without provocation, and not out of any sense of nervousness, Chief popped up on all four legs. Acting instinctually and knowing the exact moment that was his to take, Chief conquered the wave with the nonchalant confidence of the most advanced maverick rider. Sean's and Tom's mouths dropped in unison as they watched Chief ride the long board all the way to shore.

"That's my dog," Sean said proudly, puffing out his chest.

Then the wave curled and hid Chief from view.

"Shit!" Sean panicked. "What if it takes him under? Will he know to pop up?" Sean stared at the wave, hoping to see Chief emerge. A surge of worry rose through his chest, warming his center. "I love this damn dog, Tom! If something happens to him, I don't know what I'll . . ." And before Sean could finish his sentence he saw Chief's nose high in the air, catching the breeze as he floated out of the curl.

Tom, shaking his head in disbelief, said, "I don't believe it."

"Believe it, bud. The dog can surf!" Sean said, laughing in relief.

"Just like that. No effort at all," Tom said, slapping the water in front of him."

"It's all instinct. He didn't overthink it. His body just knew what it wanted. Oh my god, I wish James were here to see this," Sean shouted back toward Tom, slapping the water.

Tom let out a huge laugh. "The dog knows more than we do."

"That's not sayin' much, Tom." Sean winked and dove

back into the water and swam vigorously toward the shore where Chief was hopping back and forth and then in tight circles waiting for Sean to come to him.

When Sean pulled his body toward shore, Chief pounced on him and covered him with grateful licks before dashing off toward the board. Then, using his nose, Chief pushed the board over toward Sean.

"My turn?" he said and turned, looking at Chief. "Not me. Not today. I am not ready. My body will know when it's ready. Today's not that day."

Chief nudged the board again.

"Oh, oh, I see how it is. *You* want another ride? Ah, the surfing bug has bitten. You will never be the same again, ol' sport. Lucky for you, I like it, too. Come on, let's go," Sean said, patting the board and signaling for Chief to get on.

Tom, Sean, and Chief spent the next two hours taking turns swimming Chief out on the board over the swells and pushing him at the precise right moment. Sean never thought he'd ever find it possible to feel so much joy by simply watching another embrace his own. He'd thought those days were over. But it was possible. Anything was possible. Angels. Second chances. Colm. Chiara's love. And, yes, even surfing dogs. All of it. He could have all of it.

❧ Chapter 19

I T WAS PAST SUNSET BY THE TIME TOM DROPPED SEAN off at his apartment.

"I can't come up, Sean. I'm already running late. Told Melissa I'd be home for dinner. Do you mind if I hang on to the boards? I'd like to take my girls out one of these nights."

"That would be sweet. They'll love it. Go for it. I won't need them for a while. Come on, Chief, come on," Sean said, beckoning for the damp dog to come to him.

"All right. Get some rest tonight, Sean. James is coming over, right?"

"That's the plan."

When Sean and Chief exited the elevator and walked down the hall toward the apartment, they found James, disheveled, with his uniform shirt unbuttoned and slumped down by the door holding an open empty box of pizza.

"James? What's going on?" Sean said, approaching as quickly as he could, hopping along with his cane.

"Don't act like you don't know, Sean," James said, his mouth full of the last bite of pizza.

"What are you talking about, James?"

"Really? That's how you're gonna play it? I've known from the beginning. Ever since I saw you look at her that you wanted her. And you couldn't let me have her. Jesus, Sean. I was your friend."

"I'm sorry. What are we talking about, James?" Sean said, confused.

James stood up and the empty pizza box landed by Sean's feet.

"So I stop by Libby's on my way home from work today to see if she wants to come over here with me. She's crying, Sean. Sobbing actually. I couldn't make any sense out of what she was saying. Man, she was a mess. And she keeps saying some bullshit about being sorry. So sorry, sorry, sorry. And she says she didn't mean to hurt me. She didn't mean to mess things up. I told her it was impossible for her to mess things up."

"Whatever she told you, James, it wasn't me. I didn't do anything."

"Oh, you didn't? Really? She said she slept with someone, Sean. Told me how sorry she was and that she had to end it with me. Said I deserved someone better. Said that she belonged with an *addict* like her. *That once an addict always one.* Then she said some crap about all she would ever end up doing was hurt me and she told me to get out. And I started putting two and two together. She was here with you every night I was on duty. And you two are always going on and on about those dumb meetings. You two and your rehab stories. You two and your dogs. I asked her point-blank: 'Was it Sean?' And you know what she did when she heard your name? She started crying, man. She just started sobbing and could barely speak. I got my answer. So here I am. I want to hear it from you. I mean, Jesus, Sean, I am your friend. I've been there for you, man. Really there for you. I loved you like a brother, man. How could you?"

"James, you have the wrong idea. Totally wrong idea. She came here last night and told me the same thing. She was talking about her ex-boyfriend. Some junkie. I told her to tell you everything and that you would forgive her."

"Bullshit. Don't go giving me this. I knew all this Chiara crap was too good to be true, nobody acts like that anymore. Nobody goes holding candles for long-lost loves. All this time you were just feeding her lines that would get my girlfriend to fall for you. *Isn't Sean just so romantic? Isn't Sean just so wonderful*. Please. Save it. Quit lyin' to yourself. Quit lyin' to me."

"James, listen to me. She loves you. She does. She was crying when you said my name because I was an ass to her yesterday. I was mad at her for something she said to me about Chiara, and of course, I was mad because of what she did to you. But, James, she loves you. She does. She deserves a second chance. She messed up. Listen to her. Go listen to her. She'll tell you everything. It wasn't me."

James had been crying and wiped the tears rolling down his cheeks, and the red sauce from the corners of his mouth.

"I ate your dinner, man."

"That's okay. I wasn't hungry."

"It sucked. Worst pizza I ever tasted. I spared your ass," James said, chucking a piece of crust onto the box.

"Good," Sean said with a smile and patted James on the back, leaning in for a hug.

James shook his head over and over. "I said some horrible things to her, Sean. I called her a junkie. I was so pissed. I said you two deserved each other. I told her she would always be a screwed-up junkie. I was just so hurt. So mad. I didn't know what I was saying."

"Jesus, James."

"I messed it up. She won't forgive me."

Sean shook his head. "I don't know, James."

"I'm worried about her. What if—what if she's doing something awful because of what I said?"

Sean nodded, thinking the same thing. Sean knew the feeling. Falling down and trying to get up was like walking on sand, the earth moving beneath you, the muscles inside you contracting and making it even harder to push, and only wanting some relief, any, to feel as though you're on firm ground again.

"Where did you leave her, James?"

"Her place."

"You want me to go with you?"

"Would you?"

"Sure."

Just as Sean, Chief, and James turned to get on the elevator, the doors opened and Tom stepped out.

"What are you doing back here, Tom?" Sean asked. "I thought you had to rush home."

"I have Chief's leash and bag," Tom said, holding up the blue service-dog bag. "We took it off him at the beach and I realized that I left it in my truck."

"Oh, yeah, thanks," Sean said, reaching for it.

Tom looked at James and back at Sean. "Something going on?"

"We're worried about Libby," Sean said. "She and James had a bit of a misunderstanding today."

"We have to go to her," James said anxiously. "Now."

"Want me to come along?" Tom asked, looking at the distress on James's face and feeling his sense of urgency. "It's no trouble, guys. I'll drive you both over in the truck. I can call Melissa on the way and tell her something is wrong with Libby. She'll understand."

"Thanks, Tom," Sean said, whispering. "I don't think he's in any condition to drive."

"She's probably fine, James," Sean said, trying to reassure James.

"I know. But I've never seen her so sad. So messed up," James said, shaking his head.

Sean winced thinking of what he'd said to Libby and what her face had looked like when he said it. She looked like Colm had when Sean had lost his temper at him all those years ago. She looked broken. And there was no putting the pieces back together. How cruel he'd been. He wished he could take it all back. She had been nothing but kind to him. She didn't have to be his friend. She didn't have to care for him. But she did. He didn't even know her a year ago, but now she was like family. She came over every day. She made sure he had food in the refrigerator. She brought bunches of flowers and set them in vases throughout the apartment. She brought his dead plant on the balcony back to life. She and James sat with him for hours on end and watched old movies just to make sure he wasn't alone. Even when he could tell they would rather be alone, they sat with him. Yes, she had messed up, but Sean knew she was a good person and his friend. Sean thought of her past. Her drug abuse. And he shuddered. Sean himself had relapsed over much less. Time and time again he went back to the bottle just because it felt so good to disappear and not to feel anything at all. It felt good not to cry. It felt so good not to feel like he had disappointed anyone—his nephew, his sister, his mother, or his friends. It felt so good to taste the burn. He remembered the first sip. The warming of the esophagus. The loosening of each limb. The sense he always got after the alcohol settled through his body that he was flying. He was free, like an angel set forth on the world to bring not only light, but this message, the same simple message that every drunk from the beginning of time had slurred before passing out: *It will all work out. It will all work out.* Heroin did that, too. It did it for Libby once, and Sean knew it wouldn't take much for Libby to get her hands on it and for it to work its magic again. Sean's steps quickened. Forgetting the pain he felt when he walked, Sean picked up his pace down the hall to catch up with the men and said, "It'll all be okay, James. It'll be all right."

❧ Chapter 20

WHEN SEAN, TOM, AND JAMES APPROACHED THE tiny yellow bungalow with the fenced-in yard in Silver Lake, everything that had once seemed fuzzy about Libby came into focus. Her life of contradictions extended far beyond the sleeve tats and bubble gum pink lipstick, the cruddy wardrobe and the beautiful body, the tough talk and the gentle touches, the longing for romance and the falling for a guy like James, the prep school education and the dog-training career, the helping others when she was clearly incapable of helping herself.

The broken and paint-chipped porch swing that was hanging by one solitary broken chain was the first giveaway. The second was the overgrown ornamental grasses and weeds that grew up alongside the house and blocked off half of the steps and walkway leading to the front door. Then the stacks of unopened newspapers lining the porch and the mail bursting out of the mailbox was the final indicator. Libby was not in full control of her life, and probably hadn't been for some time, perhaps even before James.

"Jesus, James. How often do you come by here? You guys don't pick up newspapers, cut grass?" Tom said harshly. And almost reflexively, Tom got out and reached into the bed of his truck and grabbed his medical bag, then walked over to the passenger side to help Sean out.

"I don't know. Never occurred to me. We spent most of our time at my place or in restaurants. Movies. The beach. Sean's place. She didn't like coming here too much."

"I can see why," Sean said in a whisper.

James hopped out first and ran down the narrow and uneven concrete steps that sloped a bit to the left and led to the house that sat at the bottom of a hill.

James heard Mirabelle barking frantically from inside the house. He knocked on the door and shouted, "Open up, Libby. Open up. It's me, James. I'm sorry. I was an idiot. I had no right to say those things to you."

There was no answer. James looked back at Tom and Sean, by the truck, and nodded for them to both come down.

Tom took Sean by the waist and helped him to the steps and let him use his body as leverage as he took each step.

"We're coming, James. It's okay," Tom said reassuringly.

"Maybe she's not home," Sean suggested hopefully.

"That's her car," James said, pointing to the green Prius parked on the street in front of Tom's truck.

"Okay. Maybe she went for a walk." Sean offered another suggestion, though his stomach was starting to turn.

"Without Mirabelle? I don't think so. She's freaking out in there. Can't you hear her barking?"

"Maybe she's freaking out because three men are walking toward her house?" Tom added calmly, though he was feeling nervous now, too.

"Libby, open the goddamn door!" James shouted while banging furiously.

"James, I don't think that's the best way to try to get the girlfriend you just pissed off to open the door," Sean suggested as he approached the steps to the front porch and pulled himself up by using the unstable railing as leverage.

"Okay. You try," James said, raising his arm toward the door like a flight attendant pointing to the exit.

"Lib, it's me, Sean. Open up. Tom is here, too. We're just worried. Let us know you're okay and we'll leave."

There was no sound coming from the house now. Mirabelle stopped barking and they could see her face peeking through the window behind the forlorn porch swing.

"She couldn't have gotten drugs and OD'd in what, an hour and a half?" Sean looked at James, trying to calculate the time.

"It's been more like three," James whispered.

"I thought you said you just came from here and went straight to my apartment?" Sean asked to clarify.

"I stopped for a couple of bites on my way to get your pizza."

Sean nodded and understood. He would have stopped off at a bar a few years ago, too.

"Should we break in?" James asked.

"James, did you try turning the knob? Maybe it's open?" Tom said.

When Sean did, the door gave way.

"Genius," Tom said.

"Whatever, Tom," James spat back.

The three men walked in and Mirabelle immediately turned and left the living room as if instructing the men to follow her.

James ran after the dog. Tom ran after James. Sean stood still and took in the room, the single beige love seat alone in a vast white undecorated room. In the kitchen a small IKEA bistro table with two bright yellow chairs, covered with stacks of clothing and unfolded towels, blocked the sliding doors that led to the patio out back, which was also covered in over-grown grass and weeds.

"Jesus, Libby," Sean said aloud to no one.

He walked across the room, and on the mantel above a bricked-in fireplace were four framed pictures. One was of her and what appeared to be her parents, their arms wrapped around her on her graduation day from dog-training school or rehab, he wasn't sure which. Mirabelle was at her feet. Both Libby's and her father's hands were patting Mirabelle's head. In another picture, James was hanging outside his fire station, in his blues, his hands stuffed in his pockets and smiling a wide, banana-shaped grin. Another was of Libby, a younger version of herself, no more than fifteen or sixteen, and a girl who looked every bit like Libby's mirror image, save for the blond streaks in her hair. Libby had a sister, Sean realized. A twin. They were wearing matching maroon-and-gray plaid kilts and tweed blazers with matching crests. Their arms were pretzeled together and their hips cocked in opposite di-rections. A giant WELCOME BACK banner attached to a school building hung behind their heads. Libby never mentioned her sister. And a thought, brief but heart-wrenching in its realization, came to Sean. She wasn't doing drugs to impress her friends. *It wasn't chemistry.* It was, as it often was, because of pain. Trying to dull the unrelenting pain. Somehow, Sean knew without even hearing the story, he knew that Libby's sister was gone. Then Sean's eyes darted to the picture of all five of them together smiling—Tom, James, Libby, Sean, and Chief, wearing sombreros and holding maracas. "Shit," Sean said quietly to himself before hearing what he knew was coming.

"Oh God, no! No! Libby! I am so sorry, Libby!" James shouted from a room at the back of the house.

Sean fumbled with his cane and limped back down the hall, following James's screams. When he arrived in Libby's room, he saw Tom on his phone, probably calling 911, and James in the tiny bathroom pulling Libby out of the bath and dragging her to the bedroom where he placed her on the floor.

Wake up. Wake up. Wake up.

Sean grabbed the phone from Tom. "I got this. You get down there and help James."

Tom opened his bag and pulled out his portable shock paddle kit. While James leaned over Libby's naked, wet, lifeless chest and pulled her up to hug her, Sean, watching in detached silence, saw that tattooed on Libby's back was a set of angel's wings whose feathers were falling off in pieces down her back. Sean opened his mouth to speak but no words came out. James placed her flat on her back and began breathing deeply into her mouth.

"She'll come back, James," Sean said, waiting for the 911 operator to pick up, as much to reassure James as to reassure himself.

James looked up at Sean as if he was deranged or didn't quite understand what was actually happening and then quickly snapped his attention back to Libby, shouting, "Don't you die, Libby. Don't you dare."

Sean spoke the address into the phone and explained the scene to the always surprisingly unruffled operators. "We think she overdosed on something. She was in the bathtub. We've pulled her out. We have a registered nurse/physical therapist as well as a registered EMT performing CPR. The nurse is going to administer the paddles from a defib kit." Sean spoke with the calm facility of a pro. He realized he had missed the sense of calm that came over him in a crisis.

"It's okay, James. It's okay. She'll come back," Sean said, pulling the phone away from his mouth. "They're coming. They're on their way."

"Come on, Libby," Tom kept shouting.

"What did she take?" the operator asked Sean.

"I don't know. I have no idea."

"Can you look in her bathroom or on her nightstand?"

Sean limped across the bedroom and peeked into her bathroom where he saw the rubber band. The needle and glass vial on the sink. His stomach turned. "That asshole," Sean said aloud, thinking immediately of Libby's ex.

"Excuse me?" the operator asked.

Sean shouted into the phone, "It's heroin, goddammit. She OD'd on heroin. That useless son of a bitch," Sean screamed, looking for Libby's cell phone and hoping to find his number. "When I find him, I'll kill him."

"Excuse me?" the 911 operator asked again.

"Her ex. I'd bet my life on it. She got the stuff from him."

Tom looked up at Sean and James did, too.

Putting the phone to his chest, Sean said, "She told me her ex came back and she hooked up with him, but he was looking for money, looking to score. I should have known. She was coming down off something. She was a mess last night. Crying and acting crazy and accusing me of using. She was. She used with him. I should have known." Sean shook his head.

"No one could have, Sean," Tom said, shaking his head and standing over Libby to shock her heart. "Clear," Tom warned.

Again.

Nothing.

"Clear."

Nothing. And then, "We got a pulse!" James shouted. "We got a pulse!"

Tom pulled out his stethoscope and listened to her heart. "It's beating. He's right. She's okay. It's weak. But she's okay."

"Do we have any idea how long she was out?" Sean asked, repeating the 911 operator's question.

"No idea," Tom said.

"The ambulance is on its way," Sean said, relieved. "Good job, guys," he said, as if to say "All in a day's work."

Sean looked down to see James holding Libby in his arms, holding her and rocking her. "You're going to be fine. I've got you now," he repeated over and over.

Tom kept his hand on her pulse and was monitoring her vitals while using his free arm to grab the bedspread from the bed and cover her.

"It's a miracle you were here, Tom," James said finally.

"What?"

"If you hadn't come off the elevator when you did, if you hadn't driven us, if we didn't have your medical bag . . ." James shook his head and started crying. "We'd have lost her."

"But we didn't, James. We didn't," Sean said now, calmly. "You guys were fantastic."

"This never would have happened if I wasn't such an ass," James said, shaking his head.

"It would have happened no matter what," Tom said. "From the looks of things, she already had the stuff here. Whoever she was with must have brought it and taken off. She's lucky she has you, James. This is heavy stuff. Really heavy stuff. You sure you can handle this? It's so damn, I don't know, complicated. Life shouldn't be this hard."

"It's not. It's simple. I love her."

"Well, she's lucky she has you," Tom said, shaking his head.

"No," James said, "I am lucky to have her. We all are. Period."

"Ya know, guys, I know you all think I'm crazy. But I'm going on record with this one: I don't think luck has anything to do with it. You were here for a reason, Tom. And you, too, James."

"Not now, St. Francis, not now," Tom said, holding up his hand. "Not now."

Chapter 21

B Y THE TIME THE EMTs ARRIVED AND MOVED LIBBY to a gurney, her eyes had opened. James had already hopped into the back of the ambulance and Tom was making his way to the truck to load his bag. Sean, standing beside Libby on the gurney, took her hand and said quietly, "I'm so sorry. I didn't know. I should have known better. I should have helped you. You're going to be all right. James will take good care of you. I'm so sorry I said those terrible things to you the other day."

Libby blinked back a tear and it rolled slowly down her face, landing in the crease of her upper ear.

"It's okay, Libby. I know. You're going to get better. You're going to be great. We all mess up. We all deserve a second chance. Today you got one. I got one, too," Sean said, leaning in to kiss her forehead.

Beneath the oxygen mask she mouthed two words, "My angels," and squeezed Sean's hand.

"What did she just say?" James shouted from the back of the ambulance. "What did she just say to you?"

"It was nothing. She's going to be all right." Sean made a thumbs-up gesture to James and winked.

"We'll follow you guys and meet you at the hospital."

After the ambulance pulled away, Tom came over to Sean to help him walk to the truck.

"Do me a favor, Tom."

"Yeah, what is it?"

"Can you run back down to the house and grab those pictures on the mantel above the fireplace? I think she should have them with her. I need to take Mirabelle home with me, too."

"You can't handle both dogs, Sean."

"Sure I can."

"No, let me help. My girls will love watching her."

"What about Melissa?"

"She'll understand. They're my friends, too. Sean, I want to help. Please let me do this."

"Of course. You've done so much, Tom. Still don't believe things happen for a reason? James is right, if you weren't here tonight . . . it would have turned out so differently."

"I don't know, Sean. I just don't know. And to be honest, I don't care. I don't question things like you do. I am just glad she's okay. Jesus. The messes people make of their lives. You think you know someone . . ."

"It's not that simple, Tom. She can't help it. Addiction is a disease, and she's vulnerable to begin with."

"I know. It's just that I don't understand this, any of this. This life she lives. Drugs. This dump of a house. Why can't people just figure this shit out? Why can't they just get up, live, work, and power through it?"

Sean shook his head in disbelief. "You're unbelievable, Tom. Unfreakin' believable."

"What?"

"You can be a real ass. She is sick and hurt. And you're wondering why she can't power through it? Like you, Tom? Like you? How does that work out for you? You think you're different? You think you're better? Really? How's *powering through it* working for you? How's that chiseled body and those torn-up legs you hide under those jeans? How's your nine-to-five work gig that you spread out to seven to seven and then sometimes eight? How's leaving your pretty wife and two kids at home alone working for you? Don't go deluding yourself. You're no better. And you're every bit as messed up as Libby is. Your obsession just falls off the radar. You might not get arrested for it. But it's taking its toll on you, your marriage, your life. Your quest for *perfection*. For *work*. *Work. Work. Work.* You may not see it or admit it, but it is. Someone like Libby *feels* shit. She feels it deeply and she can't just *power through it*. She can't just wake up, down some raw eggs, and press three hundred pounds. She's got nowhere to go with all that pain. She counted on us, Tom. We were her friends. And we missed it. I didn't see it. I didn't want to see it. But just because we can't see someone else's pain doesn't mean it's not there. Doesn't mean we can assume stuff about them."

"I'm sorry, Sean. I didn't mean to upset you."

"No, I know you didn't. But you want to know what I don't understand, Tom? I don't understand how after everything that just happened today, you can't just admit that sometimes miracles happen. Good stuff happens out of the garbage of everyday life. Like seeing a dog surf or being in the right place at the right time so that you can actually save a life. Or admitting, just admitting once, that life is more than just work, it's about the people in it," Sean said, limping over to the truck. "And if my leg didn't hurt so badly, I'd walk my ass to the hospital, but I can't. So go grab the dog and those pics, and let's go."

"Sean?"

"What?" Sean snapped.

"I wish . . . I wish . . . ," Tom stammered and then shook his head hopelessly.

"What?" Sean said with a final exhale of exasperation.

"I wish I could see things the way you do. I wish I could believe everything has a purpose. I wish I could believe we each have an angel looking out for us. I do. God, I wish I could. But I'm sorry. I'm sorry, I just don't."

"That's all right, Tom. It's not fair of me to lash out at you. I'm just so angry."

"Me too, Sean. Me too."

After Tom had dropped the pictures off at the hospital, checked in on James, and found out Libby was stable, he ran back to the truck to drive Sean home. The two barely spoke the entire way, until Tom pulled his truck up in front of Sean's building.

"Been a long day," Tom said finally.

"Yep."

"See you tomorrow? Back to the gym?"

"I don't think so, Tom."

"What?"

"I think I'm done with PT. I can take it from here. I can get around. Probably could for some time. I just milked it longer than I should have. Should have stood up and walked a long time ago. My legs are plenty strong enough. I don't need a hired hand hanging out with me."

"Sean, I am more than a hired hand. I hope you know that."

"I know that, Tom. I know. It's just time. I need to get control of my life. It's time I start the rest of it. Playing the invalid is getting old. And today showed me that life is just too damn short. Too damn unpredictable. I'm not taking any more chances. I'm not wasting another minute of my life. I'm ready. I was great in the water. And I realized when I was on the phone with the 911 operator, I'm not done. I still want to help people. I may not be able to climb ladders or hose down buildings, but I can do something. And I want to get started. I have to. For myself. For my own sanity."

"I understand."

"Gaspar will pay you out for the month."

"He pays the VNA. I'll have other patients to see," Tom explained.

"Of course. Other patients," Sean said, nodding.

"We can still hang out? You, me, James, and Libby—when she's ready?" Tom said, staring out through the windshield. "We're friends, right?" Tom asked quietly.

"Sure, we'll all get together again," Sean promised. "When I get back."

"Are you going then? To Italy? Next month? Should I tell Gaspar?"

"I think you know the answer to that. And I'd appreciate it if you don't. He won't think I'm ready and he'll try to talk me out of it or come with me."

"So you really think you were spared to say sorry to this girl? You think an angel came down from heaven just so you could go tell some girl you're sorry?"

"I don't know. I won't know if I don't go. And no matter what, I won't be able to live with myself if I don't. I made a promise. A promise to myself and to God, Tom. And I am not backing out of it. I'm alive today because of it. I believe it. I believe it with all my heart."

"I just don't get how you can be so sure," Tom said, still shaking his head. "I hope she's worth it."

Sean turned his entire body toward Tom's and looked at him intently. "Tom, *everyone is worth it.* Don't you get it? Every single person is worth it. Libby is worth it. James is worth it. Christ, you're worth it. And, so yes, Chiara is worth it. She's worth the trip. You're worth the trip. The whole entire world is worth it, Tom. She doesn't owe me anything. She doesn't have to be perfect. She's not some prize. The world doesn't owe me anything either. Doesn't owe you anything. *I* owe her something. I owe the *world* something. I owe myself something, goddammit."

"Okay, Sean. Okay."

"I need you to get this, Tom. I need you to understand this. I need you to understand."

"Why? Why is it so important, Sean, what I think? Why do you even care?"

"Because, Tom, I care about you. You're my friend, like it or not, and I care. I need you to see what I see. I need you to see that promises matter, people matter, second chances matter. I need you to see your patients for more than their broken bones and atrophied muscles and the work they need to do to prove themselves to you. I need you to see them as possibilities. As hope. As light. I need you to see that you survived for a reason, too. It wasn't just to work. It was to be a husband to your wife; a father to your girls; a friend to me, James, and Libby; a savior to so many people who struggle every day to get up and keep walking. I need you to see that you matter, Tom. You do, too."

"Why? Why me?"

"I don't want you to have to learn the hard way, Tom. Like I did. So many times. I doubted and I was snarky and dismissive of people who believed. It was safe. It was easy. And time and time again . . . life came around and kicked me in the ass and showed me how wrong I was. I don't want you to have to lose what you have—a wife and children—because you can't get over yourself. You can't see how amazing your life is and the people in it."

Tom exhaled and looked up at the sky as if it held the answers he was looking for. But there was no denying Sean's truth. Every word stung him. He had been ungrateful. He hadn't noticed how many chances he'd been given—over and over—first his life, then his wife and his kids.

"Sean? How? I mean how did you get like this? And why does it all matter so much to you?"

"It's simple."

"Oh?"

"Someday you'll see. It may not be today. It may not be tomorrow, but someday you'll be sitting where I am and you'll see so clearly what it is that you need to see. And once you see it, you want the whole world to see it."

"Magee, you're a goddamn mystery."

"Tom, for once, embrace it," Sean said, wrapping his arms around his friend before turning and opening the door to leave. "Embrace the mystery, dammit."

"You'll tell me what happens," Tom said as Sean was about to close the door.

"Sure."

"You'll call me?"

"Ye of little faith, my doubting Thomas," Sean said, shaking his head and slamming the door.

❧ Chapter 22

LIBBY WAS SITTING IN A CHAIR BESIDE HER BED AND was swaddled in various hospital issued–blankets when Sean walked into her room with Chief two days after he, Tom, and James had found her.

"Where's James today?" Sean asked, limping into the room with his cane.

"He had to work. I told him he couldn't avoid it. He has to go back. My parents are coming down today from San Francisco. They're going to take me home for a while and check me into a rehab up there," Libby said quietly.

"How's James taking it?"

"It was his idea. He wants me to get better. I think he realizes better than anyone, even better than I was willing to admit, that this is above his pay grade. To be honest, we were both in over our heads. He thought he could fix me. I thought I could love him the way he deserved."

"He loves you, Libby. You make him happy," Sean said,

pulling a chair up next to her. "I saw him eating broccoli yesterday. No cheese. Said he was trying to go through detox with you."

"One man's downfall is heroin, for another it's cheese." Libby laughed and then dipped her cheek into the side of her shoulder and wiped away another tear, holding her head there as if listening to something deep inside her shoulder. After she cried quietly and pulled her hands out of the blanket, she rubbed her eyes with her palms. Her hands covered her eyes and forehead.

"Lib? Come on, come on. You're going to be okay."

"I've messed everything up. My job, James, and my parents. Don't get me started on my poor parents," Lib said, shaking back and forth.

"You're still here, Lib. They're happy about that. I am sure."

"You don't understand, Sean. You don't. They've already lost one. And I am such a screwup."

"Your sister? She's the girl in that picture, right? Did she die?" Sean said, pointing to the picture Tom had taken to her the night she was admitted.

"Yes, we're twins. She was my best friend, Sean. We did everything together. She was always so much cooler than me. Even though we looked exactly the same, she had that invisible magnetic charm. Boys just went crazy over her. They were always chasing her around, and she was always dragging me with her. And then one day I decided I didn't want to be the third wheel. I just wanted to do my own thing. Wanted to be my own person. I was tired of being her mirror image.

Looking just like her, but feeling so different inside. So that day she got in a car with this cool hotshot. You know the type. He took her joyriding. Asshole was going ninety miles an hour when he crashed her into a pole."

Sean shook his head and looked up at Libby to see her staring at her sister's picture.

"I should have been there with her. It should have been me in that mangled hunk of metal. It should have been me. She belonged in this world. Not me. She did. She had so much more to offer it than me. A junkie. A screwup."

"Lib, Lib. Come on. You can't blame yourself. You can't say those things."

"You know how hard it is to look in the mirror and see your dead sister staring back at you? See what could have been? Every day?"

"Is that why you got all the tattoos? The piercings? Keep your hair short?" Sean asked, already knowing the answer because the puzzle that was Libby was finally coming together. The corner pieces were all in place. All he had was to stick in a few more pieces to see the complete picture.

Libby shrugged. "You know what the last thing she said to me was, Sean?"

"I have no idea."

"She said, 'Lib, it won't be the same without you. Nothing's the same without you . . . ,'" Libby trailed off and cried again.

"Oh, Lib."

"And after they told me that she died, I kept playing those words over and over in my head. Because it wasn't the same.

It wasn't. Nothing was ever the same again. Why can't things ever be the same? Why can't we go back to that spot? That sweet wonderful spot where we started from?"

"Oh, honey," Sean said, wanting to reach out and hug her, wanting to tell her he'd been asking himself the same question for months, but she pulled farther back into the chair. "I know. I know," he consoled her.

"It was like someone took a knife and cut me in half. Carved me right down the middle. It made no sense why she died and I lived."

"It never does."

"And I couldn't take it, Sean. I couldn't take it. The ache inside. The guilt. I just wanted something, anything, to make it all go away."

Sean took Libby's hand in his.

"I just want to feel whole again, Sean. And the drugs did that for a while. And then love did," Libby said, looking past Sean's shoulder at her reflection in the window.

"Libby, you will feel whole again. You will. Not now, not today, but someday. You have parents who love you. James loves you. I love you. Tom loves you. Mirabelle loves you. You have so many people who just want you to feel better. And here is a little secret: Everybody wants to feel whole. Everybody with a pulse gets a piece of them ripped out if they live long enough. We live, we love, and we die. And sometimes people we love the most die before us and it hurts like a mother. It hurts worse than falling three stories after nearly burning alive. It hurts worse than withdrawing from smack. It hurts and it hurts and it hurts. And just when you think you couldn't hurt anymore, your body finds new ways to hurt. New nadirs—lower, darker, more abysmal than before. I know. But I know this, too, Libby. I know that we hurt because we loved and that is pretty awesome. When you think about it in reverse, it's pretty goddamn amazing. If you rewind through all the hurt, and you go back in time and find the moment when that love you felt lived and breathed inside you and filled your soul up with light, you realize just how amazing this life is. And what's even more amazing? You know what, Lib? You can go back to those times at any moment. You can go back to it now. You can take it with you forever. It lives forever. And the opposite is true, too. You can also fast-forward. One day, though you can't see it now, Lib. You can't, but you're going to be so happy. You'll be married. And you'll be holding a beautiful baby and you won't believe how all that joy could be yours. But if you rewind that moment all the way back, you'll see this moment. You'll see this pain. You'll see how hurt and sad and lonely you were and that out of that pain and hurt, you grew strong. You got better and that pain brought you that joy you'll be holding someday in the future."

"Oh, Sean, I miss her," Libby cried. "I miss who I was when I was with her. It's just not the same."

"I know what you mean. I do."

"I know you do," Libby said and squeezed his hand.

"You have to believe in second chances. You have to believe that there is a reason why you're here today. Think of your parents, think what life would have been like if both of you were in that car."

Libby nodded.

"Think of James and how happy he is just to be in a room with you. Think of the fun you two have. Think about how much he adores you. Loves you. *How he chose you.* Expects nothing from you. How simple and true his love is."

Libby smiled, thinking of him and looking at his picture beside the one of her sister.

"And think of all those dogs, all those guardian angels, you bring into people's lives every day and the smiles they put on people's faces, on faces like mine," Sean said, smiling widely.

"How can you be so sure, Sean? How can you be so sure we all have a reason and a purpose?"

"Because I've seen it with my own eyes."

"Are you talking about that angel again?"

"No, it's not just the angel. I know because I've loved so many times, and have lost so many times, but I keep moving. I keep breathing. I keep remembering. And I see it makes a difference. We each make a difference. If it weren't for thinking of Chiara, I don't think I'd be here. If it weren't for James, I wouldn't be here. If it weren't for Gaspar, I wouldn't have met Tom, and I don't think I would be walking today without him. And if it weren't for James and Tom, you wouldn't be here. So we each matter. And then if it weren't for you and Chief walking into my room, James and you wouldn't be together. And if you, James, and I didn't hang out so much and talk so much and help Tom see the error of his ways, maybe Tom would be on his way to a divorce instead of running home each day to get to his wife. And if Tom hadn't taken Chief surfing like he did the other day, then he wouldn't have forgotten Chief's leash in his truck, and he wouldn't have ended up in an elevator bringing it to me and James at the exact moment we thought to come and get you, and without Tom and his medical bag, you wouldn't be here, and your parents wouldn't be coming down to visit you today in a hospital where you're alive and on your way to getting better. It's not just a random stream of coincidences. Life's not just a bunch of disconnected events and people. There are reasons, and we may not know them or recognize them and we may not understand them, but we have to trust that there are reasons beyond us, because I've seen it work out enough. It doesn't mean we will all live forever. It doesn't mean bad things won't happen or we won't feel sad sometimes, but it does mean that we can't discount the miraculous in the mundane. It's the only way to make this shit bearable."

"Sean, how did you get like this?"

"What do you mean?"

"So damn sure of yourself."

"I wasn't always like this, Lib. I spent a lot of time lost in the dark. Wallowing. Blaming. Drinking. Getting high. Blocking myself from any sort of happiness."

"And then the fire?"

"Sure."

"What does that mean?"

"Sure, the fire changed me. But if I had to be honest, I changed before that. I had turned my entire life around three years before that, but I just lost my way again. It happens. And the fire, the angel, all of it reminded me of something I had already figured out."

"What's that?"

"I used to fight the fire—the fire burning inside me and the fires outside me. I used to fight everything. I was always so angry, so bitter, so pissed off at the world. I didn't understand why kids like my nephew had to suffer, why people like my sister and mother had to endure so much pain, and why I couldn't be with the one I loved. I fought it for so long, I pushed it out. So much so I turned out the light inside me."

"And then what?" Libby asked.

"Then one day, three years ago, I saw something amazing, Libby. And it changed me. I saw my sister holding her son—my nephew, the boy I loved and raised like my own son—dying in her arms. And there was nothing I could do to stop it. I couldn't help my sister. I knew there was nothing I could do to protect her from the pain coming for her, from the brutal, torturous suffering of my nephew. It ripped my heart out. I thought I'd never be able to breathe again, walk again, stand, go on, live. I thought right then and there: *If this boy dies, I die. It's over. I am done with this crap-ass, nonsensical world.*"

"What happened?"

"I was watching it all unfold, as if in slow motion. My sister's face changed. She looked transfixed, like she had just seen heaven itself. Like a goddamn angel. It was like she realized while holding her son, finally at peace, that she didn't need to get to heaven to see that it existed. She didn't need to see or touch God to know he existed, she held it all in her arms. She had been holding on to heaven, the goddamn universe, right there in her arms, his entire life. All the while, like Dorothy clicking her heels or something, it was right there in front of her. And I swear that my nephew, even as the light was going out inside him, looked at her in the same way. I will never understand why he had to suffer. Why she had to suffer. I won't, and I don't think anyone will ever be able to, but I know this—love. Love is what makes all this possible.

All of this bearable. Love does. It matters. We matter. Each
and every one of us matters."

Libby reached now for Sean and held his forearm, squeezing as he spoke.

"I knew in that moment, whether he lived or died, every
single thing mattered. Every little, seemingly insignificant
thing mattered, and I didn't need to keep fighting this fire
inside me. I had to walk beside it. I had to walk with it. It was
a light. Like Colm was a light. Like Cathleen. Like Gaspar.
We all were each other's guides. Each other's light. Angels.
Heaven. Whatever you want to call it. We came to set the
world on fire."

"Oh, Sean, the way you talk. I don't know. I don't know
what to do with it all. I don't know how to wrap my head
around it." Libby sighed.

"You know that angel I thought I saw that day up in that
burning house? Well, I'd seen her before. I saw the angel right
next to my sister and Colm, the same damn one that came to
me the night of the fire. It was clear as day to me. The light
around her was so bright, it made everything around her disappear."

"So it was like a hallucination?" Libby said, disbelieving.

"Sure. No one else saw it but me, so yeah, I guess it was.
But it was enough. It was real to me. The next thing I knew
or remembered was waking up in the hospital. My sister and
Gaspar were standing over me. They said I had passed out.
That I was so overcome."

"Did you tell your sister what you saw?"

"No. I couldn't. I didn't understand it then. So I blocked
it out. But it wasn't until I saw again what I'd seen before

that I realized there was a reason I was here. So that's how I know, Lib. I know all the way down to the studs that this fire exploding inside me is out there, too. It's in all of us. And it's in you, too, Libby. We just have to tear down the walls and let it out."

Libby nodded. "Wow."

"You think I'm nuts, don't you? A few years ago if I had heard the same thing, I would think I was nuts."

"I'm not in any position to call anyone nuts, Sean," Libby said, lifting both her tracked arms in surrender.

"Everybody has a bit of crazy in them, Lib. It's the only thing that keeps us sane in this bizarre world."

"You're funny, Sean Magee." Libby finally cracked a smile and wiped away her tears.

"I try," Sean said weakly.

"You're gonna go to her, aren't you? There is no stopping you?" Libby asked quietly, changing the subject.

"Yes, Lib."

"I'm sorry about what I said to you the other day. I know you're not going to rip her life apart. I know you know what you're doing. It wasn't fair of me to assume that just because it didn't work out for me it wouldn't work out for you. You both deserve a second shot."

"Thanks, Libby."

"I mean it. I really hope it works out for you, Sean. You deserve to be happy."

"So do you, Libby. So do you."

"Just be gentle."

"Excuse me?"

"Just be gentle with her. Eleven years is a long time. She's probably been through a lot. It probably took her a long time trying to get over someone as special as you, Sean. She probably woke up every day saying your name, and then spent her days looking for you on street corners, and came home tearing through letters hoping to see your handwriting on just one. She probably lay awake at night and imagined you coming to her, kissing her, holding her. And then one day, probably after a couple of years, she stopped. She got up and went about her day and realized, only as her head hit the pillow at night, that she hadn't said your name, missed you, or ached for you all day. And then she would cry, not because she felt victorious for finally reaching the point where she could move on, but she would cry because she did manage to forget you. And for her, forgetting you was worse than anything because it meant she'd lost hope. She'd lost everything she believed was real and good and right," Libby said, wiping a tear from her eye.

"Oh, Lib."

"Just be gentle. Understand that this isn't just about you. This isn't just about your second chance, or you getting over your own me-over-you moment. It's actually not that simple."

"Okay, I promise, Lib."

"And don't get too beat up if she turns you away. Promise me that. Promise you won't be an idiot like me? That you won't go hunting down a drink after a broken heart. Be stronger than that? Okay?"

"I will."

"And promise me, if you do get a second chance with her, if you do get to build a life with her, you never forget me, forget James, forget Tom, forget all the people who brought you to her. Because I won't forget you, Sean Magee. I won't."

"I won't either."

"Good."

"Thank you, Lib. You'll never know how much you've helped me."

"So this is a good-bye? Isn't it?"

"I made a decision, Lib. I am not waiting till next month. I'm leaving tonight, Lib. That's why I came today. This is good-bye."

"Are you going to say good-bye to James and Tom?"

"I said my good-byes to Tom. Don't you think James will try to stop me?"

"James won't. He wants you to be happy."

"I can't risk him saying something to Gaspar. I just can't risk it. I have to do this now. I've waited long enough. I can walk now. That's what I was waiting for. I am not waiting another minute to start the rest of my life."

"Be careful, Sean."

"I'll have Chief with me. He's on the NSAR list, so I can take him with me on the plane. He'll be by my side the entire time."

"He's such a good dog," Libby said, looking at Chief, who had become in some ways such a part of Sean she could hardly separate the two.

"He was trained by the best." Sean smiled and mimicked a punch to Libby's shoulder.

"Dammit, Sean. I'm gonna miss *you* now."

"Aw, it's all right. I'll be back."

"It's different. Everything will be different. That's the trouble with loving people. Friends. Family."

"How's that?"

"Just when you get used to how great it is, life ups and changes on ya."

"Ah, Lib. I'll be back."

"I'll say good-bye to James for you. I'll wait till your plane takes off."

"Thanks. I owe ya."

"No, you don't. Cross my name off your list."

"How did you know I keep a list?"

"We all do, Sean. We all do."

Sean leaned over and kissed Libby's forehead and said, "I better be going."

As he walked out the door, Libby called after him, "Sean?"

"Yeah, Lib?"

"It won't be the same here without you."

Sean forced a small, weak smile that actually pained him. A large lump rose in his throat. "You're gonna be all right, kid. You will."

❧ Chapter 23

SEAN CHANGED HIS MIND ABOUT LEAVING JAMES without a good-bye. Libby was right. He owed him that much.

After he left the hospital, he took a cab to his old station. When Sean limped into the garage and took a whiff of the oil, damp hoses, and engine exhaust, he knew he was home. The feeling had escaped him for months. He didn't know what he was missing until it was there, right in front of him. He had missed it all. Mostly, he missed the guys, who had been leaning propped up on chairs against the garage wall listening to the radio and didn't even notice him when he came out from behind the ladder truck.

"Magee!" James shouted, seeing him first. "What are you doing here?"

"Came for a visit."

The men leaped from their chairs and swarmed Sean,

giving him hugs and high fives, one man getting on his knees to pet Chief.

"Miss us?" his lieutenant asked.

"Of course. You guys busy today?"

"Nah, a couple of false alarms. Car fire on the 405. The usual."

"You're not missing much, Magee. How ya' feeling? Can't believe you're walking already."

"I am doing great. Legs are getting stronger every day. Burns are pretty much healed. Just scars now," Sean said, turning his head to show the smooth, stretched skin that wrapped his ear and neck. The swelling had gone down, and the hair along his new and receded hairline along the edge of the burn had grown in long and wavy.

"We miss you, buddy," another said.

"I miss you guys, too," Sean said, shaking hands with each of them as they approached him to pat him on the back and give his burns a closer look. Sean didn't mind the stares. It was part of him now, and would be forever. There was no use fighting it. He would have been just as curious if the roles were reversed.

"Hey, James, you got a sec?" Sean said after greeting everyone.

"Sure. Everything okay?"

"I need to talk," Sean said, motioning outside the garage bay door.

James followed Sean.

"You went and saw her, didn't you?"

"Just came from there."

"How's she doin' today?"

"She's doing okay," Sean said, not going into too many details.

"I mean, in your opinion, as a recovering alcoholic, do you think she has a shot at beating this?" James asked while continuing to pet Chief.

"This isn't lip service, James. I think she's going to be great. She had a setback. Lost her way. That happens. But she's going to be okay."

"I know. That's what I told her. I think her parents found her a good place. A few months, maybe a year, I think she'll be back on her feet and this whole mess will be behind her."

"You willing to wait that long, James?"

"I'd wait forever," James said in an of-course-you-jerk tone.

"Good. She loves you, James. She feels bad. She deserves a second shot. Drugs, man. They mess with you. Old friends you know who did drugs, too. The two together are lethal."

"I should have known."

"James, you couldn't have known."

"It's rough. This living thing is rough. I used to think it was so simple," James said, squinting and staring at a point somewhere behind Sean's head.

"It is simple, James. Don't lose that. Don't lose that belief. Don't lose what you've got that keeps you strong."

"I know. I just feel helpless. First you, now Lib. It's just hard on a guy like me. I never had it too rough. Not like you guys. I had a good family. We ate a shitload. But we loved each other. We didn't get ripped up by life like you and Libby did. This is all just a lot for me to handle."

Sean looked at Chief and Chief looked up at Sean as if he knew exactly what he was thinking. Chief, as if anticipating Sean's words before he could speak them, started to do the two-step backward. It seemed as if Chief could tell Sean had changed his mind about taking him to Italy with him.

"Come here, Chief, come here, boy," Sean said, and then to James, "I have a huge favor to ask of you, James. I need someone I trust completely."

"Whatever it is, shoot."

"Since Lib is going to be away for a while, and well, I'm going away, I'm going to need you to watch Chief. Keep an eye on him while I'm gone. Just a couple of weeks, till I figure out my next move."

"But don't you need him? Where are you go—" James stopped. And shook his head. "No. You're not ready, man. You're not ready. You passed out a few days ago. You're limping around. No. You can't even bend over. What if you drop your cane or something? You need Chief."

"I'll be fine. You need him. He'll look after you. Besides, he needs a coach."

"A coach?"

"Yeah. Tom and I taught him to surf. He's a natural. Found the moment, and hopped right up. Just like you taught me."

"You're kidding."

"No, I meant to tell you. But then that night . . . Libby . . ."

"Man, that's amazing. Amazing. Two amazing things in one day."

"I know, James. I know," Sean said, smiling, always so pleased to see how easily James embraced the amazing.

"Sure, I'll take him," James said to Sean, and then turned to Chief. "So you can surf, man? That's wicked cool, my four-legged friend."

"I'm leaving tonight. All of his food, everything he needs, is at my apartment. Here are my keys. Come after your shift and get him. I'll have walked and fed him."

"You gonna be all right over there? By yourself? You won't need Tom?"

"Nah, it's time Tom and I went our separate ways. He got me where I need to go, and I'll take myself the rest of the way."

"You're sneaking out, aren't you? You don't want Gaspar or your sister to find out?"

"I don't."

"What do I tell them if they call looking for you?"

"The truth. By then, they won't be able to stop me."

"You know what you're doing? You think this is smart?"

"James, I made a promise. I am alive today, I believe, because of that promise. And I have to go to her and make this right."

"Well, we'll be here when you get back. Tom, Chief, and me. We'll be here. No matter what."

"I know you will."

"Sean, man?"

"Yeah, James?"

"This is gonna sound really queer to you, but I need to say it because I feel it."

"It's okay."

"I love you."

"I love you, too, James."

"I want to hug you, man. Would you let me hug you?"

"That's cool."

"Cool," James said, reaching forward and wrapping his arms around Sean, who stood stiffly, accepting James's hug. "You're like a brother, man. I don't want anything bad to happen to you. So you be safe. Got it?"

"Got it."

"You call me if you get into trouble or need anything. I'll come. I am due for some time off and I've never even left the state of California. So it would be good for me. You know?"

"Yeah, man. I know. I'll be safe. I promise. I better get going. I have some packing to do. You won't forget to come and get him?"

"Cross my heart, Sean," James said making a giant X over his chest. And with that Sean said, "To hell with it," and leaned in and returned James's hug with a big, tight squeeze before slapping him on the back.

"Get outta here, man," James said, wiping his eyes.

✍ Chapter 24

B EFORE SEAN WENT UP TO HIS APARTMENT TO GRAB his bag, he crossed the street and the walkway and walked Chief to the beach. It was unseasonably hot for November. The beach was packed with weekenders trying to store up some sun before being trapped again in their offices and cars all week. Sean walked until he found an empty park bench and could sit down and look at the ocean and say good-bye to one last friend.

"So, Chief," Sean started, "James is gonna take good care of you. It will only be a couple of weeks."

Chief growled and dropped on his two front paws, resting his head and looking out at the water.

"It's crazy, isn't it? I didn't even know you a year ago, and now I am just leaving for a little while and I feel like I am leaving my family all over again."

Chief popped his head up and looked back, seemingly disapprovingly, at Sean and turned quickly away and plopped his head back down between his paws.

Don't even talk to me right now.

"Aw, don't be like that, Chief. You're gonna love James. He can take you surfing every day. You know I couldn't have come this far without you. And now James needs you. He doesn't know it. But he needs you. He needs you more than I do right now. He's gonna need a friend. With both me and Libby gone, he's gonna need someone to look after him. Bark at him if he eats too much Thai food, you know. Make him run after you on the beach. Now I know what you're thinking. You think I am passing you off. I'm not. I just have to go and do this. Find out if what I saw that day in the fire was real, that everything I believe is real. I just need some proof that I am not crazy. That what I saw up in that fire was real. That I made that promise to find her and survived for a reason."

Chief stood up again and placed his head on Sean's lap and let Sean pet him. "I'm gonna miss you, boy. I will. And honestly, I don't know what I am doing. I really have no idea. I don't know what I expect. You think she'll even remember me? You think she'll give a damn? Maybe Lib is right. Maybe I am going to do nothing more than mess up Chiara's life. Maybe this is selfish of me. I don't know. I can't explain it, Chief. I can't. But I just know if I don't do this, if I don't play this thing out, I will always wonder. I've never stopped thinking about her. And since the fire, she's all I've been able to think about. These legs are working today because I wanted to get up and walk to her. And I hope you know, Chief, I couldn't have done it without you. I hope you know that I couldn't have done it without any of you."

Chief barked at Sean in reply.

"I know you get it, man. I know you do. And who knows,

maybe if things don't work out with Chiara, maybe I'll find that other thing I was looking for. Maybe I'll find that spot I've been looking for since the night of the fire—that place where I started from, and maybe I'll have a shot at getting better for good. Or maybe I'll find out that I was hallucinating up there after all, and that there aren't really angels out there looking after me, looking after everyone."

At that, Chief turned, as if suggesting that Sean get up and walk toward the water with him. Sean couldn't be sure, but it seemed to him that Chief understood every word. Sean struggled for a bit, but eventually he stood and led Chief to the water's edge. When they reached the cool slaps of water, Chief offered up a wet paw and Sean bent as far as he could to take it in his hand. And if Chief could talk, Sean knew he would have said: *Here's your proof, Sean. Here.*

✳ Part 3

Yes, love indeed is light from heaven;
   A spark of that immortal fire with angels shared . . .

—Lord Byron

✿ Chapter 25

THE FLIGHT TO FLORENCE DAMN NEAR KILLED SEAN. His legs throbbed. The pain in his back was excruciating. He knew he should have sprung for first class. But when he got to the counter and saw how much the tickets cost, he couldn't bring himself to do it. He needed to stretch his cash in case things worked out and he would need to stay longer.

The pain had gotten so bad, Sean began eyeing the small bottles of vodka and whiskey on the beverage cart the flight attendant had pushed past him earlier.

It took everything he had not to raise his hand and order. It would be so easy. One bottle and the pain might disappear. He would be able to stop, he told himself. It was just for the pain. *Just this one time. A self-administered dosage. I could taper. I did it before.*

He fought the urge. He circled back to his meetings. The Big Book. The mantras. If he could get through this five minutes of pain, he could get through the next five minutes. And the next. And the next after that. And it would all add up. It was better not to think of the entire flight, the endless hours, the stifling cabin, the fact that nothing was holding the plane up, nothing but thirty thousand feet of air and miles of water below that. It was better not to think of the snoring passenger beside him, the overwhelming cologne barely covering the putrid body odor of the man sitting in front of him, whose chair was reclined and resting on Sean's knees. *His knees.* It was better not to think of them, and the femurs that were attached to them and that ached.

Sweat poured down Sean's back. His forehead glistened. His pants were soaked through.

He eyed the drinks cart again. *Just one. It would only be one.*

His teeth had formed a solid wall behind his open lips when a flight attendant approached him and asked, "Sir, is everything okay? Can I get you anything?"

He began to raise a finger to point at the small bottle of vodka he saw on an open tray table across the aisle, but he caught himself. *I didn't come this far. I didn't make it this far to fall off the wagon now. To screw up now. Screw the pain. You've been through worse, Magee. Pull your shit together.* Panic seized him. *What if he Tom, James, and Libby were right, what if he wasn't ready? What if something terrible were to happen to him up here?* He couldn't take it any more so he did what his meetings taught him to do: talk.

"I broke my legs. I broke my back, too, and burned my arms and face," Sean said, lifting his arms up and unaware of why he felt compelled to talk, to tell someone this, but he knew it was coming from somewhere deep within him. If he didn't, he knew he would ask for a drink. "I'm an alcoholic. I can't drink. I can't take anything for my nerves. For my pain. I can't take pills. I don't know how I am going to make it through the next few hours. This is hell. Hell. I can't take it," Sean said breathlessly. Panting out the last few words, *I can't take it.*

The flight attendant leaned over and in a stage whisper asked, "Sir, do you think you can stand up?"

"Yes, I think I can," Sean whispered back.

"Follow me," she whispered, quietly this time, putting a finger in front of her lips.

Sean braced himself and pushed out of the minuscule chair that had pinned his hips. "Ahhhh," he cried out, briefly waking the snoring passenger, who gave a final snort and flopped her head over in the opposite direction.

Sean limped slowly behind the flight attendant, using each row of seats as support down the long row and through the curtains to first class.

"We have one available. I was supposed to sit here, but you can take it," the flight attendant said, pointing to what appeared to be a wide fold-out bed. "It's a recumbent chair, folds out like a bed so you can stretch your legs and sleep."

"But where will you sit?"

"Back in your seat during landing. I'll be okay."

"Why? You don't know me."

"It's okay. You need this more than me. Get some rest. Sooner you sleep, sooner you'll be where you want to be."

"Thank you," Sean whispered. "You have no idea what you just did for me."

"I just gave you my chair."

Sean wanted to say, *You just saved an old drunk from possibly blowing everything he spent the past eleven years trying to fix.* But instead he said, "What you did was huge. Huge."

"Come on," the flight attendant said, swatting him. "It was nothing."

"Nothing to one person can mean the world to another," Sean said, shaking her hand before falling into a deep, fast sleep that took him exactly where he wanted to go.

❧ Chapter 26

D ESPITE THE ABILITY TO STRETCH OUT, THE PAIN
never left Sean's legs, even after he stepped off the
plane. Even after he walked through the gates and out
of the airport, a throbbing, tight sensation wrapped his left
calf. No matter how he stretched, he couldn't kick it. The pain
radiated up his legs and his chest. He felt anxious, afraid. His
old *I can't*s and self-doubts crept in. He was standing on the
ledge of a window all over again.

Jump, dammit. Jump.

Sean stood motionless at the curb outside the airport in
Florence for several minutes, contemplating his next move.
This was so stupid. Every instinct in him was telling him to turn
around, get back on the next plane, and go home. *The entire
trip was a terrible idea.* Everyone had been right to warn him, to
try to stop him. He stood with his back to the road and looked
up at the airport, deciding whether or not to go back inside
and forget this foolhardy decision. Just as he was about to step

forward and return through the doors, a large woman with a rolling suitcase knocked Sean's cane from beneath him and threw him off balance. When he regained his composure, he was facing a taxi that had pulled up alongside him.

Sean fought the instinct to retreat and stepped off the curb.

"Duomo," Sean instructed the driver curtly.

"*Si, si*. Do you speak English?" the cabdriver asked in a thick accent.

"*Si*," Sean said.

"Lucky for you, I speak it. First time in Firenze?"

"No, I lived here many years ago," Sean said while fumbling with his bag and handing it to the driver to put in the trunk.

"I can help you, sir. Please, sit. Sit." The driver held Sean's arm and instructed him to get in the car.

"You don't look so good. Are you sick, sir?" the driver said, leaning in before shutting the door.

"No. Yes. I don't know," Sean mumbled in confusion.

The driver dropped the bag in the trunk, ran around the car, jumped in the driver's seat, and adjusted the mirror in Sean's direction. "I will take you to the doctor? Hospital?"

"No, no. The Duomo *per favore*."

"I know sick. You are sick. Very sick. Your face has no color. You are sweating. I must take you."

"I had a long night and a long flight. I came from California. My legs . . . they were cramped for so long. That is all."

"You should go for a walk. You might feel better." The taxi driver looked at Sean in the rearview mirror again. "Why are you back in Firenze? That's a long trip to just see the *David*, no?"

"I came back for a woman."

"Ah, always a woman. *Si, si.* She is *bellisima*?"

"*Si.*"

"What is your plan? Stay here? Take her back to America and buy her a big house? Fancy white sneakers?"

Sean laughed and shook his head. "I just hope she'll want to talk to me."

"Ah, ah. *Il mio consiglio* . . ."

"Your advice?"

"*Si, si,* my advice."

"I don't need any more advice," Sean said, shaking his head.

"No, no. You must take this. You must. I can see you need it."

"First you said I looked sick and now you say you see that I need advice?" Sean laughed again

"Maybe your heart is sick? Eh? Maybe this old man can teach you some things?"

"You don't know me," Sean said, staring back at the driver's eyes in the mirror.

"I know love."

"Oh no, here we go," Sean said, rolling his eyes. "Another human, another opinion. Shoot."

"It is very, very simple," the driver said, holding up his pointer finger for emphasis, *"Ascolta,"* the driver started.

"I am listening," Sean said, adjusting his legs again in the backseat.

"No, that is my advice. *Listen.* Everyone needs to shut up. Shut up. Shut up. Just listen. You think you have so much to say. You probably flew all this way, and I wager this: I wager that you thought about all the things you wanted to say to the girl. You thought, *I will say this, and then she will say that.* But life never goes like you think it will. If you think it, then it does not happen. That is just the way. It is God's way to show us who is the boss. Our minds don't control what others will say and do. So shut up. Believe me. You listen and you will hear. You stop talking and you will see. You be still, and you will know," the driver said emphatically.

"Do I have to tip you more for the *consiglio*?" Sean asked with a smirk.

"No charge. I give my genius away for free. It's an added bonus for ride with me." The driver smiled and winked in the mirror back at Sean.

For the rest of the ride through Florence, Sean shut up. He listened to the taxi driver talk about his wife and children, his long hours in the cab, his mother suffering from Alzheimer's, the cost of gas, the economic crisis, and the rising crackdown on counterfeit wares. "Don't buy a cheap purse for your girl. You will get arrested. *Si?*" Sean nodded and tried to do as the man instructed; he tried as hard as he could to not create scenarios in his head of what would be, how it would all turn out. He tried to stay present. He tried to do what James had said and wait for the moment. Wait for the right time to rise and soar.

When the taxi came to a halt at a stoplight a few blocks from the Duomo, Sean tapped the driver's shoulder. "I'll get out here. I'll walk the rest of the way."

"Did I talk too much? Did I bother you?"

"No, you've been very entertaining. I just have to walk. My legs," Sean said, tapping them with his cane.

"*Si, si.* Are you going to meet *la bella* here?"

"No, she doesn't even know I am here."

"Ah, you Americans. Too many movies. Too much hope. Happy endings. You all think life is a Sandra Bullock movie? Eh? But in real life there is only one ending. In the ground. And it's not so happy. Not so much a Sandra Bullock movie."

Sean laughed, pulled out his thick wallet, and counted out one hundred euros. "Keep the change, doc. Take your *bella* out to dinner." Sean was always so tight with money when it came to himself, but never thought twice about giving it away for another's benefit.

After stuffing the money in his jeans, the driver leaped out of the car and grabbed Sean's bag. "Here is my card. If things don't work out with the girl, you call me. Just me. I'll pick you up anywhere and I can drive you anywhere. I have a lot of advice I can give."

"Thanks, I am sure you do," Sean said, taking the bag and the card.

Sean turned slowly, adjusting his cane to the cobblestones, and crossed through the piazza, pulling his bag, which bumped along loudly behind him. When he reached the Baptistery across from the Duomo, he stood and stared at it for a long time. The driver was right. He had played the scene over and over in his head. He imagined running into her as she came walking past him. He imagined all the things he would say to her. *Dammit.* He was a fool to think he could come here, just show up, and everything would go as he had imagined, as he had planned and dreamed, simply because he had some dumb hallucination on the night of the fire.

Sean fought another urge to turn around and tell the driver to stop, but instead walked toward the entrance of the church.

Chapter 27

THERE IS AN UPRUSH WHEN ONE WALKS THROUGH THE door of the Basilica di Santa Maria del Fiore. One half-expects to be assaulted by an opulent interior, one at least befitting its over-the-top exterior. But walking through the doors, Sean felt exactly how he had over eleven years ago, when he first set foot inside the gargantuan, stark nave. He felt swallowed. Infinitesimal. Insignificant. And yet, he felt connected . . . connected to everyone and everything. The vast open space filled with light and people made him feel that he was intimately connected to the divine architect, and all the men who'd made it, too, who worked for centuries to build the structure. It took thousands of men and women to build the structure, brick by brick, and none of them knew the lives they'd touch. Few of them probably knew that the magnificent structure would stand for centuries, long after they lived. Invisible to him now, the spirits of those people reached out and touched Sean as he walked. He just knew it. He'd felt them with him eleven years earlier and he felt them now. As he walked through it again, he felt like a maverick wave was hitting him and taking him to the cold depths of the ocean floor. A weight heavier than he'd ever felt pressed on his chest. He inhaled deeply and tried to catch his breath. He reached for a mask that was not there to pull off.

Breathe. Breathe. Breathe.

When he reached the front of the church, and stood beneath the colossal dome, he suddenly remembered something he'd forgotten. A found memory, the kind that happens only when looking through old boxes in cobwebbed basements, where suddenly a long-forgotten and unseen picture conjures it all up and worms its way through one's subconscious. Like a few months ago when he'd come upon a photo of Cathleen and himself at the Bronx Zoo back when they were kids. He could have been no more than nine or ten years old. He could smell the camel they were riding. He could see their mother waving at them. It had been a day lost until found decades later in a box. And just like when he saw that picture and remembered, he saw the dome and could see Chiara stop him, take his hand, and say to him in impeccable English, "Do you know how they built that giant dome, Sean? It had never been done before. Nothing this magnificent had ever been created. The closest thing was the Pantheon in Rome, but the architects of the Pantheon didn't leave instructions, of course, so no one knew just how they created it. The people of Florence felt hopeless. They didn't think that their church, which took centuries to build, would ever get the promised dome. But eventually the genius architect Brunelleschi solved the problem of building a dome on such a gargantuan scale. It is still somewhat of a mystery and argued about in certain circles, but the gist is that by creating an intricate web of chains and iron rods, he was able to build a somewhat flexible but strong structure that would eventually form the bones of the dome. He made a series of them and formed them in the shape of an octagon to hold the shape," Chiara said, pulling Sean's arms with hers and interlocking them to demonstrate how the chains were pulled taut. "It took eight sides to create the strength to support it," Chiara explained further. "Masons reinforced the structure *as* they built it with an ingenious bricklaying method—interlocking them in a herringbone pattern. The cross ties of the iron chains and rails were woven together and then were covered with the bricks and mortar of the inner dome. The bottom chains can be seen protruding from the drum at the base of the dome. The others are hidden. Can you see?" Chiara asked, breaking their taut circle of arms and pointing up.

Sean nodded, but he didn't see.

"They never even needed scaffolding. They just stood on the web of chains and built from the inside out."

"So there are iron rods and chains still up there?" Sean asked.

"Yes, the clay bricks were formed in fire, Sean, and then formed the body of the dome. And the inside was reinforced with metal."

Formed in fire and reinforced with metal. Sean dropped his cane with the memory and looked up toward the small windows cut into the dome.

"And all of it was created so that at the top of the dome, a circle of windows could be installed, to let the light in. So that through the fire, the hard metal, and the heavy stuff of this world, the light could come shining through," Sean remembered Chiara saying and pointing.

"All that for a little bit of light," Sean said, looking up at the dome and then back at Chiara in disbelief.

"Yes, Sean. A little bit of light makes all the difference. How else would we be able to see the angels?" Chiara's head fell back and she pointed up to the frescoes painted on the interior of the dome.

"How do you know so much? So much about the light?" Sean asked her, taking her by the hands and looking deep in her eyes.

"I was named after it. Sort of. My father . . . he brought me here as a child and he told me the same story I just told you. He came here every day and prayed under that light for a daughter. My mother was old like him and they wanted a child. And he made a promise to the angels and the light above that if he was granted this request, he would name me after the light they pointed to. He would spend his life in service to it."

"Wait, I thought Chiara meant Clare?" Sean asked.

"*Chiara* means *clear*—so light may pass, so that it may enter," she said, smiling and pointing.

"All this for a little light." Sean laughed and hugged her close. "Little Chiara," he said, kissing the top of her head.

Sean, overcome by the memory, caught his breath and looked up at Vasari's, Zuccari's, and Cresti's frescoes, painted over the course of eleven years. Each building upon each other's work, where one left off another began. One informed the other, making each consecutive fresco more beautiful, more alive. Each added their own version of light to the entire dome, covering the fire-burned bricks, chains, and metal with beauty, essence, and spirit. Each interpretation wholly different than the other but together working to tell a complete story of the world, creation, judgment, hell, earth, and heaven. Each used their divine talents to fill the giant, empty white dome with beauty and light.

Sean saw Cresti's *Choirs of Angels,* which encircled the dome. Their wings spread wide, and their arms pointing to both the light above and the people below. He thought of Chiara, the light, and the eight sides that helped strengthen and reinforce the dome. *Eight.*

He looked at the angels above and then started another mental list, slowly whispering each of their names aloud:

> *Mom*
> *Cathleen*
> *Colm*
> *Gaspar*
> *James*
> *Libby*
> *Tom*
> *Chiara*

He envisioned each of their faces in the faces of the angels above him. And he was overcome by the thought of the eight people who held him up, pushed him into the light.

Sean fell to his knees.

Chapter 28

A N HOUR AFTER LEAVING THE DUOMO, SEAN STOOD
outside the Montanari family apartment afraid to
knock. Despite what the driver had warned him not
to do, he stood planning what his explanation might be to
Chiara's father and just how he might elicit her whereabouts
from the protective man. He had not seen him since the last
Sunday dinner he had been invited to. Just days before he left
Chiara and Florence for good.

Sean had held his arm up in preparation for a knock when
the door opened in front of him. A skinny teenage girl with
heavy eye makeup stood before him. She was small in stature
like Chiara and had Chiara's hair color and amber-colored
eyes, but she was more angular and dark.

"Lucia?" Sean asked in disbelief.

"*Si?*" The girl looked at the man, confused for a moment,
and finished pulling on her jacket and grabbed her bag off the
chair by the door, giving him a suspicious once-over.

"It's me. Sean Magee? You were a little girl, no more than three or four, when I saw you last. I dated your sister, Chiara. A long time ago. Do you remember me?" Sean asked.

"Sean? Magee?" Lucia's eyes squinted suspiciously. "You're real?" she said in perfect English, like her sister.

"Of course."

"You're alive?" she said, poking Sean.

"Yes, of course, why . . ." And then Sean remembered. It had never occurred to him, it never crossed his mind for a second that Chiara would have thought he died or that that would even have been a possibility.

"She said you disappeared. Poof. Gone. One day here, the next day gone. I don't remember much of it, but I remember being sad for her, because she would spend hours curled up on her bed holding your picture," Lucia said, not holding back in the least.

"God, I am so sorry," Sean said to her, realizing that his leaving affected more than just Chiara.

"She got over you. So don't get too sorry. And you don't have to pretend *sorry* for me," Lucia snapped back again. "You grown-ups are so full of shit."

Teenagers scared Sean. They said exactly what they thought. Social media had made it even worse. It made him uncomfortable. They all felt entitled to share their opinions and highlight perceived grown-up hypocrisy. Half-truths and hypocrisy were the bane of every teen's existence and had been since the beginning of time, long before they could tweet it or post it. He remembered his own teen years well. He remembered when his idea of truth was more prized than another's pain, sacrifice, or closely guarded secret. Teens felt for lies and deceits like Sean felt for fire behind thick walls and they rejoiced in finding and revealing them. More than anything, they enjoyed crashing through them with axes of perceived truth.

"I'm not pretending," Sean said.

"Really? Then why are you here? Do you just happen to be in the neighborhood? Since when did New York City move next door?" Lucia asked, using her thumb to point to her neighbor's door.

"Los Angeles actually. I came from Los Angeles," Sean corrected her.

"Well, you're out of luck. You came a long way for nothing. My sister, Chiara, she's not here," Lucia said.

Sean's shoulders dropped and he turned.

Lucia looked at Sean's ear as he turned and then noticed his scarred hands and his cane. "Did you fight in the war?" she asked, staring.

"What? No. Why? What war?"

"Any. All of America's wars. You're a soldier? You're injured," she said, pointing to Sean's ear and then his hands.

"No," Sean explained. "I am a firefighter. Well, I used to be."

"Ah, ah," Lucia said, softening at the sight of Sean's melted ear and what looked to her like a lame attempt to cover it with long hair that had been brushed forward to hide the burns.

Sean, feeling her stare, put his hands up to push his hair forward and realized it only brought more attention to his burned hands. He felt his face flush with embarrassment and turned again to leave.

"Hey! Hey! Where are you going?"

"I'm sorry. I shouldn't have come. I probably look and sound very foolish to you."

"No, I'm sorry. I was rude. It's just that . . . I wasn't expecting you . . . or your . . . well . . . how you look now."

"Yes, I see that."

"Sean, do you want to come with me? I am going to see her. We have lunch plans."

"Wait. I thought you said she wasn't here. She is still here—in Florence?" Sean asked hopefully.

"*Si, si.* She is not home right now. She works at the Art Institute. She is a curator. She lives here," Lucia said, pointing back into the apartment. "Our father died right after our mother did. Cancer and a stroke. They were old when they had Chiara and practically ancient when they had me and Franco. So she got stuck taking care of us. She knew it would end up like this."

"So she's not . . ."

"No, no, no. No husband. No boyfriend. She's what you call in America a single white female."

"We don't actually call anyone that. One movie did, a long time ago." Sean felt suddenly light and jocular, brimming with the hope that he might actually find Chiara today. He pulled himself together to ask Lucia when her father passed away.

"About three years ago. My sister was in Rome living with a boyfriend. She came back to take care of us and the boyfriend wouldn't follow."

"That's too bad," Sean said, feigning sympathy.

"He was an asshole. Don't feel too badly," Lucia dead-panned.

"So you're going to see her, right now?" Sean asked, trying to clarify whether the invitation still stood.

"You know Chiara will fall over dead when she sees you. You know she still keeps your picture in her jewelry box. I see it every time I steal her earrings. You used to be hot," Lucia quipped, coming out of the door and closing it, then slipping in her keys to turn the series of locks.

"And I'm not anymore?" Sean said, looking worried.

"No one your age is hot. You and my sister are old."

"The thirties are not old," Sean corrected her.

"It's twice as old as me. So you're super old. Do you think sixty-year-olds are hot?"

"Point taken," Sean said, hobbling behind the girl, who walked quickly ahead of him.

"You coming?" she asked, turning around.

"You're gonna have to be patient, Lucia. I'm an old man," Sean said, limping behind her.

Lucia stopped and grabbed his arm and guided him down the steps, saying, "Oh, I love an adventure. Life is so boring."

"It's really not," Sean said.

"When you're a kid, it is. It's so boring, I want to do outra-geous things," Lucia admitted with a shout and swung her arms out wide, almost knocking Sean over.

"You and every other kid. Just don't be an idiot. You'd be amazed by how much of your life is determined by the stupid things you do to break up the boredom. In fact, most of life is determined by the stupid things you do. The split-second, rash decisions are the ones that make all the difference between whether you end up on either Savile or death row."

"You sound like Chiara."

"She's smart. Always was."

"She thinks she knows everything," Lucia said, rolling her eyes.

"She's *old*, so she knows more than you. A wise man once told me the key to life and love is this . . . ," Sean said, turning to the girl.

"What?" Lucia said as she pushed through the apartment building door and spilled out into the street.

"*Listen*. Listen to your sister. I wouldn't have gotten in half as much trouble in life if I had listened to mine," Sean said, coming up behind her.

"Yeah, but I bet you were never bored," Lucia said smartly.

"Point taken," Sean said for the second time since they met.

"Are you nervous, Sean? Because you look nervous," Lucia said bluntly, tearing through his truth with her teen ax.

"Yes, Lucia, I am," he said, inhaling. "I'm nervous and excited. You have no idea how long I've waited for this moment. What it took for me to get here. To this day," Sean admitted.

"Well, don't be disappointed. She's changed a lot since then."

"We all have. I have, too," Sean said.

"She's tough. She used to laugh so much. She doesn't anymore," Lucia said while fumbling with her iPod and inserting her earphones as she walked.

"Life is tough, Lucia. From the sound of it, it's been especially rough for her," Sean said, pulling one of the earphones out as he spoke to her.

Lucia nodded, looked up at the sky, flipped her long hair to reinsert the earphone in defiance, and said, "You know, Sean, she'll kill me for this, but here's what I am going to do. You and I both want something. So I'll make you a deal. You want to see my sister and I could use a break from my sister. She's both *boring and old.*" Lucia feigned a yawn and then laughed. "So you go to lunch with her. She'll make you eat lettuce and won't let you order a cappuccino. But she'll be at this café on this street around the corner from the Art Institute," Lucia said, writing down the address and name of the café on a piece of paper she had pulled from a notebook in her purse. "And in exchange for this address, you will tell her I went to the library to study," Lucia said, stuffing the address in Sean's jacket pocket and patting his heart.

"Are you going to get me in trouble, Lucia?"

"Probably. But better you than me," Lucia said, swinging the bag over her shoulder and taking off down the street.

"Jesus," Sean said, shaking his head. "Kids today."

❧ Chapter 29

As Sean sat waiting for Chiara to arrive, he tried his best to do what the cabdriver had instructed. He tried not to think of all the things he would say to her. He would try not to come to her with excuses. He tapped his foot and adjusted his legs under the table several times. He looked at every woman who passed by on the street and thought each one might be her. A chubby woman with blond hair: *Maybe she gained weight and started to dye her hair?* A tall, gamine woman wearing bright red lipstick: *Maybe she had a growth spurt?* Then he panicked and thought she wasn't coming at all. He thought that Lucia had never been going to meet her sister. That it was all a big joke on his account. *Ha-ha, you dumb American. You freaky stalker, you. Like I'd ever give you my sister's whereabouts? Scram, loser.* After fifteen minutes of destructive self-talk, Sean grabbed his cane and tried to stand. Pushing himself up, he bent down over his cane and hoisted himself into a standing, though bent position. When he finally stood up straight, Chiara Montanari was there before him.

Her amber eyes grew as large as quarters and her mouth quivered when she locked her eyes with his. She was trying to form words, Sean could tell. He wanted to say his name, finish her thought for her: *Yes, it's me. Sean Magee.* But he remembered to shut up.

"Sean? Sean Magee?" Chiara finally whispered. Nearly inaudibly, as if she'd just remembered the precise location of a lost set of keys. *I just set them down over there. Yes, that's where I left them.*

Sean matched her whisper. "Yes."

"But, but, I, I . . . why? Wait. What is going on? Where is Lucia? Why are you here? Why are you in Florence?"

Sean pointed to the chair. "Would you like to sit and talk?" he said.

"I am supposed to meet my sister," Chiara said, still not fully comprehending what she was seeing before her.

"She's not coming, Chiara," Sean said, his heart fluttering as he spoke her name. "I went to your apartment. She told me you would be here. I came looking for you. She went to the library to study."

"You came from where exactly?" Chiara asked, stepping back.

"Los Angeles," Sean said.

Chiara's head cocked to the left and then the right. "I don't understand."

"Please sit down, Chiara. Let me explain."

Sean pulled out a chair for Chiara and she fell into it. As if someone had taken a feather and tapped her. She was ready to be blown over at any moment. She stared for a long time at him as if running through an inventory.

Sean hobbled a bit and sat back down in his chair, wincing as he did.

"Your legs? Your hands? Your ear? Burns?" Chiara could only put together singular words, not quite full sentences as the shock of seeing him overtook her.

"Yes," Sean said, self-consciously moving the hair over his ear and neck and then dropping his hands to his lap. "I was in a fire."

"Is that why? Is that why you didn't . . ." Chiara's mouth opened in horror and she covered it. Tears were welling up. "My God, I am so sorry. All this time, I, I, I . . ." Chiara's head shook.

"No, no, no, please, Chiara. Don't apologize. No. You're so, so good. So kind. Don't go thinking that I am a good person. That the reason I left you was that I was injured . . . this happened later, much later, recently actually," Sean explained.

"So you . . . you just left then," Chiara's head dropped. Sean noticed small gray roots protruding from the burgundy waves that had, for the most part, remained unchanged. Everything about her looked the same, except for her eyes, which were darker and more deeply set. Her cheekbones were more pronounced. Age had made her even more striking.

"Yes," Sean said. "Yes."

Chiara's head popped up quickly and she clasped her hands together on the table. "So let me guess. You are here to explain," Chiara said in an exasperated tone.

Sean nodded.

"And I bet you're here to tell me how sorry you are," Chiara said.

Sean nodded and tried to open his mouth to speak, but Chiara cut him off.

"Save your breath, Sean. I don't need to hear your excuses, your reasons, your apologies. We were kids," Chiara said dismissively. "Foolish, foolish children," she said, raising her hand for a waiter. "I hardly ever think about you anymore. I mean, it hurt at first. But everyone hurts for a while after a breakup. It was just part of growing up. It's all ancient history. Honestly, I have had boyfriends who I wouldn't give a second glance to if they walked by me on the street," Chiara said coolly.

"Oh, oh, I, I, well yes. We were just kids." Sean tried, faintly, agreeing with her. *A boyfriend she wouldn't give a second glance to.*

"Two cappuccinos, please," Chiara said to the waiter in English as he passed, never losing eye contact with Sean.

Sean smiled.

"What? Why are you smiling at me like that?"

"Lucia said you wouldn't let me have a cappuccino."

"I don't let *her* have them. Caffeine makes the girl act like a madwoman. She has enough nervous energy as it is. Someone has to be the grown-up," Chiara said, rolling her eyes. And Sean felt like the comment was aimed more at him than it was at Lucia.

"Chiara, I need to tell you—"

"Please, Sean. Please. Let's make this pleasant. Let's pretend you and I are old friends and we just bumped into each other. Let's pretend things didn't end the way they did. Okay?

You've been through a lot. I've been through a lot. Come on. Don't be melodramatic."

"But we were more than friends," Sean said, leaning toward her. "Right?"

Chiara shrugged. It was the same shrug from eleven years ago. The same one she had when he would come to her place drunk, slurring his words in front of all of her friends. "You're fucking embarrassed by me, Chiara. Admit it. I am just your drunk American boyfriend." She shrugged then, fighting back the tears, the hurt.

Sean's stomach lurched. It was all an act. He could tell. She was fighting it all back. Just like she had back when they were a couple of kids.

"I was terrible to you, Chiara," Sean said abruptly. "I said terrible things to you when I was drunk, and I treated you unfairly. I made you promises. I told you that I wanted to marry you. I promised to take you to America. To put you through art school. I promised you—"

The waiter dropped two cappuccinos in front of them and stood for a moment staring at Sean and the heavy layer of smooth flesh stretched taut between his ear and neck.

"*Grazie*," Chiara said, taking the coffee and sipping it.

Sean became entranced while watching her drink and remembered their early days—sitting beside her in café after café, talking and talking and talking. There was no end to what they could discuss.

"I don't drink anymore," Sean said, trying to explain.

Chiara nodded and said, "Good for you, Sean."

"I'm an alcoholic," Sean said, realizing that he had in fact practiced saying that line, that exact line, every day for years.

Chiara nodded and took another sip as if to say, *And what does that have to do with me?*

"I said and did a lot of horrible things, Chiara, to you and to a lot of people I love, because I drank," Sean continued.

Chiara's eyes narrowed. Wrinkles creased around her eyes and she furrowed her brow.

Sean could see a hint of anger rising in her, but thought perhaps he was misreading her emotions and continued. "I drank because I thought it would lighten me up. I thought it would make it easier for me to talk to you, keep up with you and your friends . . ."

Chiara put her hands up to stop him. "So it was my fault? My fault you drank? That you're an alcoholic? You came all the way to Florence to blame me for your stupidity? To blame *m*e for your decisions, for *you leaving me*?" Chiara asked incredulously.

"No, no! I got it all wrong. It came out all wrong," Sean said, wishing after all that he had actually practiced what he was going to say.

"Then what? What are you trying to say? Go on!" Chiara, waving him on, demanded. "Go on!"

"I drank before you. I drank in high school. I drank whenever I felt like I needed to feel that feeling, you know, when everything just falls into place. I was always looking for that peaceful moment when I could just feel okay in my own head. In my own skin. I always felt broken. Weak. I don't know, *less than*. I thought it was because I didn't have a dad. Then I thought it was nine/eleven. Then I thought it was my mom dying. And then I thought it was because I was just so damn useless. No good at anything. And I wanted to be. I wanted to be great. I wanted to do something with my life. Have a purpose. And then I found you, Chiara. And you actually liked me. You loved me. *Me?* I didn't understand it. I hit the self-destruct button, you could say. I did. I destroyed what we had because I was an idiot. I thought I wasn't good enough for you. But I was. I could have been. By the time I figured that out, I'd already messed up your life, my life, and so many other people's, too. It took me a long time, Chiara, to get sober. To see things clearly. And that's why I am here. I am here to make amends. I am here to tell you I am sorry, truly sorry for hurting you. I know I did. I was weak and foolish."

Chiara stared at him for a long time and said nothing. "So you alcoholics, you keep these lists? You make lists of people whose names you need to cross off when you make amends to them? Is that it? It makes you better? It heals you? I bet my name is on a list."

Blood rushed to Sean's face. He burned hot in embarrassment.

Chiara's mouth spread wide in a smile. "Ah, that's it," she said, pointing at him. "I am a name on a list somewhere in your pocket," she said, smiling.

"My wallet actually," Sean admitted.

"Well, that's a shitty thing, Sean. A very shitty thing." Chiara's face fell.

"What? To say I'm sorry? To try to make amends? Make up for what I did?" Sean asked, surprised, not at all expecting this response. Not once when he imagined saying he was sorry to her did he expect her to utter those words. No one ever had.

"No. *Sorry* is not shitty. *Making things right* is not bad. It is *why* you do it that is shitty. You think this will heal *you*. This isn't about me. It is about *you*. Once again. *You*. This is about what *you* want. What will make *you* feel better. It has nothing to do with the other person. What the other person wants or needs. Once again it is about *you*—*you*, no doubt fulfilling some promise to yourself or God, *you* taking the 'steps' *you* need to stay sober, *you* getting what you want once again," Chiara said sharply.

Sean inhaled and realized how right Libby had been. *Be gentle*. He realized how right Chiara was, too.

"You're right. I'm sorry," Sean said. "I never saw it that way. I never realized how selfish I was being."

"Okay. Go on."

Sean's eyes lit up when she opened the door for him to keep talking. "I want to fix this. For you."

"You can't fix it, Sean. You can't go back in time and fix what you broke. Hearts don't just get whole again after you say *I'm sorry*. They stay broken. They get thick and hard from the scars." Chiara's voice trembled and then softened. "I . . . I . . . I . . . loved you," she whispered into her chest and then wiped a tear from her cheek quickly, as if hoping Sean wouldn't see.

"Chiara, I was an idiot, but you're all I've ever thought about . . . when I was in the fire and I thought I might die, it was your name, Chiara, yours that I spoke. I thought of you! You," Sean said finally, lifting his burned hands to the table and reaching for hers.

"Well, isn't that rich. I am supposed to feel better because you didn't think of me for over a decade, but only thought of me when you might die? What about all that time in between, Sean? Did you ever think of me? Ever? Just once? Because I thought of you. I didn't understand it. I couldn't understand it. I thought we were happy. I thought . . . we . . . I thought we'd grow old together. You made me believe that."

"I'm sorry, Chiara. I was stupid and young."

"I was young, too! You weren't the only one!" Chiara snapped. "Men are so selfish. So selfish. All you think of is *you*. As if this just happened to *you*. You've been tormenting yourself for years, but it's really been about *you*. Not me. *You*. Because, if you thought for one second about someone besides yourself, you would have written me a letter. Called me. Reached out and told me it wasn't my fault. Because that's what I thought: You left because of me. Because of something I said. Something I did. I kept playing it over and over in my head."

"What? What did you play over and over?" Sean asked.

"The last time we saw each other. You had spent the night. I made you coffee. We read the paper. I told you I was going to paint at a vineyard nearby with my class and you were going to go to mass. That was the last time we spoke. The last time we talked. The last time we touched. I tried to remember if you kissed me good-bye. If you knew it then, that moment. I wondered for years if you knew you were going to leave me that morning. And I was so angry for so long because I couldn't remember . . . I couldn't remember if you kissed me. I wanted to. I wanted to think of you as Judas, kissing me and betraying me all in the same day. It would have been easier for me to hate you. But I couldn't remember. And it killed me. I just wanted one last memory. One last kiss to hold on to and remember and you stole that from me, too. I looked for you. I went to church. I went to the library. I went to all of our places. I couldn't find you. You didn't answer my calls. You didn't check your e-mails. I went to the police. And after a couple of days they said your passport had been stamped and you had left the country. And I knew right then and there: you'd left me. And so of course I thought it was something I'd said or done. What else could it have been? What?"

"I can't imagine what I put you through. I am so sorry."

"You keep saying that. Stop saying that, goddammit. Stop making me feel sorry for you."

"I'm sor—" Sean stopped himself. "You're right. You have every right to be upset with me. Go on. Let me have it."

"You treated me like a stranger, Sean. Like someone you met on the train and swapped stories with about your hometown and talked with about the weather, and then at your next stop you went on your merry way."

"You're right," Sean said, shaking his head.

"Before I found out you left the country, I thought you were dead, Sean. I thought that could have been the only thing to keep you from me. Death. But no, you just up and left me. Like a half-sipped cappuccino left on a table. Up and gone. You'd had your fill."

"No. No. No. It wasn't like that."

"Then what? What, Sean? It's been eleven years. What did you expect? Did you want me to jump into your arms and hug you? Say, hey, ol' pal, where ya been hidin'?" Chiara said with a mock American accent.

"No, I don't know." Sean trembled and started to sweat.

"I can't understand this, Sean. I can't."

"I was so weak, Chiara. I was weak then and I am getting stronger. It took me years to see that. I spent the past decade

in a haze. You deserve an explanation. You deserve so much."
Sean reached across the table and with his burned hand tried
to touch Chiara's.

Chiara looked down at his thick scars and recoiled a bit,
then looked up at him.

"This is too much, Sean, it's too much. I can't," she said,
standing up suddenly and turning, and then dashed toward
the door to leave.

❧ Chapter 30

A SUDDEN SURGE WENT THROUGH SEAN'S BODY. Now that he had Chiara so close, he felt the distance all the more acutely as she stood to leave. He felt a tear at his heart. As if their two hearts were connected by a web of chains, holding and reinforcing him, and when she stood to leave she pulled and broke it, and with that break he felt his entire structure, including the tiniest shard of light that came through it, about to collapse and envelop him in darkness. It unraveled him with every step she took toward the door. Sean hopped up quickly and shouted across the café, "Wait! Wait! Don't go! Chiara! Stop! Don't leave! Please, give me another chance!"

Every patron in the café turned and looked at Sean and then at Chiara. Chiara's face reddened. No doubt everyone in the café was thinking that she was leaving an invalid.

Sean tried to walk, but when he moved his leg forward he kicked his cane and it fell to the ground. Unable to bend and get it, he stood, motionless, staring at Chiara, knowing there was no way for him to catch her, to keep up with her.

Chiara turned and saw Sean struggle to move forward and

put up her hand to tell him to stop. "Don't move, Sean, I've got it," she said, walking over and bending to pick up the cane. "Here," she said, putting the cane in his hand with hers and their hands touched.

Sean took her hand and held it. "I'm sorry, Chiara. I am so sorry. I wish I could do it all over. I wish I could take it all away—all the pain and sadness I caused," he whispered.

"It is okay, Sean, we all suffer," Chiara said earnestly. "Some more than others, yes. But we all suffer," she said, squeezing his hand a little tighter and guiding him back into the chair before sitting down herself. "I am sorry I was so harsh. I've been holding it all in for a long time and I guess I didn't realize how much it still hurt."

"Leaving you was the hardest thing I have ever done. I didn't want to. But I thought you would be better off without me. I thought I would just bring you down with me," Sean said quietly.

"It's dangerous to think you know what is best for someone else. To make a decision for two people without the other's consent. To decide another's life for them." Chiara did not look away from Sean.

Sean nodded. "A good friend told me a similar thing not so long ago."

"He is a good friend. It is good advice," Chiara said.

"So you never married?" Sean asked, pretending to not know.

"No."

"Ever come close?"

"Not really," Chiara said. "It's not so easy when you have kids to care for."

Sean nodded. "I understand."

"Oh? You have children?"

"No, I don't. My sister was a single mom for a long time and I helped her. Her boy was like a son to me."

"*Was?* So she is married now?"

"Yes."

"So no more son?" Chiara clarified.

Sean shook his head. "No."

"That must be difficult. To love someone so much and then have to let someone else do the loving."

Sean nodded and said nothing. The story was too hard to tell. *He was so sick. So very sick. His body. His heart. None of it worked. You have no idea how hard it was.* But he couldn't form the words. Every emotion within him brimmed. He had lost so much, he could not bear, at this moment, to lose her. Not now. Not after everything he had done to get here.

"So no one special in your life, I presume. Otherwise you'd have a lot of explaining to do when you get home. Or did you take off on her, too?"

Sean winced. "Ouch."

"People stick to their routines. They do what they know," Chiara said, with every bit of nonchalance Sean had had a few days ago in his apartment talking to Tom.

Sean wanted to say, *Hey, I said that, too! See how much we still have in common!* But instead, he resisted and said, "People can change, Chiara. They can learn new ways to cope. New behaviors. Discover new ways to do things. Like how Brunelleschi discovered a new way to build a dome."

Chiara's eyes lit up. "You remembered that?"

"Of course, I went there this morning."

"It is still one of my favorite *Sean* places," Chiara said absently.

"Sean places?" Sean asked.

Chiara surprised herself and blushed. "Yes, well, there are not many places here that I don't go to and see you. See the memories we shared. It is difficult sometimes. I used to be jealous of you. That you could just walk away and forget us. But I had to walk into every church, café, bookstore, museum, park, my own living room and see you there, your memory alive and screaming at me to hold on and remember."

"I drank to forget, but never could," Sean said. "I may not have had the places to remind me of you. But you were everywhere. You still are. And you always will be."

Chiara took Sean's hand across the table and felt the scars. "How did this happen?"

"I was a firefighter. I was trapped in a building."

Chiara traced the edges of the skin grafts and flesh with her fingers. "And you survived," she said.

"I survived."

"And now you have a second chance," Chiara said, holding his hand and staring at him.

"A second chance," Sean said and nodded.

"We're both different now, Sean. We're different people. And the time is different, too."

"That could be a good thing. In fact, it's the best thing. I am better. I understand things better. I will be better," Sean urged.

"Life isn't so easy," Chiara said. "We can't just pick up after eleven years and start where we left off."

"What if we could? What if . . . all of this . . . all of our life was for this reason? This purpose? We each had to go on a different journey to do what we needed to do to be the people we are today, to be together?"

"Sean, most people who are together stay together on that journey," Chiara answered.

"But we're not like most people," Sean said, smiling hopefully.

"Sean, Sean, Sean, that old charming smile won't work on me anymore," she said, shaking her head and smiling at him.

"All right, all right. You're right," Sean said, holding his hands up.

"Do you have a piece of paper and a pen?" Chiara asked him.

"Yes, here," Sean said, pulling out the piece of paper with Lucia's bubbly handwriting and a pen from his jacket pocket.

Chiara wrote down another address, reached across the table, and slipped it into Sean's pocket just as her sister had done not an hour before.

"I have to get back to work, Sean. But we can finish talking later. If you want to, meet me at that address. If you change your mind between now and then and you don't arrive and leave me stranded again, then I'll know you haven't really changed and I won't ever make the mistake again."

"Agreed," Sean said.

"I'll see you at six o'clock," Chiara said, standing up again and turning to walk away.

"I'll see you tonight." Sean's chest expanded in relief and with possibility.

❧ Chapter 31

SOMETHING AKIN TO A DRUNKEN BUZZ WASHED
through Sean as he entered his room. He hadn't
stopped smiling since he left the café. Despite the
ever-worsening cramp in his calf, Sean walked as fast as he
could to the hotel where he was due to check in. Not only
did he have to shower and clean up before his evening with
Chiara, he had been anxious for another reason. "I have to
call home," he said aloud to himself as soon as Chiara disappeared out the door. It was primal. It was urgent. It couldn't
wait. Something Chiara had said to him stung though. *It's
dangerous to think you know what is best for someone else. To
make a decision for two people without the other's consent. To
decide another's life for them.* Yes, Gaspar had basically said
the same thing six months ago, but the way Chiara said it
made more sense. It struck him like a right hook. It came
from out of nowhere, and he was out for the count.

He pulled the pink receipt out of his wallet and the pen out of his pocket and scribbled over all the names, including Chiara's. He scribbled over all but one:

Colm.

Three years. He swallowed hard and felt the guilt rising up. *Three years.*

Sorry is not shitty. Making things right is not bad. It is why you do it that is shitty. You think this will heal you . . . It is about you. Once again . . . You . . . This is about what you want. What will make you feel better . . . It has nothing to do with the other person.

How could he be such an ass? For so long? How? He fumbled with the list in his wallet. He wanted to go back in time and make it all up. He wanted to explain, however feebly, how wrong he had been to make a decision that affected all of them—not just him, but his sister and Gaspar. He had left them. Left them all, because it was good for him. And they loved him enough to let him go.

Sean's heart raced with anxiety. He couldn't believe he had come this far. A wave of panic seized him. What if he screwed up again? What if he ran? What if he couldn't do it after all? He suddenly craved a drink. His hands shook. He was overwhelmed by his own failures. Again, and again, and again. Chiara had sliced right through all of it. Within minutes of seeing him and being with him, she could see what he had been so blind to.

Like the night of the fire, Sean spoke out loud in the darkness of his hotel room: "Help me. Please. Help me. Help me understand. Help me be a better man. Help me follow through with this. Help me be the man Chiara deserves. The man that Colm, Gaspar, and Cathleen would want me to be. Please don't let me screw this up."

Eventually, Sean's prayers gave way to sleep. Though he dreamed of the boy often, he always dreamed of him as a toddler or a preschooler, back when the boy could run and walk and talk incessantly. Sean pictured his long auburn hair, hanging out of a Yankees hat, his tiny, rail-thin body running toward him whenever Sean burst through the door. But this time when he dreamed of Colm he was older, perhaps a ten-year-old boy. His hair had darkened to brown and was cut short. He was still skinny and small for his age, but his green eyes looked as bright as ever, though older and wiser with age. Sean marveled at him for a moment. He couldn't believe how fast the boy had grown. He couldn't believe he was with him in his hotel room, sitting right next to him on his bed.

"Colm? Is that you, buddy?"

"Yes, Uncle Sean. It's me."

"How are you, big guy?"

"Good. Mom said Gaspar saw you. Said you would come home soon. Why haven't you come home, Uncle Sean? Why are you here?" Colm asked softly, as if whispering.

"Because I owe someone an apology and an explanation," Sean said. "I need to explain why I was such a jerk."

"You're not a jerk."

"I was a jerk to you and your mom, and I was a jerk to Chiara."

"Mom says you helped save my life over and over. I remember. Mom says no one else on the planet besides her and

Gaspar loves me like you do. She says you left because it was hard for you to see me suffer."

"Oh, bud."

"I understand. It's okay, Uncle Sean. I know why you left."

"No, it's not. It's not okay. I was weak, Colm. Weak. When I saw you die up on that hill, I thought I would, too. But when you opened your eyes, I swear to God I almost lost my mind. The world doesn't make any sense. Why you have to suffer—it doesn't make any sense."

"Is that why you fainted?"

"Sort of," Sean said sheepishly, not wanting to explain the apparition to the boy who for so long, so clearly and emphatically believed there was no heaven, no angels. "That day fundamentally changed me, in so many ways, and I thought I was doing you a favor. I thought that your mom deserved a life where she could just focus on you. And you had Gaspar. You two formed such a special bond over the years and your mom fell in love with him. You all belonged together in a family. I didn't belong there. I didn't. You deserved a dad, a real dad. A good dad. I'll never forget how you looked when you saw that your biological dad wasn't coming for you, wasn't there. I saw how heartbroken you were and I was so angry at myself for not doing enough to protect you. I should have done more . . . and maybe you wouldn't have collapsed . . . maybe you wouldn't have gotten so sick . . . maybe you'd be . . ."

"Uncle Sean, you did enough. You were enough. I don't blame you. I don't blame anyone." Colm came over and patted Sean's hand.

"But I couldn't give you what Gaspar could. I couldn't be

a dad. I could never be your dad. I would always just be an uncle. And your mom, she deserved to be happy. I couldn't guarantee that I wouldn't hurt her again, that I wouldn't drink again. And she didn't need anything else to worry about. She needed to start her life. Hers. The one she was meant to have. The one you were meant to have."

"I thought you left me because you were angry with me. I thought it was something I did."

Sean shook his head back and forth, realizing he had put the boy he loved so much and tried to protect for so long through the very same pain the boy's own father had by leaving him before he was born. He remembered the boy's tears mixing with his own as he held him and assuaged his hurt. *Why doesn't he love me? Does he know? Does he know how much I love him—want to know him, Uncle Sean?*

"Colm, you didn't do anything wrong. You're the bravest person I know. With the biggest heart in the world. I am so proud of you," Sean said. "I was being selfish. I see that now. I made a decision that affected both of us, and I didn't even think to ask you how you felt about it. I thought I knew what was best. It wouldn't be the first time," Sean said.

"It's okay, Uncle Sean. We just worry about you," Colm said, sounding every bit like his mother.

"I know. It's not your job to worry. You're just a kid."

"Everyone says that to us kids, but we have no control over anything. Adults have all the control. And all we have is the worry. You adults at least can do things. We can't. We sit and worry," Colm added.

"Don't worry about me though. I've got a lot of people looking out for me."

"Like angels," Colm said, apropos of nothing.

"Yes, Colm. Like angels. And since when did you start believing in angels?"

"Remember after I woke up that last time in Los Angeles? Remember how I told you I saw beautiful things, Uncle Sean? I saw this light; it was so bright. Like an angel pointing me back home."

Sean nodded, remembering the light, too.

"I think that sometimes . . . maybe . . . maybe it was a dream. Like Gaspar said the brain makes when people are dying. And maybe it was real, like Mom says. But all I know is that it was different. It was different from any other time. Every other time I just saw darkness. It was always just black. But that day I saw the most beautiful light. And I'm here now. Right here. For a reason, I think. And between you and me, I think it's to take care of Mom," Colm whispered. "She still needs lots of help with the babies and whatnot. And you know what else? I think the reason was a second chance for me, too. I didn't realize how much I loved her, how much I needed her until that day. I get it all now."

"Colm, I saw the light, too. I understand. I don't know if it's a dream. Or if it's real. I don't know what any of it means. I wish I knew. But I know what you saw, because I think I saw it, too. And it scares me."

"So you're like me?"

"Yes."

"You were in the dark and then you could see?"

"Yes."

"You were lost and then you got found?"

"Yes."

"You got a second chance to be better? To love Mom, Gaspar, me, and Chiara?"

"Yes."

"Uncle Sean, does this mean you finally believe in angels? In heaven?"

"I was sort of hoping that this trip would give me proof, but I guess I don't need it. I have all the proof I need. I guess all I ever had to do was just, I don't know, get over myself."

"So? Did you see Chiara yet?"

"Yes, today. She's older now. Not so much a girl anymore. But yes, I saw her. And she is as kind and smart and beautiful as ever. She and I have a date tonight."

"Wow! So you really found her? It really worked out!" Colm said excitedly.

"Yes, took eleven years, but I made my way back."

"How long?"

"Eleven years. I moved back home a year before you were born."

"Hmmm."

"What?"

"It's just that—remember when you, me, and Gaspar were at the Museum of Natural History a few years ago and we learned about the sun's magnetic field?"

"Yeah? What's that have to do with anything?"

"Did you know that this is the year the sun's magnetic poles are switching positions? It would be sort of like earth's north would become south and south will be north. It happens every eleven years. The magnetic poles actually pass each other through the light of the sun. It takes eleven years for the sun to change. And it took you just as long to change, too."

"What's it mean though? What's it mean for the earth?"

"You mean what does it mean for *the universe*? The magnetic shield that spreads out from the sun reaches beyond our galaxy. A change like this affects everything. The coolest thing is that the magnetic shield is so thin it's infinitesimal, basically invisible, but its reach is beyond us, beyond the outer regions of our galaxy, so we can never really measure it. No one will ever know what it touches. How this change will affect so much."

"Jesus."

"You and I are like those magnetic poles, Uncle Sean. We both changed positions. We both crossed to the other side of the light, and we'll never ever know what effect we have on the world, on the universe."

"Colm, kid, you're an angel," Sean said.

"We all are, Uncle Sean. That's the point. We all are."

Sean sat up and tried to hug the boy, but when he wrapped his arms around Colm, he woke and realized the boy was gone. Alone in the darkness, Sean stood up slowly and then walked over and picked up the pink receipt with all the names of the people he thought he owed amends to. He took his pen and scratched off Colm's name and then ripped it in half, and then in quarters, and then in eighths, and then sixteenths until there was nothing left but small pink bits covering the floor like cherry blossom petals that have fallen on paths in late spring. And then he took the address Chiara had given him and flipped the paper over. Remembering the past few hours, the past few days, the past few months, the past year, the past three, the past eleven, Sean began writing a new list:

Proof of Angels

1. Cathleen, who helped me notice the little things
2. Gaspar, who gave me his friendship and wisdom
3. James, who showed me the moment
4. Tom, who gave me back my strength
5. Libby, who showed me gentleness
6. Chief, who guarded and guided me
7. The flight attendant, who had mercy on me
8. The driver, who taught me how to listen
9. Lucia, who showed me the way
10. Chiara, who pointed me to the light
11. Colm, who gave me proof

Sean then folded the paper in half, and then in quarters, and stuffed it in the pocket by his heart. He patted the pocket, touching it as if touching all the people who had touched him, who sent him messages and helped him cross over to the light, and who would never know what effect they each had on him, on the world, on the universe.

🌿 Chapter 32

S EAN'S HEART CONTINUED TO RACE UNTIL HE STEPPED out of the cab and looked at the location of the address Chiara had written down for him. Standing before Santa Croce, he knew.

Sean knew. His shoulders relaxed. His body slowed as he walked through the open doors and the lost-but-now-found memories assaulted him. It was a *Chiara* place. Everywhere he looked she was there—looking at Giotto's frescoes, walking in and out of the chapels, standing by the tombs and monuments to Galileo, Machiavelli, Dante, and Michelangelo. His eyes traveled through the nave searching for her everywhere.

Stopping for a moment in front of Michelangelo's tomb, Sean felt a pang rise up his leg and settle somewhere in his back. He inhaled deeply and fought through the pain, the onslaught of self-doubt that always made an appearance. *What if she doesn't show? What if this was how she could get rid of me? Give me a taste of my own medicine and just disappear?*

Sean felt a tap on his shoulder and all of his doubts and fears dissolved.

"You came!" Chiara said, surprised.

"Of course. I wouldn't have missed this date for the world. You have no idea how long and how hard it was and how much help it took me to get here," Sean said.

"I can only imagine, Sean. You know you didn't have to come. You never had to."

"But I did. I could never have lived my life, the life I was supposed to live, without seeing you again. Without asking for your forgiveness, for trying to at least heal what I harmed," Sean said.

"I forgive you, Sean," Chiara said, kissing him on the cheek.

"Thank you," Sean said with his eyes closed, cherishing the touch.

"I almost didn't come, Sean. To be honest, I am a little afraid."

"I know. I am too."

"I have gotten used to being alone. I have enjoyed it. There is no fear of a broken heart at the end of each day."

"I understand."

"And I am afraid the person you remember is the person you will love. I am afraid you won't like the person I have become," Chiara said in a whisper as tourists walked by them.

"I am afraid of the same thing, Chiara," Sean leaned in and whispered back.

"You know, I didn't go back to work after I left the café."

"No?"

"No, I went to the Duomo. Something you said over lunch reminded me that I hadn't been there in a long time. I climbed to the top of the lookout. Just like we did on the day we met."

"You did? You must be exhausted," Sean said, looking her over. She didn't look any the worse for wear despite the exhausting climb to the top.

"I am tired. But it was good. I stood up there and looked out over all of Florence and then beyond. After you left all those years ago, do you know many hours I spent up there looking for you? I thought I could stand up there and see you below, sitting in a café or walking down the street. I thought all I would have to do was just see you once. Just once and I would be cured. I'd forget you. Forget your name. But I never did. So I stood up there again today knowing that you really were somewhere in this city and I could see you again tonight. And if things went well, I could see you tomorrow, and the day after that. And I started to cry because I realized that was what I wanted. I wanted that. Back then I had prayed every day that you would come back. I had bargained and promised and begged over and over. I had wanted this. My entire adult life, no matter what man I was with, I had dreamed of the day that you would come back. Have you ever gotten what you wanted?"

Sean shook his head.

"Exactly. No one gets what they want. The simple act of wishing it to come true almost necessitates that the opposite happens. The secret to life's happiness is not wanting. It's not getting what you've always hoped for or imagined. It's managing your expectations."

Sean nodded and listened. Though thousands of miles apart, she had changed, just as he had. She had come to the same forgone conclusions that he had.

"But you came. Why?" Sean asked.

"I came because for the first time in my life I realized that this was what I wanted. *This. This. You.* To hell with the disappointment. The pain. I want you. And to say it out loud and admit it to myself is proof enough."

"Proof of what?"

"Proof that my father was right. Proof that if you make a promise to the light, the light will reward you."

"What do you mean exactly?"

"I made a promise a long time ago that I would love you forever. I would say your name every day even if you didn't come back. I would say it anyway and I would l love you anyway if he just granted me this one wish: that he would take care of you and watch over you. That he would send his light out, the same light my father prayed to, and watch over you and protect you. And when I saw those burns and your cane, I knew my prayers had been answered. The light protected you. It guided you and kept you alive during something awful. God had held up his end of the bargain, and it's my turn to hold up mine. I will say your name every day and love you forever, Sean Magee."

Sean took Chiara's hand and felt it tremble in his.

"I made a promise, too, Chiara," Sean said, bursting with hope and breathless. "When I was at my darkest and lowest point, when I was lost in the fire and abandoned all hope, I thought that if I just found the space where I started from, then I'd find my way out. If I could just go back to where

I started, I'd figure it out. But I couldn't find that place. I couldn't. So I made a promise, too. I promised that if I found a way out of the fire, I would become a better man. I would find you and I would make things right. And as soon as I did, I saw this light, this incredible light, like an angel, who showed me the way out of the dark. And now I am here. I am here for you. And now I realize it was *because of you,* Chiara. All of this was because of you."

Chiara shook her head back and forth in amazement. "Do you know why I picked this place, this place of all the places we shared here in Florence? Not my home? Not the Duomo? Nowhere else but here? Right here? This place? This moment?"

Sean shook his head and listened.

"I picked this place, this moment, you—because I thought if we could just get back to where we started from we might find our way back to the light together."

✣ Acknowledgments

I WOULD LIKE TO THANK MY EDITOR, LUCIA MACRO, WHO had faith in me and this book, even when I did not, and for showing me the way to do it better. Her name means light, and she literally showed it to me when writing this book. I will forever be in her debt. And for my steadfast agent, Marly Rusoff, who could have dropped me after my epic fail, but didn't. Also, I'd like to thank the incredible talent at Harper-Collins who shepherded this book through its many stages. Most especially Nicole Fischer, editorial assistant, who took care of so many details and pointed me in the right direction more times than I can count. Dale Rohrbaugh, production editor, who kept this book on schedule. Danielle Emrich, who is not only the best publicist and champion a writer could hope for but a good friend and mother, too. Victoria Mathews, the most precise and astonishingly thorough copy editor I could have asked for, who saved me from my repetitive self count-less times, yes, countless times. *Intentional repetition in this instance. Victoria, please STET. Wink.* And last but certainly not least, Amanda Kain, cover designer, who created the gorgeous cover for *Proof of Angels*. It took my breath away the first time I saw it and still does. Thank you all.

I would also like to thank my husband for countless trips to Home Depot, Target, and the Y, just to get the kids out of the house long enough for me to scribble a few thoughts on paper, only to have him find me fifteen hours later still in my pajamas and covered in melted chocolate and coffee spills and still clacking away. Thanks for putting up with me. And thanks to my kids, who also put up with my writing, not one, but two novels in the course of six months while I started a new job, and who rarely complained when I forgot to pack their school snacks, wash their uniforms, or sign their permission slips to all of their Guardian Angel functions. You're welcome in advance for when you both become world-famous memoirists detailing your neglectful mother's many lapses.

I'd like to thank the usual suspects who have supported my writing from the beginning, most notably my sister Eileen Curran and my brother Sean Curran who read my stuff and who encouraged me to keep going and quit my *bitchin'*. Of course my parents, Maggie and Phil Curran, who gave me seven angels in the form of siblings and who have purchased and handed out so many copies of *Proof of Heaven* they could wallpaper their kitchen with the receipts. Thank you.

And a special shout-out to my favorite bookseller, Audrey Bullar at Joseph-Beth, for always passing along books that keep me inspired.

And most important, all the angels who have stood by me and urged me on, I have written your names on my own long list of proof of angels, and I carry your names in the pocket by my heart always.

And finally thank you to the Venerable Solanus Casey, who I prayed to and thanked ahead of time for the publication of *Proof of Heaven* and *Proof of Angels* and the ability to do what I always wanted to do: write. And who I promised that in return for this gift, I would say his name always and remember him daily. As a porter, he opened the door for all people and showed them the light. And he did that for me long after he left this life for another.

✣ About the Author

MARY CURRAN HACKETT is the mother of two children, Brigid Claire and Colm Francis, and is married to Greg Hackett. She received an MA in English Literature from the University of Nebraska and a BA from the University Honors Program at Catholic University in Washington, D.C. Born and raised in Danbury, Connecticut, she now lives in Cincinnati, Ohio with her kids, her husband, and her stacks of books.

About the book

Read on

Insights,
Interviews
& More ...

Q&A with Mary Curran Hackett

In your first book, Proof of Heaven, *Sean was an important but secondary character. What motivated you to give him his own story?*

The simple answer is that everyone from my editor to my siblings to my book club fans wanted "more" Sean after reading *Proof of Heaven*. He's a fun character. He's not perfect. He says some outrageous things. He messes up a lot. And for that reason, quite honestly, he was one of my favorite characters in *Proof of Heaven*, too. I love him, not despite, but especially *because of* all his flaws. In *Proof of Heaven*, he didn't accept everything blindly. He doubted everything, and everything was such a struggle and a fight for him. While in *Proof of Angels* we see him mostly on his own, in *Proof of Heaven* we see him interacting mostly in a foster-father role. He takes care of his nephew; sometimes he does the job well, sometimes he's just terrible at it and causes more harm than good. But you can't deny his love for the boy. It makes him endearing. In real life, I know so many "Seans"—so many people with huge hearts who want to do the right thing, but there is a gap between what they want to do and what they are capable of doing.

Something always gets in the way
of each of them doing the right thing.
And I have to say I get why, because
I've definitely had my own share of
"Sean" moments. I've messed up
my life and the lives of others more
times than I can count. And getting
to spend time with Sean's character
and Sean's friends made me remember
all the angels I've had along the way
who have led me back to where I started
from, so I could eventually see the light,
too. As I mentioned in the back of
Proof of Heaven, a long time ago I loved
a boy just like Sean. He was going to
be a priest. Eventually he became an
alcoholic. He struggled for years before
he got the help he needed, and in the
process he hurt himself and a lot
of other people. I had no idea how
tormented he was by a lot of things
and, quite truthfully, there are some
things I'll never understand. So in a
way, *Proof of Angels* was a way I could
explore that part of the human psyche—
the part we all have—that causes each
of us to self-destruct and, conversely,
that helps us to find our way back to
the light.

Do you need to read Proof of Heaven in order to enjoy Proof of Angels?

My agent and publisher might not like
my saying this, but no, you don't need
to read *Proof of Heaven* to enjoy *Proof of
Angels*. When I did allude to Sean's past
in this book, I tried, wherever I could, ▶

3

to fill in the blanks. This may seem a bit repetitive to those who read *Proof of Heaven*, but I hope I told a different enough story. (Though I highly recommend that you do read *Proof of Heaven*, if for nothing else but to find out more about Colm, Cathleen, and Gaspar, who are mentioned a bit in this book but not fully explored here.)

Was it difficult to give those who hadn't read* Proof of Heaven *enough backstory about Sean without overwhelming the work and alienating readers who already knew about him from that book?

I thought it was going to be difficult at first, because *Proof of Angels* is really all about what makes Sean the person who is Sean. And I couldn't possibly tell the story without mentioning so much of what happened to him in *Proof of Heaven*. In *Proof of Heaven*, we learn he's an alcoholic, and he struggles with his faith; he has a hard time accepting his sister's faith and her means of trying to save her sick son. We also see how lonely he is, and in many ways, how tormented he is by his past. I was worried that by repeating that backstory, I might lose readers. But, at the same time, *Proof of Heaven* was much more about Colm and Cathleen than it was about Sean. In *Proof of Heaven*, we really didn't know much about what made Sean who he is— there were still a lot of holes there that needed to be filled. So with *Proof of Angels*, I could go deeper and find out more about him. We didn't know much about what happened to him in Italy in *Proof of Heaven*, nor do we know what happened to him after Colm's final collapse on the mountaintop in Los Angeles. By giving Sean the opportunity to start his life over without his sister, brother-in-law, or nephew around, I was forced to think about him in a new way and see the kind of life he could build for himself without them. Also, in *Proof of Angels*, we got to see what he was really made of. He is the one struggling and suffering in this book, and he's the one who has to figure out what he believes.

Why did you have Sean move to Los Angeles of all places?

I picked Los Angeles because it is the "City of Angels" and therefore the name would lend itself to the total theme. But more than that, it was a place that held special significance for Sean. It is the point of transformation for his sister and himself. Three years earlier his nephew had his final collapse in Los Angeles. So much for Sean changed during that trip. He witnessed something miraculous (again, regardless of whether Colm lives or dies, the experience itself changed him fundamentally). Another reason was that in *Proof of Heaven*, Sean expressed a love of the water, as well as the need to be free and get away. He had a pattern, "a routine" rather, of running when life got tough, and how much farther could he have run from New York than across the country? I also wanted to incorporate my own love of the water with Sean's. And while it's true that New York City has water, I don't know many New Yorkers who get on the train and ride an hour to Coney Island every day to hit the waves each morning. By living right on Venice Beach, Sean could literally walk out of his apartment and be part of that water. I also chose Venice Beach because it, even if Sean wasn't aware of it himself when he picked the area, had a deep connection to Italy. Venice Beach was originally designed to have canals much like Venice, Italy. And whether Sean was aware of it or not, he was always, in some way, trying to get back to where he was most happy, most alive. And for him, that was Italy, where Chiara was.

How did you pick your epigraphs?

Oh, I love this question. I love to read. I love words. (Go figure.) And over the years, I have collected many quotes that have resonated with me. In fact, *Proof of Heaven*, in many ways, came about because of the epigraphs that open the book. Those quotes inspired and framed the entire story. Similarly, the quotes that open this book, "Go forth and set the world on ▶

fire" by St. Ignatius of Loyola, "Angel came down from heaven yesterday/She stayed with me just long enough to rescue me" by Jimi Hendrix and "The golden moments in the stream of life rush past us and we see nothing but sand; the angels come to visit us, and we only know them when they are gone" by George Eliot, set a spark in me and made me think about my story on three different levels. St. Ignatius Loyola's quote really got me thinking about Sean, who embodied fire. He is the epitome of "live by the sword, die by the sword." He is so fiery, so temperamental, and in the end it gets the best of him but also, conversely, saves him. If he could just learn to harness that fire and put it to good use in the world, he would find he has the power to not only change his own life but the lives of everyone he touches. I work for a Jesuit institution now, Xavier University, and I have learned a lot about Ignatius Loyola's belief that the divine is in everything and that it is our job as humans on earth to look for the miraculous and, when we find it, share it with the world.

Jimi Hendrix's "Angel" is not only an amazing tune, its lyrics always struck me. In it Hendrix talks about an angel that came down from heaven and stayed long enough to rescue him. I've often thought about what that meant to Hendrix, and even wondered about what it meant for me. Did I ever have an angel come down and stay long enough to rescue me? So I wanted that experience to happen to Sean. I have met so many people who speak of their guardian angels as if they are real and present, and have helped them in difficult times, and equally I have met others who speak of "real-life" angels who have swept in and helped them out when they are in need. This book explores both sets of angels—the seen and the unseen. And I guess it provokes the question in the reader: What do you believe?

And finally, George Eliot's quote encapsulates everything this book is about—our angels, whether seen or unseen, only stay for a little while, and we often don't know how profoundly they changed our lives until they are gone. Another one of my favorite quotes in the book is Tennessee Williams's "If I got rid of my demons, I'd lose my angels." I mean, how true is that?

Sometimes we don't know who are angels in our lives until we have totally messed up. In fact, I don't think we know who are true friends until we have become so unlovable and difficult to be around. It's then that we see who is strong enough and compassionate enough to stick around and love us despite our demons. That is when we truly know who our angels really are.

And finally, I'm a huge Mary Karr fan. Her book *Lit* in particular struck several chords with me—as a writer, a mother, a teacher, and someone who has struggled with depression and dependence. Her epigraph that opens the prologue is precisely what that entire section, and hence the book, is about: When we see the light, we often don't know what we're seeing or experiencing. We're disorientated, lost; it takes us a while to get our bearings, and find our true path, and in this book that is precisely what Sean, and everyone else, really, is trying to do.

At one point you say that "dogs are like guardian angels." I think many people would agree, but can you explain why you think so?

I think so because I've experienced it myself. I was born into a large family—there were eight children when all was said and done, but even before I was born, my parents had a menagerie of animals, one of which in particular holds a special place in my heart. Chief was our yellow Lab mixed breed. He was part of our family from the beginning. Wherever we kids went, Chief followed, and more often than not, he led the way. He played with us in the river behind our house, chased after us as we rode our bikes around town, and tramped through our neighborhood with us all summer long. (I don't think there were any leash laws back then, and if there were, we never abided by them. I don't ever remember our parents using a leash, or a fence.) At dinnertime, my father would whistle for us kids to come home, and we would pour out of the trees in the woods behind our house, or the backs of our neighbors' yards, and come running home. To this day, ▶

I can see Chief, running down the center of our street to meet us in the driveway and head in with us to dinner, like he was one of us kids. He posed with us in family pictures, slept at the end of my brother's bed each night, sat beside my grandfather in front of the fireplace every evening, and guarded whatever newborn baby came into the house by sleeping next to the bassinette. When it was time to put him down, my father took him to the vet three times. Each time my father took him, Chief rallied. He stood up and ran around the room, and my father couldn't do it. It went on like that three times, and so by the last time, we all expected my father to come home with Chief. We never really believed Chief would die, that he would leave us. But he did. We wept and carried on as if we had lost a sibling. And in many ways, Chief had been one. He looked out for us. We each had a story about how Chief looked out for us and loved us unconditionally. In so many ways, he taught me about unconditional love. He never asked for anything in return. He gave us rides on his back, he let us dress him up, he ate our vegetables and my mother's shoe-leather corned beef (blech) when we didn't want to. He greeted us every day as we got off the bus. We had other dogs after him, and each one taught us something new. By the time my daughter was born, my parents had a black Lab named Clancy. Clancy slept beside my daughter in her little pumpkin carrier and guarded her every day. He went on walks with us and let her hug him, climb on him, and play with him. To this day, my daughter sleeps with a stuffed animal named Clancy, who she swears carries the soul of her beloved Clancy, who passed away several years ago.

And I guess the idea of a service dog for Sean came out of not only my love for my dog Chief, but in part after observing one of my neighbors, who is blind, for the past eight years. His yellow Lab walks beside him to the bus every day. The love that dog has for my neighbor is absolutely visible. I am sure not a moment goes by that my neighbor doesn't think of his dog as a guardian angel. I can't help but think of it every time I see the two of them together.

The real Chief, the "mayor" of our neighborhood, coming home when called for dinner.

Storytelling is such a strong part of the Irish heritage, and your Irish background clearly influences your writing. Who are the writers—Irish or not—you love to read?

I have too many to count. And my favorite writers—or even genre—seem to change annually. Every week I am discovering someone new to love. Of course, I love the classics. I cut my proverbial reading teeth on Dickens. I read and read and then reread his books. My favorite of his to this day is *A Tale of Two Cities*. And then Dickens led me to the Russians—Chekhov, Tolstoy, and Dostoyevsky. And of course, what self-respecting female reader didn't fall in love with Austen, the Brontës, Alcott, and Eliot at some point in her high school years? Those were ▶

Chief and my brother Sean posing. Chief was photobombing before all the cool kids were doing it.

the books I grew up on and loved. When I got to college, I became obsessed with Irish writers—I began with Joyce. I think I must have read *A Portrait of the Artist as a Young Man* five times one year. I ended up reading all of his works, except *Finnegans Wake*; it was impossible for me then, as it is now. Then I moved on to Shaw, Beckett, Behan, and Friel, and read everything I could from each until I discovered the contemporary writers—and that's when I fell in love with Roddy Doyle. (I ended up writing my master's-degree thesis on him.) Then one day at the library, quite by accident (I received someone else's book order), I discovered Edna O'Brien and my mind was blown! Blown. That's the only way to describe it. Here was this Irish woman, writing about sex and love and life and I could hardly breathe or put it down. It was just magnificent. There was something about the Irish voice that resonated with me. It was an old-fashioned way to tell a tale, spin a yarn, whatever you want to call it, but it came with a bite. It always came with a bite. And I loved it. It sounded very much like my own kitchen table. And I also love William Trevor and Colm Toibin. (I actually named my son, in part, after him. I was reading a *New Yorker* story by him when I was pregnant with my son and said to myself, "That's a cool name," and the more I learned about St. Columcille and what Colm meant in Gaelic, the more I was convinced I needed to name my son Colm.) I also adore Colum McCann. (He spells his Colum with a "u," and McCann himself tried to convince me to add a "u" to my son's name one night when I spoke with him after one of his lectures.) His book *Let the Great World Spin* is probably one of my all-time favorites, though his recent *TransAtlantic* is magnificent. And I love Mary Karr, Billy Collins, the late Frank McCourt, and Seamus Heaney. I have taught Irish and Irish-American literature, poetry, and drama on and off for the past ten years, so it is impossible for me to list all of the stories, plays, and poems that have informed my writing and my soul (mostly my soul, my writing will never measure up to any of them). I try to stay current and read as much as I can, and I rely on the recommendations of my various book clubs, Goodreads, *New York Times* book reviews, and my most trusted source, my siblings, to read what is "hot" right now. My favorite book last year was *The Light Between Oceans* by M. L. Stedman. Occasionally, I will read a historical biography, but it is rare. (Lauren Hillenbrand's *Unbroken* was the last one I read and it was fantastic.) I love poetry, too, and try to follow various journals to see what is new. I also think of music as a form of reading. So much of writing is about following a tune. When ▶

Q&A with Mary Curran Hackett *(continued)*

I write, I often feel a rhythm and I realize it often reflects whatever music I am listening to. When I listen to John Prine, Steve Earle, Johnny Cash, Bob Dylan, Emmylou Harris, Mumford & Sons, the Avett Brothers, or Alison Krauss, I am listening to the story they are telling me as well. In my mind I see the story play out, just as I would if I were reading a book, and there is something beautiful and magical about that. Whether I am listening to the radio, reading a book, or watching a film or a television show, I am always on the lookout for a great story. I read using every single kind of media you can think of. I download e-books from my library, iTunes, or Amazon: I have at least two e-books going at any one time. I also borrow audiobooks from the library, some of which I keep on my iPad and listen to while I am at work or lying in bed. I carry an MP3 with me everywhere with an audiobook loaded on it, and I always have a library book or purchased book in my purse, by my nightstand, and in my car. I also make a point to stop by Joseph-Beth Booksellers in Cincinnati and look for my favorite bookseller, Audrey, who I like to think of as my very own "personal bookseller." She has never steered me wrong. I ask what I should read next and she always gives me the best books.

No matter where I am or what I am doing, I try to squeeze in reading. When I sit at the Y and watch my son's swim practice, I often have an audiobook playing. When I go on walks I take the audiobooks with me (and I've been known to walk and read an actual book at the same time). I read before bed and when I get up. I sneak writing in here and there, but my first love will always be reading. I love it so much that when I think of hell, I don't think of it as a place of fire, but as a place devoid of books. And when I think of heaven, I envision an infinite bookshelf with no shortage of overstuffed couches near sundrenched windows, hot cups of coffee, and bowls and bowls of M&M's. In so many ways, I think of books as my own guardian angels, showing me the light time and time again and leading me in the right direction.

What is the story behind this story? How did you get the idea to write it? Have you always thought about angels?

I saw the image above for the first time in an art book and became mesmerized with those little thinking angels who sit at the bottom of the larger Raphael painting. I loved the image so much, I ordered a print and hung it my college dorm room. (I know what you're thinking: How many college kids have angels hanging on their walls? If it makes me sound any less lame, I hung it just above my posters of Bono and U2.) I was totally captivated by these winged creatures—not just Raphael's treatment of them, but the notion of angels themselves.

Though I was raised a Catholic and we prayed to angels as children ("Angel of God, my Guardian dear . . .") and I had seen angel pictures and statues in abundance in my childhood home—especially around Christmas—I really had no idea what these ▶

About the book

things were. I always thought that when people died they became "angels" who then watched over us here on earth. I later learned from a supposed expert on angels (yes, there are people who claim such expertise, I discovered, to my surprise as well) that the term *angels* suggests that they are not nor have they ever been earthlings, rather they are thought to be messengers from heaven. They also don't always appear with wings. They can be radiant light, breath, and only sometimes appear with wings. They also only take on human form when necessary. (Duh! Explains Clarence in *It's a Wonderful Life* then!) According to this expert, the "laws of angels" makes it impossible for angels to interfere with human destiny unless instructed to do so (just like Clarence!). Makes sense (if this sort of thing makes sense to you to begin with). Angels are assigned various tasks, too, such as fighting evil; protecting humanity; safeguarding and watching over children; inspiring beauty, art, and poetry; healing; and even helping humans cross over to heaven. Almost every faith has angels—Hindus, Buddhists, Christians, Jews, and Muslims all do. And recent surveys have shown that over 80 percent of Americans believe in some form of angels. Angels like Raphael the archangel are mentioned in the Jewish Torah (in Deuteronomy), in the Koran, and in the many texts of the Christian Bible. According to some angel experts, each of us is assigned two and both guide us from life to death and only interfere when, according to God's plan, it is "not our time." Good to know all that fuss, "to leave space for your Guardian Angel," when I was a kid in church was not for naught.

Good to know, sure, but in the end, to be honest, I just thought the poster was pretty. Eventually, like all of my college days' fleeting passions (boyfriends included), the poster didn't last long. I went on with life. And soon my nineties faddish obsession with angels disappeared along with my grungy plaid shirts, Birkenstocks, and bottles of ck one (thank God).

Fast-forward twenty years: I am no longer a college freshman. My novel *Proof of Heaven* is released and I am visiting book clubs and attending signings. Everywhere I go (it's really not many places, only from St. Louis to Connecticut to D.C. and places in between), the people who were kind enough to read my book want me to write a sequel to *Proof of Heaven*. The only problem is: I don't want to write a sequel. I have no intention of doing so. Nevertheless, readers want me to tell them what happened to Colm. But I don't want to tell anyone anything. That wasn't my goal. My goal was for people to decide for themselves where Colm went (or didn't go). I wanted people to go on a journey with him and come out on the other side a little closer to what they believed—not what I believed.

Then one night while I was at a book club sipping wine and laughing with a bunch of women, a reader turned to me and said, "You should write about Sean. I want to know what happens to him. You should follow up with all the characters." As most writers will tell you, after writing, rewriting, editing, and proofing, and then talking about the same characters for years, you're over it. You want to move on, explore other stories. I said, "Thank you for the suggestion; I'll definitely keep it in mind," and moved on to the assorted cheese tray, forgetting about it by the time I shoved the warmed Brie in my mouth.

Meanwhile, something was happening to me—to my marriage, to my life. The year leading up to the publication of my novel was, to put it mildly, one of the worst years of my life. And let's just say, I've had some doozies along the way. So that is saying something. And it was made all the more terrible because I didn't tell anyone how awful I felt, how miserable, sad, scared, lonely, and depressed I was. Everyone around me was telling me: *Wow, you're getting published! All of your dreams are finally coming true! You'll be rich and you can retire on the Riviera!* Some others, more passive-aggressive types, would chime in, *Must be nice to have all that time to write and chase your dreams.* I always just smiled and nodded while thinking, *Yeah, by "time," do you mean the hours I spend writing when you're sleeping?* No, I didn't actually say that. Uncharacteristically, I bit my tongue. I was having a really, really crappy year. I was working around the clock—at not one, but two jobs—an editor by day at a nonprofit and an ▶

underpaid, overworked adjunct professor by morning and night. I was writing, quite literally, in the middle of the night, whenever I could sneak away, all the while being a wife, working every day, and raising my two kids. I honestly didn't think life could get any more difficult or more lonely.

Then the phone rang.

My daughter Brigid's school had called to tell me that my daughter was paralyzed on her right side. *What? You've got to be kidding me?* She could not move the right side of her body. She was having difficulty breathing. *This is unreal.* She was due to go onstage for her first school play that night, so I immediately thought: *She's just panicking. She's fine. She's suffering from stage fright. She's going to be just fine.* Only she wasn't fine. After a day and a night in and out of the hospital and exam rooms at the Cincinnati Children's Hospital, a doctor sat my husband and me down and showed us a film with what appeared to be a Ping-Pong-size mass growing in Brigid's lung. I was incredulous. I sat in disbelief, shaking my head. My husband and I looked at each other. We thought the same thing at the same time:

No. No. No.

We asked the doctor what we should do. *When in doubt, get it out.* He told us the only way to know what it was was to either operate and remove it or conduct a bronchoscopy to extract and biopsy the "neoplasm growing in her lung." A euphemism, we would soon discover, for, *The stuff we have no idea what to call that is growing in your daughter's lung.*

At some point in the days that followed, I said to my husband, "Greg, the doctor is right": *when in doubt, get it out.* He knew I was referring to the large black mole that was spreading on his arm. He'd assured me he'd have it removed once already and the test had come back saying the mole was benign. I asked him, for me, to go and get it checked. We didn't need to take any more chances or test fate anymore.

On April first, like some sort of cosmic April Fool's joke, Greg received a call from his doctor, who explained that the lab she had sent his skin biopsy to a year prior had made an error. It was not benign after all. After a few days, we got another call. Greg had, at the least, stage 2, possibly stage 3, malignant melanoma. Anyone who has gone through a melanoma diagnosis knows what this means. If it's stage 2, you're saved; if it has spread beyond the lymph nodes, you have months to live. A couple of years if you're lucky. We both felt like we'd been punched in the stomach. Greg needed to have a large section of the skin and tissue on his arm removed. He needed to have a sentinel biopsy and the lymph nodes removed. More than anything else, he needed to have the uncertainty and fear of impending death removed. But that, we could not take *that* off him with a scalpel. His own mother had died, under similar circumstances, of cancer when he was a child. She had had her breasts removed and had been told she was cancer free, but the doctors had missed the cancer growing in her lungs and she had passed away soon thereafter. Needless to say, Greg was rightfully overcome by fear and anxiety. There is no way to overstate the black hole he was in.

We scheduled his surgery.

To say the next few days went by in a haze is an understatement. I still had to work. I had edits due for my book. I had kids to feed. I had a husband who very well could die if his cancer was not caught in time. A daughter who wheezed at night and cried in pain as we tried to rid her of what was growing in her lung with antibiotics, antiviral, and antifungal meds—for what turned out to be not a bacteria, virus, or fungus after all. I honestly didn't think life could get any harder. (Though, thanks to ample amounts of literature and the nightly news, I knew that life could always get harder. Life has boundless opportunities within it to get even harder still. So it's not that I was comparing it to others' tragedies; it was, for me, as tough as it gets.)

We scheduled my daughter's bronchoscopy and biopsy, too. Greg and Brigid were both operated on within weeks of each other. On the day of Brigid's procedure, we woke at 3 A.M. and dressed in old bridesmaids' gowns and tiaras, and sipped tea while we watched Princess Kate and Prince William marry in ▶

Q&A with Mary Curran Hackett *(continued)*

Westminster. She told me she would grow up to marry Harry, and I wished for all the world for that to be true.

In the days that followed, waiting for results from both procedures, I can honestly say I came very near to complete physical and emotional collapse. I had never felt so alone and so terrified in my life. My fate rested completely in the hands of fortune or God or chaos. It made no sense to me whatsoever. If tests came back any way other than negative for disease, I very well was facing a world without half of my family. Honestly, I never said it out loud, but I felt it over and over: *I just can't do this. I am not strong enough to do this. Please take this cup from me.* I prayed. I bargained. *Give me cancer instead, God. Let me be the one to die.* I felt somehow at fault. Blindsided. I had written a novel about a boy who dies and causes his mother immense heartbreak. *Was life imitating art? Had I conjured this up? Caused this? Was my fixation and anxiety over almost losing my son Colm several years earlier causing me to now pay by losing my daughter and husband? Did the universe act in such a way? Could God be so vindictive?* I admit it, I thought it. I am not saying it was right or good, but I felt totally responsible and yet totally powerless at the same time.

I couldn't sleep at night. Neither could Greg. He paced. We didn't speak to each other. The gulf between us was growing wider and wider. We learned something monumental about each other that we hadn't known until true crisis befell us. When our fear response in our amygdalas kicked in, he was all flight and I was all fight. He wanted nothing more than to go to our room, close the door, and lie in bed for hours. I wanted nothing more than to face everything and everyone head-on. I thought if I made enough phone calls, looked up enough facts on Web sites, made enough dinners, folded enough laundry, wrote enough words, I would somehow defeat cancer—defeat this black cloud that had descended on my family. I thought if I stayed busy—made sure everyone got to where they needed to be, every blogger got their article I was writing to promote my book, everybody I worked for during the day received my assignments on time—then all would be well.

But I was growing resentful and mad. I didn't understand how or why he was so ready to give up, so ready to accept that the cards had been dealt and this was his fate.

I called my mother.

I remember it like no other memory from that time—as fixed and real—because I know that up until I made that call, I was on the brink of a nervous breakdown.

It was in the middle of the day on Saturday and Greg was having an especially horrible time. I didn't want the kids to see him like this, and if I had to be honest, I also didn't want to see him like this. There is a reason, I thought, that some wise person made couples vow to sustain their love and marriage even in sickness and health. You don't know your partner, *you don't know love*, you don't know commitment until the person you love is so ill and so far gone that they are completely unlovable. Unable to face him, unable to face cancer and all that it might take from us, I packed our kids into our car and headed to the movie theater. (I swear we watched every animated movie we could during the months of March, April, and May of 2011.) I didn't make it a mile from my house before I felt the wave of anxiety, fear, exhaustion, and sadness overwhelm me. I knew at any moment I was going to cry, scream, or crack in two. I pulled into a gas station, stepped out of the car and started to fill it up with gas, and dialed my parents' home number.

"Mom, I need you."

I felt it completely. I wanted my mom. I was a thirty-five-year-old wife and mother of two and I wanted my mommy. I wanted someone to tell me I wasn't alone. I wanted someone to tell me I could handle this. I wanted someone to tell me this would all work out, that in a few years it would be nothing more than a memory. I needed her to remind me of my wedding vows— in sickness and in health. I needed her to tell me what I knew already—that I needed to stick by my husband, that I needed to give him hope, even if he didn't have any. Even if I, a skeptical cynic, didn't think he had much reason to hope.

I can't remember any specific words she said. All I remember ▶

is my hands holding the gas pump, clutching it for dear life. As if that nozzle filling up my tank was the only thing holding me to the earth. I remember crying, *I can't do this all alone. Help me.* I remember hearing her voice, and feeling, no matter what the words, that I wasn't alone. I do recall, vaguely, her reassurances that I was doing the right thing by taking the kids out of the house, taking care of myself. I remember her telling me she loved me. It felt as if the arms of an angel wrapped around me and calmed me instantly. Just minutes before, I was so desperate, so alone, and then suddenly, because of her, I knew I had the strength to carry on.

There would be many more days like that. Eventually Brigid's neoplasm disappeared as mysteriously as it had arrived and Greg's cancer was completely removed and he had only to go in for checkups every six months now. (It will always be, for me, one of those mysterious miracles. If Brigid had not gotten ill, we would never have noticed Greg's arm, would never have pushed to have the cancer taken out. Brigid, in the end, was fine, and so was Greg.) In the meantime, my book hit the bookshelves and as happy as I was to celebrate my lifelong dream come true, I have to admit it was something of a letdown. (Don't get me wrong, I know how incredibly blessed and lucky I was and am, and I know ten years earlier I would have given a limb if it meant I would be published.) But in my, admittedly, CRAZY mind, I felt like I was an epic failure. I had imagined the moment of my debut as something so much more than it was. There was no starred *Kirkus* review. (I had some lovely reviews, I will admit that.) I had no Debut Author feature story in *O, The Oprah Magazine.* No review in the *New York Times.* No worldwide book tour, film rights, foreign rights packages. Oprah didn't call me personally to tell me how awesome I am. Go figure. It sold decently, but it was, for me, not enough. It didn't soar on the *New York Times* bestseller list. I know all of these are just the fantasies of every budding writer. These are things every naive writer thinks are going to happen once they get that elusive pub deal. Instead, the reality of publishing was surprisingly less dazzling. And I felt like a fool publicizing it on blogs and my Facebook fan pages. In a world that measures success by how many Twitter followers or Facebook fans you have and how much money you've earned, I was coming up slightly smaller than a centimeter. I was nothing. A nobody. My book a pretty dust collector on my shelf. I lived my entire adult life struggling to fit writing into my two kids/two jobs life, and I was looking for a break, something, anything, to make my—no, my family's—life easier and I had failed them. In fact, I had made their lives harder. When I should have been taking care of my husband and daughter and devoting all my time to them, I was working and writing and editing. And for what? I thought. Nothing special. Some bloggers and Amazon reviewers said nasty things, and I felt like calling them and personally chewing them out. *Do they have any idea how hard I worked? Do they have any idea how much of my heart, soul, and life I put in that work?* I have to admit it was crushing. Soul crushing. The entire year leading up to the publication of *Proof of Heaven* and the months following were rough. There is no way to pussyfoot around that fact. We were overwhelmed with medical bills and debt. And then I was laid off. Perfect. Just perfect. Now I had no income. Then to add salt to the wound, another book with the same name, *Proof of Heaven*, by Dr. Alexander was soaring on the bestseller charts. Granted, his was a true account of his near-death experience, but I still couldn't help but feel slighted. By whom? What? I had no idea. I know the universe owes me nothing. I know that, but still, every time I got an e-mail or Facebook comment from someone telling me they loved my book, only to realize they were talking about the other *Proof of Heaven*, I very well wanted to scream: I wrote my book first! I am not Dr. Eben Alexander! Can't you read a book cover?

But every single time I was about to lose it, crack, come undone, call it whatever you want, something miraculous would happen. Over and over and over again, it happened. An e-mail would appear in my in-box. I would open it and it would be from someone who happened to have read my book—usually ▶

by mistake. The writer of said e-mail would explain how they were looking for Dr. Eben Alexander's book and brought home mine by accident. Nevertheless, they stuck to it and discovered that they didn't hate it. (Thanks!) In fact, many wrote to me to tell me how my book had affected them, changed them, and in some ways comforted them after the loss of a loved one. I was touched. Overwhelmed. But, more than that, I took these notes as some sort of sign of encouragement that I needed to keep writing. Despite however badly I thought I had failed or let myself or my family down, I needed to keep writing. It happened more times than I could count. I would be frustrated and lonely and feeling like a complete loser, and someone would stop me in my kids' school parking lot and tell me they'd read my book. It was like they were *angels*, messengers who knew how to reach out and touch me at the exact moment I needed them most. Many of these angels had a singular message in common: all of them wrote to tell me that they had lost someone close to them, usually a child, and in a couple of instances more than one child, and many faced unspeakably difficult challenges along the way, and all of them had a deep and profound sense that they were not alone. They felt compelled to tell me that, like the characters in my book, they felt that someone was with them every day, watching over them, and that there was hope that they would see their loved one again. Some admitted that they had their doubts, but more often than not, readers felt strongly that those who had gone before them were watching over them and loving them. They had all the proof of heaven and angels that they needed.

And so I started writing *Proof of Angels*—a very different book from the one you now have in your hands. For months I was having visions of a woman, Birdie, who came to me in dreams—she was the first thing I thought of when I woke up in the morning and the last person I saw before I fell asleep. I felt like I was having long conversations with an old friend. And I realized something—I not only understood Birdie, I just might be a bit like her. I knew what it was like to have a vision of what your life would be like and then for reasons beyond your control, things just didn't work out the way you'd hoped. So you got a little bitter. A little hard. Not just hard on yourself but hard on others for no reason other than that life was hard on you. I knew what it was like to be a single mom, a hard worker, and have this calling to create and make things beautiful—make art. I also got my character Claire, who was completely unprepared and torn by her modern life—juggling a career, her children, and her husband—and feeling completely overwhelmed by the crushing daily responsibilities.

I thought I'd written my best work. I was so proud. So full of myself. So certain. *This is it. This is the book.* Three months after pushing Send, to my editor, I received a call from my agent. The news was grim. The book was unreadable. Not good. Nothing like they had hoped or expected. One reader stopped reading just a couple of chapters in. I tried to remain calm. I took the criticism for what it was: criticism. Meant to make me better. Meant to push me further. I had two options: throw in the towel and give up on writing, or write a new book. Instinct told me to do the former, but I knew not to give in to that self-destructive urge. I knew I needed to keep at writing. Fortunately for me, my kids and Greg were at my parents' house for the week. I could cry at night without having my kids hear me. I could process all the range of emotions I felt. I felt like a giant failure. A huge loser. I had created characters that had become like family to me and others didn't like them. It's nothing personal, but it is *totally* personal. It was personal to me. But it was also an opportunity. A second chance. My editor was giving me a second chance. Not many people get them. She owed me nothing. And yet she believed in me and I didn't want to let her down. I didn't want to let my family down. Myself down.

My mind circled back that week to all the people I had talked to over the past three years since publication, all of the stories of angels people had shared with me and all the requests to find out more about the characters who lived and breathed inside *Proof of Heaven*. To Lucia, my editor, it seemed simple, really: tell what happened to all of them, through Sean. After a couple ▸

Q&A with Mary Curran Hackett *(continued)*

of false starts, I pitched the idea of the entirely new book you have now to my agent and editor. I wanted a book about second chances—about failure and forgiveness, about doubt and faith, and about all the angels who touch us along the way, the ones who might just bump into us long enough to nudge us on our way and the ones who stay in our lives forever and guide us indefatigably toward the light. It took me a long time, and a lot of wasted energy, to see what was so clear and simple right in front of me: write a sequel. I couldn't have done it without Marly and Lucia. I couldn't have seen through the darkness without their light. And what seemed difficult was in fact simple after all.

We're not alone. Angels are among us. They are right here, every day, all around us, guiding us, guarding us, and lighting the way. I guess you could say this cynic, like doubting Tom and bullheaded Sean, who had to find out everything the hard way, finally believes in angels. ◠

Reading Group Discussion Questions

Just as *Proof of Heaven* was a story about a big question, "Where do we go when we die?" *Proof of Angels* continues in that thread and asks another thought-provoking question: Why are we here and what is our purpose? Each character in *Proof of Angels*, especially Sean, struggles with that fundamental question, as well as several others: If he was spared, why him? Why not others? What does that mean for his life?

1. *Proof of Angels* opens with several epigraphs: which one resonated with you? Why? How do you think these quotes relate to the book?

2. Each character has a different approach to life—Sean, James, Libby, Tom, Chiara, and even Chief have certain ideas about why they are here and what their purpose is. Whose approach do you most relate to? Does anyone's belief upset you? Why?

3. Do you see yourself or any of your loved ones in these characters? If yes, who? And why?

4. Do you think Sean really saw an angel? Or do you think he was hallucinating and got lucky in finding his way out of the fire?

5. Do you believe in angels? ▶

Reading Group Discussion Questions
(continued)

6. There are two types of angels discussed in this book: the type that is the mysterious "being" that supposedly points Sean to safety, and then all the angels in his life who challenge him, push him, support him, and give him insights, or rather, illuminate the truth of his life. Which type of angel are you more apt to believe in?

7. Have you experienced a miraculous or unexplained event? Have you ever felt the presence of an angel or a messenger? When? What happened? Could you rationally explain it, as Gaspar tried to get Sean to do? Or did you feel strongly that it was truly a miraculous intervention?

8. Have you had transformational moments when you saw the light? When you were saved? Or when a friendship or relationship made all the difference in your life?

9. Sean tells Tom at one point that everything in life happens for a reason. Tom doesn't feel this way. Do you feel more like Tom or Sean? Do think that there is a purpose for everything, even if it is beyond our own understanding? Does every life have a special purpose or mission?

10. Both Sean and Libby must overcome their demons. They are, for the most

part, their own worst enemies. Do you think people who are "repeat offenders" at the game of life deserve a second chance? Would you forgive Libby or Sean for what they did to their loved ones?

11. Why do you think Chiara is so quick to forgive Sean? Do you think it's possible for time to heal wounds and to just grow up and move on? Do you think that she took pity on his injuries? If he wasn't injured, do you think she would have been so kind?

12. Chiara tells Sean: "It's dangerous to think you know what is best for someone else. To make a decision for two people without the other's consent. To decide another's life for them." Do you agree? Has this ever happened to you?

13. Sean forms a few new friendships in this book; which one particularly resonated with you? Why?

14. In the end do you think Sean found proof of angels? Where? When? How?

15. What's your proof? Or do you even feel like you need it? ∿

Have You Read?
More from
Mary Curran Hackett

Joseph Moss

PROOF OF HEAVEN

A mother's faith, a child's courage, a doctor's dedication—a moving and thought-provoking tale of hope, love, and family.

He might be young, but Colm already recognizes the truth: that he's sick and not getting better. His mother, Cathleen, fiercely believes her faith will protect her ailing son, but Colm is not so sure. With a wisdom far beyond his years, Colm has to come to terms with his probable fate, but he does have one special wish. He wants to meet his father, who abandoned his beloved mother before Colm was born.

But the quest to find the dying boy's missing parent soon becomes a powerful journey of emotional discovery—a test of belief and an anxious search for proof of heaven.

A magnificent debut novel, Mary Curran Hackett's *Proof of Heaven* is a beautiful and unforgettable exploration of the power of love and the monumental questions of life, death, and the afterlife. ❧

Don't miss the next book by your favorite author. Sign up now for AuthorTracker by visiting www.AuthorTracker.com.